IT ROSE FROM THE ASHES

TAYLOR FENNER

ALSO BY TAYLOR FENNER

It Rose From the Ashes

First Edition
Copyright © 2024 by Taylor Fenner

Edited by Hana Blue C/Charshade Press
eBook Cover by The Cover Collection
Dust Jacket Layout and Hardcover Design by Taylor Fenner
Hardcover ISBN: 979-8-218-45147-9

First Publication September 2024

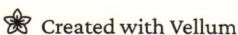 Created with Vellum

For my late great-uncle, Robert Fenner.
1923-2006
Thank you for sharing your love of history with me.

A
NOVEL OF THE
PESHTIGO
FIRE

IT ROSE FROM THE

ASHES

FROM THE AUTHOR OF NO CHECK OUT
TAYLOR FENNER

TRIGGER WARNING

It Rose From the Ashes is a romantic suspense featuring a shy woman on the run from her past and a gruff cinnamon roll biker who helps her heal. Some story elements may not be suitable for some readers. Flashbacks of domestic physical abuse, explicit death on page (based on a historical event), stalking/harassment, and gore are present in the novel. Readers who may be sensitive to these elements, please take note.

PROLOGUE

S moke swallowed the skies as the world bowed to the blaze. Acre after acre of tinderbox-dry landscape was devoured whole by the greedy tongues of flames. Sporadically, dark figures blotted against the inferno, performing a sensual dance; colliding together and breaking apart as their screams fought to overshadow the crackling of wood.

Beyond the banks of the lobster-boiling pot that the Peshtigo River had become, a lone figure stood at the shoreline, watching. The ravenous inferno reflected in the dark nothingness of his pupils. His cracked, blackened lips peel back in a smirk, his chortle lost beneath the surrounding cacophony. A few desperate souls, skin blistering and peeling from bone, spotted him from where they bobbed in the current; reaching out, crying, begging for salvation from the waters meant to be just that. The man merely kicked at a burning log and turned his back on them, disappearing into the flames that knew better than to lick at his heels. He wasn't done yet; not even close.

He'd appeared in town a week prior; walking up the middle of the road with an ominous cloud of dust trailing in his wake.

The man had a name; surely he did. Everyone does.

No one knew him, or else, if they did, they would have greeted him as the townspeople filed out of church that unseasonably hot October morning. Collectively, they watched the gaunt-looking man with black hair, longer than what was fashionable, and torn threadbare clothes, walk straight through town, and up to the most prominent house as if he owned it.

He paused there, head tilted back, admiring the house. Then he climbed onto the porch and knocked on the door. Three sharp raps echoed through town like gunfire.

No one walked up to Zachariah Sorenson's house and knocked on the door uninvited. But this stranger did. Surprisingly, he was let inside.

If the season hadn't already been cursed with drought and extreme heat, some could say this was when everything went wrong.

Now, the man with coal-black eyes stalked through a clearing, flanked by mighty pines rising forty feet into the air; flames turning them into shuddering beacons in the night, threatening to collapse at any moment. Just past the clearing sat Zachariah Sorenson's house. The grandest house in town, ask anyone. Or it was.

The stranger's focus narrowed on that grand house, nearly engulfed in flame. Pleasurable tingles flooded his skin.

The stranger had always liked fire; it spoke to him like a seductive lover. Fires sprung up mysteriously everywhere he went, and by the time suspicion fell on him, he was long gone.

His current masterpiece, the grand house in the middle of town, devoured by the hungry flames, would be no different. If any of them survived this night, the townsfolk would blame it on whatever was causing the rest of the village to burn. Another victim of nature's cruel fate.

As the stranger smiled from his hiding place among the trees, the owner of the house, a young man in his middle thirties, came stumbling out. Flames encompassed him as his painful cries sounded above the chaos of the townsfolk back by the river and beyond.

"Help...me..." He choked before he sunk to the ground in defeat, his lungs so battered from smoke inhalation that they simply stopped.

"Papa!" Zachariah Sorenson's young daughter scurried out from the shadows, crying out for her father. Before she could reach him, she mistakenly misstepped and fell into the open metal well. Her shrieks grew louder when she hit the water. The heat from the ground made the well a boiling pot, scalding her to death almost instantly.

He smiled as he recalled living out east, and how he used to love lobster boils. You dropped the live lobsters in the pot of boiling water, and they came out dead, red, and delicious. Just like the little girl.

Seeing that his work was finished, the stranger walked out into the chaos of East Front Street, whistling a tune as he went along.

CHAPTER ONE

SEPTEMBER 12, 2023

POPPY

Poppy tossed the map onto the passenger's seat. It was no help in finding her exit off the interstate. Poppy couldn't understand why anyone would want to bypass the small town of Peshtigo. It looked charming from the overpass, but she supposed most travelers just wanted to get to their destination. No one appreciated the journey anymore.

The trip north was gorgeous. Poppy passed cheery, roadside farm stands selling Indian corn, gourds, squash, pumpkins, and apples. She'd also passed more cows than she'd ever seen in her entire life. The trees,, set back from the interstate, exploded in a sea of reds, oranges, and yellows. It made her feel warm and welcome, as though it were a sign that she was making the right decision. Finally, she spotted the off-ramp, nearly hidden from sight, and swerved right onto it. Other cars honked at her, and she lifted her hand apologetically to the window as they sped by.

County Road Y took Poppy into the heart of town, merging into French Street. Small businesses popped up here and there, decorated with hay bales, scarecrows, and pumpkins. Following the directions the realtor sent her when she bought the house from the online listing alone, she crossed the river, staring in awe as vibrant red maple leaves reflected on the surface of the Peshtigo River. This time, she slowed at the second street crossing the river and signaled properly before turning.

Five minutes later, Poppy reached the end of a small lane and checked the address on her printout. The sprawling Victorian mansion stood at the end of a forty-foot-long driveway, cresting a sloping hill she wasn't sure she wanted to navigate in winter.

Though the house needed extensive repairs, landscaping, paint, and hours and hours of work, it had fantastic bones. Something Poppy noticed immediately when she saw the listing online. It even had a turret. Behind the house, down the slope of a hill and a thicket of trees, ran the river.

Poppy could already picture herself sitting on the back porch next summer, drinking coffee, reading a book or a magazine, and listening to the sounds of nature as the babbling river acted as a soundtrack in the background. Maybe she would cut down a few trees to get a better view of the river.

When Poppy questioned the realtor on the home's low price, the realtor told her that the house had been vacant for nearly forty years; the deed reverted to the city when the last owner's descendants were all gone. As it was a historic home, the city wished to sell the house - at any cost - rather than tear it down.

The photos had not done it justice, Poppy thought as she pulled into the drive and parked in front of the detached garage. She had expected a simple, two-story home in the center of town. This home seemed to have been the city's crown jewel.

Poppy stepped out of her car, jingling the keys nervously as she approached the front porch. Yes, the porch joists were leaning and would need to be replaced. The boards beneath her feet were splintered and creaked ominously as she stepped on them and the paint was peeling everywhere; but this was the type of house, the type of project Poppy had been looking for.

"What do you want with those old houses?" Poppy's ex-fiance, Jack's, condescending voice crept up from the dark recesses of her memory. "They're nothing but fire traps that deserve to be burned down. You're so fucking stupid wasting your career trying to fix up dumps like that. I can't believe I ever saw anything in you."

Poppy took several deep breaths and forced the words to blow away in the breeze. She shivered briefly as the memory of Jack beating her spilled free from the little box she stowed all her pain and suffering. He'd broken her eye socket that time, and the bruises on her face and neck took several weeks to fade. She had to fake Covid to take time off work and didn't leave the house for those weeks.

Shoving the memory back into the box, Poppy opened the door and let it swing wide, giving her the first glimpse of her new home. Dead leaves crunched beneath her feet as she stepped inside. She noted that the seal beneath the front door leaked, adding to the already long list of things that needed repair. Once she had a better idea of all that needed to be done, Poppy would make a list, starting with the most urgent repairs and ending with minor cosmetic work.

A grand, though neglected, foyer welcomed her into the home, boasting a narrow staircase and natural wooden accents. Thick chair rails lined the walls, a compliment to the carved crown molding. Delicate floral wallpaper wrapped the walls, torn and peeling at the seams.

Part of the railing on the stairway had broken off, a loss from vandalism or time. However, the stairs seemed intact and in good condition, despite the red damask and floral patterned runner, which had faded to a pale pink with age. All the woodwork would need re-varnishing, and the walls would need scrubbing and re-papering, but overall, it wasn't as bad as Poppy had expected. She'd walked through homes completely ripped back to the studs and left bare, but this house appeared mostly intact.

Poppy flicked on the light switch next to the door, pleased when the small overhead chandelier lit without hesitation. The condition report provided during the closing promised that all the wiring and plumbing in the house had been updated within the last five years, so at least that was something Poppy could cross off her list.

For now, Poppy would bring in her cleaning supplies and make the space liveable. Then she would look for a cheap, used furniture store and see about finding herself a job and a few groceries. She wouldn't attempt to stay on the second floor until she had time to assess things.

The sun was setting and grime covered Poppy from head to toe. A streak of gray matter coated one cheek and part of her forehead from where she'd wiped at her face. But the living room, dining room, and kitchen sparkled; smelling strongly of the natural cleaning solutions she used.

To Poppy's dismay, the kitchen had been updated to the 1970's finest, but there would be time to work on that later. The refriger-ator cooled, and the stove turned on as it should, and that's what mattered for now.

Poppy was pleased to find the previous owner left some furniture behind, which was in surprisingly good shape. There was an antique wooden bed frame, though she'd have to find a mattress, and other odds and ends. In the meantime, there was an antique-looking couch that she could sleep on until she could find a decent mattress in the next city over. In the dining room, two wooden chairs were pushed up against the wall, missing a table. But that was no matter, she could sit on the couch or floor while she ate and made her notes.

The bathroom on the first floor was the worst room to clean. Rust lined the rim of the claw-foot bathtub, which took more than a little elbow grease to scrub away. A colony of spiders had turned the toilet bowl, empty from disuse, into a den that reminded Poppy of The Forbidden Forest. A restrained scream, a flush of the toilet to get the water running again, and a thorough scrubbing made it good as new, though the pull cord for the flush made Poppy laugh. She hadn't seen one of those in ages. The only thing she couldn't remedy was the mirror above the pedestal sink, which was shattered, some pieces were missing entirely, and the entire piece would have to be replaced.

Poppy's love of old houses had been instilled in her during her childhood summers spent at her grandmother's home in southern Illinois. For three months every year, she would soak up the sunshine by Crab Orchard Lake until her pale skin threatened the fragile balance between light glow and lobster red to match her hair. In the evenings she'd come running through the backyard, emerald green eyes alight with mischief as she threw herself into her grandmother's waiting embrace. People had always commented about Poppy's eyes, even before she started wearing colored contacts to conceal her identity - commenting on how wide and curious they were. Later, kids in high school were afraid of her, like she could see through to their souls and learn all of their secrets. The freckles on her cheeks popped up like the fireflies they would count once night fell. It had been the happiest time of Poppy's life, but it had come to an abrupt end when her grandmother passed away the fall that Poppy started college. She'd been chasing that comforting feeling for the last twelve years and this was the closest she'd been to feeling it.

"Breathe," she ordered herself as she gripped the edges of the sink. "It's only day one. There is no rush."

Once she had calmed, overwhelmed by the ever-growing list of things she had yet to discover about the home, Poppy stripped down and turned on the shower. The pipes creaked and groaned, and a steady stream of red liquid shot from the faucet and shower head before turning clear. As soon as the water was hot enough, she climbed into the tub and stepped under the spray as she pulled the yellowed, circular shower curtain closed. The water was a soothing balm to her aching muscles as she lathered her hair with the shampoo she'd brought in, along with her other toiletries, when she dragged in her box of cleaning supplies.

The water temperature fluctuated several times as Poppy cleaned herself before turning ice cold. She yelped and turned the taps off. Stepping out of the tub, she grabbed the towel she left on the toilet seat on top of a fresh set of clothes.

She quickly dried her hair, skipping the hairdryer and toweling it dry before working it into a loose braid. Once dressed, she padded into the entryway, slipped on her well-worn sneakers, grabbed her keys from where she'd hung them off the bottom of an ornate wall sconce, grabbed her purse, and set off back into town.

A quick trip to the Dollar General filled the back of Poppy's car with more cleaning supplies, a few dry good food staples to get her through a few days, and a cheap fleece purple throw blanket patterned with jack-o'-lanterns to keep her warm until she purchased a mattress and could unpack the old bedding she'd managed to find when she cleaned out her storage unit.

Poppy's stomach growled insistently as she drove back through town. Scanning French Street, her gaze landed on a small diner. Conveniently, an old black truck, pocked with rust and trailing part of the undercarriage, was pulling away from the curb, so Poppy signaled and parked out front.

Looking out onto the road, the sign above the windows read, Della's Diner. The facade was clean, with decorative red shutters adorning the windows. Beneath the windows, wide window boxes burst with bright yellow mums. Framing the door were two bales of hay and an arch woven from dried corn stalks. Pumpkins and gourds of all shapes and sizes spilled over the edges of the hay bales A scarecrow, with a cheerful smile and bits of stuffing protruding from beneath the brim of his straw hat, stood vigil next to the door with a wooden "welcome" sign curled into one gloved hand.

Poppy smiled at the display, tugged the strap of her purse up onto her shoulder, and pulled open the door.

Three older men, sitting at a long counter, turned to look at her as she walked in. One glanced at her over the top of his spectacles; bushy eyebrows slanted down as he squinted to look at her through the sunlight streaming through the open door. The second man, who looked much like Santa Claus, leaned behind the first man's back to get a better look. The third man's glance was the shortest as he resumed shoveling a piece of pie into his mouth.

Poppy looked around the diner and smiled. The old-fashioned black-and-white checkered floor gleamed, still slightly wet from washing. Pale yellow and green Formica tables were arranged in the middle of the diner while three sides of the restaurant were packed tight with booths; their shiny blue bench seats shining in the fluorescent lights overhead. An older woman in a flannel shirt stood behind the counter, refilling one of the older men's coffee mugs while the cook on the other side of the pass-through window rang a silver bell and announced, "Order's up!"

Noticing Poppy hovering by the door, the older woman looked over and smiled, "Take a seat anywhere, honey. I'll be right with you."

"Thanks," Poppy murmured. A chunk of curly, mousy-brown

hair had escaped from her ponytail, and she tucked it behind her ear self-consciously. Shuffling to a booth by the front window, she felt the lingering gazes of the customers following her.

"You must be new in town," the older woman commented as she placed a dark green menu in front of Poppy. She nods slightly, trying not to draw more attention to herself. "A quiet one, huh?" The older woman said a little too loudly. Poppy shrunk in on herself. "Well, welcome to town, honey. Can I get you something to drink?"

Mentally, Poppy calculated the balance in her account, minus the supplies and the money she needed to save for expenses and repairs. *Maybe eating a meal out wasn't such a good idea.* "Water is fine."

"Alright, then," the woman's smile was friendly, as though she saw through Poppy and already knew everything about her. "I'll be right back with that while you look at the menu."

Poppy opened the menu and scanned it. Her stomach rumbled louder and her cheeks heated. She glanced around, but luckily, the other patrons seemed to have returned to their conversations and meals. The phone rang behind the counter, and the older woman set Poppy's water down on the countertop to answer it.

"Della's Diner," the woman answers, "this is Della speaking. What do you mean you're quitting?" The woman, Della, raised her voice, which grabbed Poppy's attention. "Well, congratulations," Della rasps, sounding aggravated. "Of course, I'm happy you're getting married, honey; I just don't know what that has to do with you quitting."

Della listened to whoever was on the phone as one of the older men at the counter coughed and shook his head. The trio hung on every word as they eavesdropped on the call.

Della sighs, "You're leaving me in a real bind here, honey."

The call lasted a minute or two longer, but Della couldn't convince the employee not to quit. As she hung up the phone, Della muttered, "Kids these days."

"Lazy generation," one of the old men agreed. "All they want to do is sleep all day and play video games while collecting a government check." His companions grunted in agreement.

Della shook her head, picked up the glass of water, and walked back to Poppy's table. "Sorry about that, honey," Della slipped on a smile. "What can I get you?"

"I can help," Poppy blurted; the idea only half-formed in her mind.

"What's that?"

"Your waitress just quit, right?" Poppy asked, suddenly feeling like she couldn't sit still. "I'm new in town like you said. I don't have a job yet. I could waitress if you're looking."

Della narrowed her eyes slightly, considering. "Do you have any experience, honey?"

Poppy nodded, then bit her lip, "a little. I worked at a pizzeria for a year in high school."

Della hummed thoughtfully, "Why don't I get you something to eat while I think about it?"

"Okay," Poppy nodded eagerly. "I'll have a bowl of soup and a club sandwich."

"Chicken noodle or cream of broccoli?" Della asked as she scribbled Poppy's order down.

Poppy considered it for a moment, "cream of broccoli."

"Alright, I'll get that going for you." Della wrote it down and walked back over to the counter.

Now that Della was gone, Poppy wondered what the hell she was thinking. *A waitress? In a small town where everyone seems to know everyone? Talk about a stupid idea.* It was about the furthest from laying low and staying under the radar as Poppy could get. *Maybe Della will say no.* After all, even though Poppy looked young, it was easy to see that it had been more than a few years since she wore a waitress's apron.

Nerves fluttered like moths in the pit of Poppy's stomach, anxious for the hopefulness of light but afraid to burn from it. The feeling lasted through Poppy's meal. She barely picked at her lunch, even though her stomach begged to be filled.

As Poppy finally forced herself to eat the last few bites of her sandwich, Della approached the table once more. "Can you start tomorrow for our opening shift?"

"Absolutely," Poppy replied.

"Alright. I'll go get the forms and go over everything with you. First things first, what's your name, honey?"

"It's Fal-" Poppy coughed and caught herself. "Poppy. My name is Poppy Isles."

"Welcome to Della's Diner, Poppy."

She felt guilty lying to Della, but according to all her documents, Poppy was who she said she was. That old name was nothing more than a ghost; the identity of a dead woman. Poppy had buried that name the day she'd traded her bright red hair for mousy brown and placed gray contacts over her green irises.

Della returned with a stack of standard employment forms and Poppy began to fill them out. She pulled her new social security card and banking information out of her purse. Della cleared the empty plate from the table and then slid across from Poppy.

"The diner opens at 6:00 AM despite the efforts of those old coots behind me to get me to open earlier," Della explained as Poppy filled out the first tax form. "My husband Len and I get here around 5:00 AM to get things going and I expect my morning waitresses to get here by 5:30 AM."

"Makes sense," Poppy agreed.

"We don't have a uniform, just an apron over your clothes," Della continued. "I'll warn you, it starts off cold in here first thing, but with all the walking around that will wear off fast, so dress accordingly. And be sure to wear comfortable shoes."

"Got it. Wear light layers and good sneakers." Poppy scratched out an error with her account number before handing the next few forms to Della.

"Where are you from Poppy?" Della asked as she scanned the forms.

"Chicago," Poppy replied.

"What brought you to Peshtigo?" Della's stare is more curious than critical but it put Poppy on edge.

"I just needed a fresh start," Poppy explained. "I was getting sick of the city."

CHAPTER TWO

POPPY

Poppy's alarm woke her minutes before five in the morning. She was replacing one of the morning waitresses. Her shift would run from the diner's opening at six in the morning until two in the afternoon.

Poppy was used to getting up early. Jack expected a full breakfast before he left for work: pancakes, sausages or bacon, eggs, and coffee at precisely the perfect temperature. And more times than not, he'd take two bites and turn his nose up at her offerings, leaving her to clean up before she left for work.

This morning, Poppy awoke on the cramped couch, her neck bent awkwardly, and her body aching. The fleece throw she'd bought lay in a heap on the floor. The house had been so warm that she'd kicked it off. She would have to check what the thermostat was set at and turn it down. It wasn't far enough into fall to need the heat turned on just yet.

Poppy shifted upright, planting her feet on the hardwood floor.

She rubbed her neck to work the soreness out when something on her arm caught her attention.

A thin cut ran diagonally from her wrist to her elbow. Poppy's brow wrinkled in confusion. *Where did that cut come from?* She was positive it wasn't there when she went to sleep, so it couldn't have come from cleaning.

I must have scratched myself in my sleep. Poppy rationalized. A niggling objection fought to the surface. Poppy's nails were always short and blunt. They'd had to be. In her old life, she'd been so hands-on at work that anything longer would have become broken and ragged as she remodeled homes from the studs out. Either way, Poppy could not think of any better explanation and didn't have time to fret about it more as she crossed to the bathroom to shower and prepare for the day.

Poppy worried she wouldn't be able to fall back into the nearly decade-forgotten pattern of waitressing. Still, once Della explained the ticketing system and showed her the section she would be working, Poppy stepped back into time. As though she were sixteen again, minus the smell of parmesan cheese and tomato sauce cloying up the air.

The diner was busy first thing in the morning. The three old-timers from the day before were seated on the same three stools at the counter. This time they were joined by several other men, all sipping coffee, talking about the good old days, and sending covert looks at the group of little old ladies who had pushed two tables together in the middle of the room.

A couple of teenage girls sat at the booth Poppy had the night before. Textbooks and laptops covered the table as the girls hastily shoved bagels into their mouths; hurrying to finish their schoolwork before it was time to leave.

Nova, one of the other waitresses, spun around the room like a ballerina, delicately performing a well-orchestrated routine. She delivered breakfast to the tables along the back wall before pausing to talk to a young mother with a chubby-faced baby chewing on her fist.

"Boys, I'd like you to meet Poppy," Della steered Poppy toward the three old-timers in the middle of the posse at the counter. "She's our new waitress, and I want you to be nice to her."

The man in the middle, who had unabashedly gawked at her the day before, scoffed as he lifted his coffee mug to his lips. "Now, Della, don't be filling this young girl's head with fanciful lies; you know we're nice to everyone."

"Yeah," the man with glasses on his right piped up, "How else are we supposed to get all the gossip before those old crones in the back?"

"We heard that!" One of the older women shouted.

The older men cackled, ducking their heads, pretending to be chastened.

"Ignore these old fools." Della rolled her eyes. "They're harmless. This here is Everett Peters, a retired school teacher."

Della gestured to the man who had paid little attention to her the night before. He had short gray hair and blue eyes that once had been vibrant and bright but had paled with age. He wore a white button-down shirt and a dark green bowtie.

"Nice to know you, miss," Everett acknowledged her before returning to the crossword puzzle next to his coffee mug.

"And here we have Alfred Upton," Della gestured to the man who looked like Santa Claus with his long white hair and bushy white beard. "He was the police chief for nearly thirty-five years, and now he likes to sit here and drive me crazy."

Poppy chuckled as Alfred fixed Della with a stony stare before a wide grin appeared beneath the white bristles of his mustache. "Your day would be boring without us, Dell."

"Maybe so." Della laughed. "And finally, last but not least, we have Father Edgar Brown."

"God's blessings be with you, miss," the old priest murmured as he studied her over his wire-rimmed glasses. He reminded Poppy of the cartoon owl in the Tootsie Pop commercial: wise but personable. Looking at him face-on now, Poppy could see the white collar peaking out of his shirt.

"Nice to meet you all." Poppy forced a smile. "Can I get you a top-off on your coffee?"

"Don't mind if I do." Alfred shoved his mug forward as Poppy reached for the fresh carafe of regular coffee.

Della smiled approvingly. "I'll leave you to it."

"Decaf for me, Poppy," Everett said as he offered her his mug, and Poppy dutifully grabbed the orange-topped coffee carafe and filled his mug up.

Father Edgar put his hand over his mug. "I'm all set for now, Poppy." Winking, he added, "I have to switch to water soon, or I'll have heartburn all afternoon and won't be able to make my rounds at the hospital up in Marinette."

"Alright then." Poppy nodded as she returned the carafes to the warmers. "Can I get you anything else?" All three men shook their heads, and she went to wait on some arrivals in her section.

By the end of the week, Poppy's feet were sore, and she added a new pair of sneakers to the ever-growing list of things she needed to buy. Every afternoon after work, she came home and worked on a few cosmetic repairs around the house, scrubbing, clearing rooms, and making notes until she fell asleep on the couch around ten at night. She would need to hire a contractor for the larger jobs but was contented in what she could accomplish alone. Her new routine was exhausting, but she felt more relaxed than she had in a long time.

At the diner, everyone was friendly. Poppy had forgotten the names of almost everyone, many of whom were regulars, but they didn't seem to mind. She just smiled and went along with their small talk.

Alfred, Edgar, and Everett came in every day. They always sat in the same spot, ordered cup after cup of coffee, and asked questions.

"Where are you from, Poppy?" Alfred had asked on that first day.

Poppy answered vaguely. "I'm from south of here."

"I hope you're not one of those damn FIBs." Alfred chuckled as he sipped his coffee.

"FIB?" Poppy echoed, unfamiliar with the term.

"Yeah, Fucking Illinois Bas-" Alfred stopped when Della shot him a sharp look.

Everett laughed heartily, an outward display that Poppy hadn't expected from the old school teacher, while Father Edgar smiled over the rim of his coffee cup. Poppy blushed a little, getting the gist of Alfred's explanation, but didn't answer.

"So how do you like Peshtigo, Poppy?" Father Edgar asked today.

"It's a nice little town," Poppy replied honestly. "Exactly what I was looking for."

"Shirl said she saw you by that old firetrap on Splake Court," Alfred commented almost accusingly. "You didn't buy that old dump, did you?"

Poppy frowned, looking at the table of older women, once again in the center of the room. In the middle was Shirley Benton, whom Poppy was learning rivaled Alfred for the town's biggest gossip.

"I did," Poppy admitted after a long pause. She wished her address could have remained a mystery. If Jack somehow tracked her down here, all it would take for him to find her would be to talk to one of the locals. But Poppy couldn't think like that. She'd been careful, so very careful. She'd changed her name and cut ties with any friends she had in Chicago. She carefully picked a town in the middle of nowhere that she had no ties to. An anonymous town that Jack would never think to look for her in. There was no way he could find her.

"Why ever did you do that?" Alfred exclaimed, pulling her back to the present.

Poppy shrugged like it was no big deal. "I like taking broken things and making them look beautiful again."

Too bad the same couldn't be said for herself. Every time Poppy looked in the mirror, Jack's words echoed in her head, reminding her of her flaws. But the house she would make spectacular again. Poppy thought of the floorboards in the study on the second floor. They were buckled and broken, rising from the floor like jagged teeth just waiting to trip her. She'd had to seal the room off until further notice.

"You've got a big job ahead of you," Everett commented.

"I know." Poppy nodded. "But it will be worth it in the end."

"You got a contractor lined up?" Everett asked as he watched her grab several plates through the pass-through and deliver them to a couple sitting by the door.

It astounded Poppy that she could already pick the couple out as just passers-through after less than a week. "Not yet. But I'm working on that." Poppy admitted.

"You should call Ev's son." Alfred nodded toward Everett. "He's a good boy; he'll give you a good rate."

"Maybe," Poppy replied noncommittally. "I'll look into him if you give me his name."

"I can do you one better," Everett told her as he reached into his wallet and pulled out a business card. "Just tell him I told you to call."

"Thank you," Poppy looked at the card before placing it in her apron pocket. It was heavy cardstock, good quality. James Peters was written in raised letters on the top of the card, and she was surprised to see that he owned one of the top companies she had been researching.

Saturday morning, the last morning before her day off, Poppy was taking an order from the table of teenage girls she'd seen studying when she heard the rumble of a motorcycle outside. Poppy had learned that Della's Diner was a staple in the community and a regular haunt for most of the members of the local motorcycle club, The Burning Blood Riders. Della also employed several of the sisters and girlfriends of the club members.

It was a beautiful fall day that felt like Indian Summer. The sun was out, and Poppy couldn't wait to get home and work on winter-izing her backyard. She'd bought some tulip bulbs to plant as well.

As the motorcycle engine cut out, one of the girls squealed a little and grabbed her friend's wrist, shaking it excitedly. Only seconds later, the bell over the door jingled and a behemoth of a man stepped inside. His long, dark brown hair was braided down his back, and the scratchy start of a beard covered his upper lip and chin. The man wore a black leather jacket covered in patches, faded blue jeans, and heavy black boots. A dark pair of sunglasses obscured his eyes, but still, as he turned his head, Poppy felt like all the oxygen was sucked from the room; he seemed to stare right at her.

His grin was wry, daring her to comment as he unashamedly took her in. And then the moment was broken; the usual sounds of the diner came rushing back all at once like she'd been underwater and broke the surface again.

The man looked away, crossing the dining room to the edge of Nova's section, and slid into a booth. Poppy was grateful. Danger and trouble hung around that man like a dense fog. His appearance screamed the *bad boy type*, and he was the type of complication Poppy could not afford.

"He's so hot," the girl who had first noticed him commented dreamily as she stared at him across the room.

Her companion snorted."He's so old."

"Nah-uh." The girl shook her head. "He's only, like, in his early thirties, probably."

"Which means he was practically an adult when you were born."

The girl looked at her friend mischievously. "That doesn't mean I can't look and appreciate."

Poppy smiled and shook her head. The first girl grinned up at her sheepishly and finished giving Poppy her order. "I'll have chocolate chip pancakes with bacon, please." She closed the menu and slid it across the table to Poppy.

"No bagel today, girls?" Poppy asked.

"Nah," the girl with her back to the door shook her head. "We save those for school days when we're in a hurry and don't have time for a bigger breakfast."

"I see. Well, I'll get this order in for you, and it shouldn't be too long."

"No worries," the girls chorus.

～

Colton

Colton "Fox" Sterling had picked the wrong day to quit smoking again. His cat, Large Marge, had chewed through the plastic outside of her dry food bag, and there was kibble all over the kitchen floor. When he got to work, the auto parts supplier had sent the wrong part for the Chevy Equinox that he'd promised the owner would be finished today. Then, when he'd crawled from beneath a Ford Taurus that should have seen the scrap yard fifteen years ago, his back screamed at him in protest.

Colton had given up and decided to take a lunch break at Della's. Della's husband, Len, had founded the motorcycle club Colton was a member of in the early 1970s and everyone in the club hung out at Della's.

His fingers itched for a cigarette as he grabbed the silverware roll on the table and began shredding the adhesive napkin ring.

On the bright side, it appeared Della hired a new waitress.

The last waitress, Birdie, had been a nightmare. The new waitress was slightly older, probably around thirty. Her long brown hair was swept back into a high ponytail, giving him an unobstructed view of her wide, gray eyes. He'd seen the look on her face when he stepped through the door. Curiosity, tinged with an underlying current of fear. It didn't surprise him.

Most women were afraid of bikers if they hadn't grown up around them, with the media and television shows giving them a rough reputation. But the Burning Blood Riders were deeply committed to charity work; and despite the leather jackets, tattoos, and scruffy appearances, most of the members were harmless as flies.

Colton felt a pull toward the new waitress. He'd love to get under her skin and see a healthy flush bloom on her alabaster cheeks. It had been years since he had more than a string of one-night stands; too long since any single woman called to him. He doubted this new waitress would be any different. Not that it looked like she was willing to give him the time of day. But he enjoyed the challenge. Now he was hungry for something more than a turkey club.

"Hey, Colton," Nova, the ever-persistent club hanger-on, purred in his ear, drawing him from his contemplation. "What can I get you?"

Colton tore his gaze away from the new waitress as he felt Nova's hand rubbing his arm. Nova was constantly trying to become a club old lady, and it looked like this month, she had her sights set on him. Her last attempt had been on Della and Len's son, Michael, the current club president. Michael "Vlad" Just, had grown up around the club, joining at seventeen and taking over as club president a little over ten years ago, at the age of thirty. Colton knew Nova had struck out with Vlad and was now on the prowl.

"Coffee." Nodding in the new waitress's direction, he asked, "Who is the new girl?"

~

Poppy

"Hydrangea, we need more coffee!" Alfred called out as he noticed Poppy walking back to the counter to put a couple of breakfast orders into the system.

"Poppy," she corrected, though Poppy suspected that Alfred misnamed her as a joke. The older man was like that.

"Close enough," Alfred grinned, confirming Poppy's suspicion.

Poppy raised her eyebrows, biting her tongue before she could ask Alfred how he thought the names were interchangeable.

As she crossed behind the counter, Poppy felt the man in the leather jacket's gaze on her again. She snuck a look as she refilled Everett, Alfred, and Father Edgar's coffee. Nova was taking his order, or maybe just chatting him up. She could never tell with that one, but the man's gaze, now unencumbered by his sunglasses, was firmly on Poppy as he said something. Nova turned to look in Poppy's direction before replying. Even as something flipped over in her stomach, she hoped that he was asking about something on the special board over her left shoulder. When Nova crossed the dining room with a knowing smile, Poppy knew she was wrong.

"Who is that?" Poppy hoped she sounded only mildly curious as she and Nova leaned over the iPad on the counter to enter their orders.

"Who?" Nova asked coyly, vibrating with excitement.

Poppy snorts. "You know who I'm talking about."

"Oh, *him*," Nova drawled. "That's Colton Sterling. But everyone calls him Fox. He's a member of the Peshtigo chapter of the Burning Blood Riders MC with Trixie's brother, Corbin. Have you met Trixie yet?"

"Yeah, briefly," Poppy said, thinking of the perky blonde waitress she'd met the day before. Trixie worked part-time during the afternoon and evening shifts. She hadn't had a chance to talk to her too much, which was fine. Already, she was afraid that she was forming too many attachments.

"Anyway," Nova steered the conversation back on track, "Fox was asking about you."

Poppy felt her blood run cold as a nervous sweat dotted her brow. "Why?"

Nova looked at her like she'd grown a second head, "Because you're new, and you're hot, obviously."

Poppy shook her head. "I'm not interested."

Nova raised an eyebrow. "If you insist. But sooner or later, you'll have to break down those walls you've built sky-high around you. Make some friends, have some fun, and smile a genuine smile once in a goddamned while." Poppy stood there stunned as Nova walked away to tend to her tables.

"Poppy, darling, could you bring us a warm-up on our coffee?" Shirley called from her usual table.

"Coming," Poppy called before taking a deep breath to collect herself.

Poppy tugged on an old pair of gardening gloves as she mentally made a to-do list for the yard work. Perched among the changing leaves of the trees lining the property, one crow cawed to another. The answering caw came a minute later, passing on information, or perhaps discussing Poppy, standing with her hands on her hips, surveying the yard before her.

One for sorrow, two for mirth, Poppy's mind supplied the old rhyme as she reached for a rake to gather the leaves that had already fallen. She worked in short, fast strokes, piling the leaves in one corner of the yard. She conjured memories of her childhood self, taking running leaps into the piles of drying red, yellow, orange, and brown leaves as her father raked them. The memory was fuzzy and faded around the edges. Her father's face was no more than a blur, forgotten over time and gone forever when she lost all of her family photos.

Leaves gathered, Poppy moved on to weeding the house's perimeter. In spring, she would landscape, plant a vegetable garden, and curate a few rose bushes in the front yard. With a fresh coat of paint and other exterior repairs, the house would return to its long-ago beauty.

A warm breeze played with Poppy's hair, pushing a few strands across her face, causing light brown cuts in her vision. Blinking and tucking the hair back into her braid, she was surprised to find herself standing in the driveway, staring up at the house.

It wasn't unusual for Poppy to get so lost in her head, picturing ideas and plans coming to fruition, that she lost track of time or physically ended up somewhere other than she last remembered being.

Jack once claimed to love that passion in her, but she'd noticed the tick in his jaw, the tightening of his mouth, the flash of anger in his eyes as he'd had to repeat something he'd said that she missed. In public, he'd laugh it off and tell his friends or colleagues that she was worlds away, thinking about her latest project like he was a proud parent discussing a prodigy child. But in private, there became no escape from his wrath.

Poppy took a deep breath, grounding herself in the present, then hurried to plant the tulip bulbs along the driveway and back-yard. She didn't notice the two crows from the trees were now perched on the house's eaves.

She didn't dream that night. She fell, exhausted, into a dream-less sleep as the couch wreaked havoc on her neck and spine. The house was fevered again; sweat dotted her brow and soaked through the thin t-shirt she slept in. She flopped to face the back of the couch and then shifted again toward the open edge, one arm draped over the side, knuckles resting on the floor.

Outside, the night was still. The streetlight across the way flickered several times before plunging Poppy's end of the dead-end street into darkness. In the distance, an owl hooted once. A light breeze kicked up, stirring a few errant leaves across the driveway. On Poppy's wrist, the seconds hand on her watch passed over twelve, and the minute hand sluggishly dragged itself from 2:59 AM to 3:00 AM.

The hour ushered in with a cataclysmic shattering of glass as a dark object burst through the bay window that overlooked the driveway, landing with a decisive thud on the floor. Poppy sat up quickly and stared in horror at the jagged remnants of the window, the hole in the middle gaping like a mouth with razor-sharp teeth. Jumping up from the couch, she flipped on the overhead light. The gold and crystal light fixture hummed in protest before flickering on.

Poppy gasped, feeling the air being torn from her lungs as she crept forward, hand clasped over her mouth as tears pricked her eyes and dripped down her cheeks. On the floor, black wings splayed wide over a thousand tiny shards of glass, and beak opened in a caw that would never be heard, was a massive crow.

Fighting back a wave of nausea, Poppy stared at the bird, waiting for it to hop up, stunned, but all right. When it didn't, she nudged it with her bare foot, trying not to gag. The bird was dead.

Poppy shivered as the dusty, old draperies began dancing in the chill breeze blowing in through the remnant of the window. She tried to ignore the ominous tone of the dead crow on her floor as she shrugged on a sweatshirt and a pair of sweatpants. Slipping her feet into her sneakers, she went to fetch a tarp and a shovel from the garage, where she'd been storing all her supplies.

Back inside, she covered her face with her sweatshirt and closed her eyes, counting to ten before shoveling the dead bird into a large black garbage bag. She jogged out to the garbage bin at the end of the driveway and threw the bag in, not wanting it near the house.

Methodically, forcing herself not to think about her task, Poppy swept the broken glass into a dustpan and dumped it into the garbage, then wiped the blood away with a cleaning rag before throwing that away, too. Finally, she grabbed a stepladder and nailed the tarp into place.

There was no avoiding it now; she'd have to contact a contractor in the morning.

CHAPTER THREE

POPPY

"You definitely have a big project ahead of you," James Peters whistled as Poppy led him into the kitchen the following day. She was grateful he had agreed to come out immediately, especially on a Sunday morning.

"I think it will be worth it," Poppy stared lovingly up at the ceiling, picturing how the house could be.

James nodded. "No doubt about that."

He was an attractive man, probably in his mid-forties. His light brown hair was starting to show shoots of gray. His green eyes were friendly, not predatory, like some men in the industry who thought they could pull a fast one on women. Smile lines framed his eyes and mouth, a testament to a happy life.

"You know, this was the house kids were always afraid of growing up."

"Really?" Poppy's eyes widened as she eagerly leaned across the counter. "Why was that?"

James looked out the kitchen window, shrugging. "I don't

know. It's been abandoned since before I was born. You know how it is when you're a kid. Your mind comes up with all kinds of sinister reasons for why a house like this would sit empty for so long. Especially with how dilapidated it has looked over the years. The city has tried several times to fix it up a little, but it still has that eerie air of being abandoned but not at the same time."

Poppy laughed as she prepared coffee. "So you're saying I'm living in the neighborhood haunted house?"

"Something like that," James said, laughing with her at the absurdness.

"Can I get you some coffee?" Poppy asked as she set her mug down.

James glanced up from his clipboard. "Sure."

"So, what are you thinking?" Poppy bit her lip. "For the repairs."

"Well, when it comes to restoring these old homes, the sky is the limit, of course," James said thoughtfully. "The good news for you is that the roof is new, so we don't have to worry about that. According to the condition report from the sale, structurally, the house is pretty sound. As you know, a few floors need to be replaced on the second floor. Obviously, the broken window needs to be replaced, but I noticed air leaks around some of the others, so they'll have to be replaced as well. The basement foundation looks good, which is a relief for you living this close to the river. In the spring, the river overflows and can creep all the way up to the tree line out back on a bad year. The porch needs to be ripped off and replaced, which I believe you had in your notes. We can update the kitchens and the bathrooms as much or as little as you like. There's a lot of cosmetic work: painting, wallpapering, re-varnishing the floors, and I know you mentioned wanting to help with some of that or do it on your own. You mentioned some issues with the heating and the plumbing as well?"

"Yes." Poppy nodded as she handed James a steaming mug of coffee and then, taking one for herself, led him through the dining room, across the hall, and into the living room to show him the thermostat.

"I thought at first the heat was just turned up high from while it was on the market to keep the pipes from bursting," Poppy explained as she motioned to the thermostat. "It's still warm enough that it shouldn't have needed to kick in much yet, but when I went to turn it down the morning after I moved in, it was set to sixty. But look at what it's registering out as."

James leaned forward, reading the balmy eighty-eight-degree readout on the thermostat. He tuts. "It could be the blower motor, or it could be the furnace. We'll have to take a closer look at that. What about the plumbing issues?"

"I figured they were connected," Poppy sighed as she sipped her coffee. "The plumbing is working all right for the most part. The toilets flush, the sink and bathtubs run. Albeit when I first moved in, the water needed a few minutes to clear the rust from the pipes, but that's to be expected. I think it's a water heater issue connected to the furnace issue. One minute, the water is fine, then it's ice cold, and in seconds, changes to so hot you could burn yourself."

"Definitely a heating issue then" James said, confirming Poppy's suspicions. "The water heater might have to be replaced altogether. On its own, they can be costly, but with the list of things we'll have to do, it's not the worst. I'll put together an esti-mate when I get to the office tomorrow, but I think we could get this project done for about one-twenty including labor and supplies. The good thing is you got this place on a song."

"One hundred twenty thousand? That's all?"

James laughed, taken aback, "Well, like I said, when restoring an old house like this, the sky is the limit. If you want it restored with exact period accuracy, the price could quadruple. Still, if all you want is a house that looks nice on the inside and the outside and is livable, I don't think my estimate is out of the ballpark."

"While I appreciate period accuracy, I'm not interested in living in a museum," Poppy said. "I'm just not used to - back home, a contractor wouldn't even walk through the door for less than two hundred thousand, and those were on homes with much less repair work than this."

"Welcome to small-town Wisconsin," James grinned. "We try not to rip people off. You sound like you have some experience in home restoration."

"A bit," Poppy hedged, silently cursing herself for the slip. She smiled gratefully and added, "Let me know about the estimate, and I can get you a cashier's check right away."

"I'll call you from the office tomorrow," James promised as they walked back into the dining room, and placed his empty coffee mug on the lone chair in the dining room.

After James left, Poppy drove to the next town over and picked out a mattress so she could set up the bed. She didn't want to chance another night in the living room with the broken window. She picked a cheap, out-of-a-box mattress and lugged it all the way upstairs. She winced at each thud of the dolly as she dragged it, and the fifty-pound box, up by the handle stair by stair.

Once she got to the landing, it was a smooth roll to the master bedroom at the end of the hall. Inside, she arranged the headboard against the wall and grabbed her toolbox to assemble the frame.

Sweat created a dew-like sheen on her skin as she worked. The upstairs was even more stifling than the main floor, so Poppy paused her work and opened one of the windows. The lock hesitated in her grip before giving way and nearly snapping off in her hand. She slid the window up a few inches and sighed as the autumn breeze flittered through the screen.

"There," Poppy announced proudly to the empty room as she stood back, admiring the assembled bed frame. It was constructed of rich, dark wood, probably walnut. It had an ornate, leaf-patterned carving on the headboard and footboard. Poppy ran her hand along the carving, admiring the craftsmanship and noting that it paid homage to her favorite season, the season of her fresh start.

She jiggled the frame, making sure it was solid before grabbing her exacto knife and slicing open the oblong box holding the wrapped-up mattress. The mattress had its own tool for cutting the airtight plastic encasing it. Poppy unrolled the mattress and positioned it on the boards across the bottom of the frame. Slicing into the plastic, a hiss of air whistled around her. Once finished, Poppy gathered the plastic and left the mattress to finish self-inflating, leaving the slicing tool and the exacto knife behind on the windowsill.

True to his word, James got back to Poppy with the estimate the following day, and by afternoon, the cashier's check was in his hand. James sent a couple of men over to the house to place plywood over the window until a new one could be ordered and the permits from the city obtained.

Poppy worked in the mornings and found herself opening up to the customers, as well as Nova and the other waitresses, bit by bit. Della told her she fit in perfectly and that she was glad to have her, much to Poppy's relief. It wasn't the type of work she was used to, or the kind of work she imagined herself earning a living on, but it was refreshingly simple.

That afternoon after work, Poppy planned to get some paint so she could scrub down the icky dust and debris coating the walls of the master bedroom and repaint the room. After a quick inspection, James signed off on the room, claiming only the floor needed to be re-varnished and the stone fireplace across the room from Poppy's bed needed to be re-stoned.

Poppy's phone rang as she walked out to her car. She pulled the low-tech pay-as-you-go device from her pocket and frowned at the display. The number looked familiar, a Chicago area code she knew she'd seen before but couldn't quite place. In the era of cell phones and technology, it was easy to have dozens of numbers stored in your contacts without knowing them on sight. Still, very few people had this number. Della, James, Nova, and Trixie - but no one with a Chicago area code.

Poppy ignored the call and waited to see if the caller would leave a voicemail. She didn't have to wait long. Unease unfurled in her gut. Hands trembling, she lifted the phone to her ear. "You think you're so clever, don't you?" A familiar voice taunted. "You think you can just up and leave and that I wouldn't find you? It's only a matter of time now that I've found this number. And when I do track you down, you're going to pay bitch."

The world crashed to a screeching halt. Poppy's heart threatened to rip out of her chest as her stomach lurched violently. Suddenly she felt a hand on her shoulder and she screamed, leaping out of reach and into the middle of French Street.

"Poppy!" Alfred cried as she spun around. The old policeman looks as startled as Poppy felt as she stared at him, chest heaving. Sensing her distress, Alfred asked, "Are you all right, dear?"

Poppy flattened her free hand against her chest as though that would calm her racing heart. "Yes, I'm sorry. You just startled me."

"Is everything all right?" Concern etched Alfred's face. "Is there anything I can do to help you?"

"I," Poppy began, swallowed hard, then tried again. "I - no, I'm fine. There's nothing wrong. I'm sorry, I have to go."

Poppy rushed around the hood of her car, head low as she felt Alfred's concerned, curious gaze tracking her every step. Her hands shook as she shoved her car key into the lock and unlocked the door. Poppy heard Everett, or maybe Father Edgar, exit the diner and ask Alfred what's wrong. Poppy tugged the door open and slipped into the driver's seat, ignoring their stares as she turned the ignition over and pulled away from the curb.

The police department was halfway between Della's Diner and the turnoff for her house. She talked herself into and out of, stopping half a dozen times as she traveled down French Street at a snail's pace. Finally, forcing herself to decide, Poppy pulled over in front of the police department. It took even longer for her to get out of the car and walk inside.

Inside, an older woman sat behind a glass window. Her gray hair was cut into a short buzz cut, and oversized glasses took up much of the upper part of her face. She wore a dark blue uniform, reminding Poppy of a meter maid of days of old. "Hi, how can I help you?" the woman asked, her tone friendly and professional.

"I'd like to speak with an officer, if there's one available," Poppy sounded scared, and she hated it. She thought she was past all this.

"What is it regarding?" The older woman wrote something on a notepad in front of her. Poppy couldn't read what the woman was writing from where she stood.

"I received a threatening phone message from someone."

"Someone?"

"An ex-fiance," Poppy clarified. "I have a restraining order against him back in Chicago."

The woman nodded. "Take a seat back there, and someone will be with you shortly."

Poppy sat down and stared at the minute hand on the clock, marching steadily onward as the woman disappeared from the window and further into the bowels of the police department.

A young, bald officer with a red beard stepped into the lobby and walked over to Poppy. "I'm Officer Michelson. How can I help you?"

"I received a threatening voicemail from my ex-fiance," Poppy repeated for the officer. "I have a restraining order against him from Chicago, and I just moved here, and I don't want him to know where I am."

"Whoa." The officer held his hands out to calm her, and Poppy realized her tone bordered on hysterical. "Take a deep breath. Why don't we step inside, and you can tell me everything?"

Poppy nodded, taking several deep breaths in and out. She followed the officer into the central part of the police department and then into an interview room. Leaving the door open, the officer turned to her and said, "I'm leaving the door open so you know that you're free to leave at any time."

"Okay," Poppy murmured as she sat across from the officer.

He pulled a yellow legal pad in front of him, then looked at Poppy. "Why don't you start from the beginning?"

So Poppy did. She told the officer about the abuse she suffered and Jack's temper. How she feared things would only get worse, and that he would kill her one day if she didn't get out. Handing the officer a copy of the paperwork, she explained the restraining order she had issued in Chicago before she fled; faking her death with the aid of a detective and changing her identity.

"I've done everything to protect myself." Poppy shivered across the table from the officer. "I don't want him to find me here. I thought I was safe in a place he'd never think to look for me."

"It seems like you've taken every legal precaution," Officer Michelson gestured to the restraining order. He chose not to comment on the channels she went through for a new name. "Just because you received a call from him doesn't mean he's tracked down your exact location."

Poppy scowled at the officer's lack of interest. Officer Michelson pointed to the flip phone, still clutched in Poppy's fist. "The good thing about low-tech relics like that is that they can't be tracked with GPS like more expensive smartphones can. Not without the cell phone company adding it on. And I assume you bought this one at a department store or somewhere? It's a pay-as-you-go model?"

Poppy nodded.

"Then you have nothing to worry about," Officer Michelson said as if that solved everything. "I'll take a copy of this restraining order for our records, and I can make up an informational report, but there isn't much we can do unless he comes to town and starts bothering you."

"Aren't phone calls part of the restraining order?" Poppy asked, feeling sick.

"We could send a referral to the District Attorney's Office for a violation of a no-contact order," he said, "but that might alert Mr. Richards to the general area where you're staying."

"No," Poppy shook her head adamantly. "I don't want Jack to know where I am."

"Then, as I said, we can keep the restraining order on file and make an informational report," Officer Michelson repeated patiently. "And I suggest you change your cell phone number as soon as possible."

"Thank you," Poppy nodded stiffly as Officer Michelson shook her hand and escorted her out of the building.

Poppy got into her car, feeling like all the energy had been torn from her body, leaving her walking husk. What Officer Michelson didn't understand, what chilled Poppy to the bone, was that this was a new number. Her old number–her old phone–sank to the bottom of the river.

CHAPTER FOUR

POPPY

Poppy slept fitfully, tossing and turning for hours, waking up repeatedly to check if the windows and doors were securely locked. The only person who had a key to the house besides Poppy was James. She left him a message with her new phone number after she changed it and he called her back. He informed her that a couple of his guys would come the next day to look at the furnace and the hot water heater.

When Poppy's alarm went off, her eyes felt dry, sore, and crusty. She dragged herself out of bed and into the upstairs bathroom; terrified by her reflection in the mirror. Her light brown hair was matted into a clump of curls from sleep, her gray eyes were bloodshot, and her skin looked sallow in the overhead lighting.

Forcing herself into the bathtub, Poppy took a quick shower. She shivered when the water turned to ice and jumped back in pain when it became unbearably hot, steaming around her. Poppy hopped out, quickly dried off, dressed, and pulled her hair back.

Half-trotting down the stairs, she jiggled her car keys. Poppy got in the car, but when she went to turn over the key, the ignition protested. An ominous thunk preceded a series of clicks. "Come on," she groaned when, after several tries, it still wouldn't start. She was on the brink of flooding the engine when she turned the key back and gripped the steering wheel, leaning her head against it.

Digging her phone out of her pocket, Poppy contemplated who to call. She would have to have the car towed to a garage, but that wouldn't solve her issue of how to get to work. Poppy's thumb hovered over Nova's name. Then she remembered it was Nova's day off, and she was going down to Green Bay for a shopping day with her sister. Poppy sighed and hit Della's contact information.

"What's up, honey?" Della answered on the first ring. Poppy quickly learned that *everyone* was "honey" to Della.

"My car won't start," Poppy sighed as she stared out the windshield, already estimating enormous figures for the repairs. "I'll start walking, but I just wanted to let you know I'll probably be a few minutes late."

"Nonsense," Della scoffed. "I'll come get you, honey. You wait right there, and I'll be there in five minutes."

"Are you sure?" Poppy asked. "It's not a big deal. I can walk. I know you have to get the diner open."

"I'm positive. Len is already in the kitchen. He can get the coffee going until we get back."

"Thanks, Della."

"Not to worry, honey."

～

"Thank you again for coming to pick me up," Poppy thanked Della as they pulled into the back parking lot of the diner.

"Honey, no need to keep thanking me," Della patted Poppy on the knee. "That's what friends are for. Any time you need anything, and I mean anything, you let me know, you hear?"

"I will," Poppy grinned reluctantly. "I promise."

"That's what I like to hear. You're a good girl, Poppy, and a great employee. You need to realize that you have a whole restaurant full of people who love and care about you."

"It's just so unusual to me," Poppy said thoughtfully, "how quickly everyone has taken me in and befriended me. I'm not used to that."

"Well, then, you've been living in all the wrong places and knowing all the wrong people," Della said as if that explained everything.

"Maybe you're right," Poppy mumbled as they got out of the car and headed into the diner.

Alfred, Everett, and Father Edgar were the first people in the door that morning, which wasn't unusual. But this morning, they gathered around Poppy, peppering her with endless questions.

"Are you all right?" Father Edgar asked first.

"I didn't mean to startle you," Alfred said, looking chagrined. "I hope you can forgive me."

"With the mug on that one, no wonder you were scared," Everett added. "Was it the Bengay? I always tell Alfred he smells like an old coot when he puts that crud on. Like a right old serial killer sneaking up on people and knocking them out with the stench alone."

"I'm all right," Poppy assured them as she poured each of them a mug of coffee. "I just received an unexpected phone call, that's all. I didn't mean to scare you, Alfred."

"Is everything all right?"

"Fine," she said vaguely.

The doorbell jingled and Colton Sterling stepped inside. Poppy felt his gaze on her back as she turned away, fiddling with the coffee carafes and straightening the sugar packets on the back counter. Since that first day, Colton had been coming in like clockwork. He'd sit in Poppy's section, trying to drag a conversation out of her. So far, she'd managed to keep the conversations to mundane things, like his order and the weather, but Poppy doubted Colton would give up that easily.

"Morning," Poppy forced a bright tone as she carried the carafe of regular coffee and a mug over to his table and poured him a cup. "Do you want a menu, or do you know what you want?"

"I thought it was your day off," Colton said as he raised the mug to his lips and took a long, slow sip. There was something about the way his bright blue eyes stared at her over the rim of the mug that made her heart thud angrily against her ribcage.

Poppy forced the feeling down. "Oh? Why did you think that?"

"I didn't see your car outside." Colton sets the mug down, giving Poppy every ounce of attention. She shrunk back, feeling like she was under a microscope.

She raised an eyebrow, pulling on a false sense of confidence and sarcasm like a security blanket. "Oh, and you know which car is mine?"

"Gray Chevy Malibu," Colton rattled off. "You always park it on French Street, just down the street from the diner."

"That's kind of unsettling that you know that?"

Colton guffaws. "Just being observant."

"If that's what they're calling it these days," Poppy said as she looked away, looking out the front window. The gray, overcast sky made it look like late afternoon instead of early morning. "My car wouldn't start."

"I could take a look at it," Colton offered. "I'm a mechanic. I work at a garage on the other side of town."

"I don't see your motorcycle here today either," Poppy said instead of answering him.

"It looked like rain," Colton said, unbothered by her diversion. "I'll get it out a time or two before the season ends, just not today. Maybe you'll let me give you a ride someday."

Poppy's eyebrows rose into her hairline at the double meaning behind Colton's suggestion.

"I meant on the motorcycle," Colton laughed. At ease and smiling; the gruff, dangerous exterior melted off of him. Mostly. He still looked as though he could knock someone on their ass without breaking a sweat.

"I k-know," Poppy stammered as she glanced down at her order pad. Unconsciously, she reached up to tuck a stray hair behind her ear before noticing none had wiggled free from her ponytail.

"I don't bite, you know?" Colton continued. Poppy looked up at him and he cocked his head. "You always look like you're afraid of me. I want you to know there's no reason to be."

Poppy shrugs, "I'm not afraid. I'm... *off* men for a while."

"I see," Colton said dryly, as if the idea were preposterous. "Well, I guess I'll have the Fireman's Special with scrambled eggs."

Poppy jotted down the order. The Fireman's Special: four eggs, any way you want them, bacon, sausage, ham, toast, pancakes, and a bowl of fruit to cut down on the cholesterol overload. Not that it was worded *precisely* that way on the menu.

"I'll get that in right away," Poppy said as she shoved the pad into her apron and turned away.

"I hope you know that whoever it is that put you off men," Colton said slowly, his tone low and dangerous. "He'll get what he deserves sooner or later."

A shiver walks up Poppy's spine as she keeps walking towards the counter.

Poppy was exhausted when she got home from work. She'd turned down Della's offer of a ride home after her shift because the diner had been busier than usual all morning. There hadn't been an open booth or table all shift. Della and Poppy had been running around for hours with barely enough time to come up for air. Even Trixie, usually full of boundless energy, had taken one look at the packed dining room and looked intimidated.

The walk wasn't as bad as Poppy initially thought. It was only about twenty minutes from the diner to the bottom of her driveway. She leaned against the mailbox as she reached in to retrieve her mail and let herself cool down. Her legs felt leaden as she trudged up the driveway, wishing it wasn't so long and steep. It had been a critical error on the original owner's part. Not that they had cars when the original house was built, but no matter.

Poppy was pleased to see that James's workers had been to the house that morning. Parts of the porch overhang had been ripped away, and parts of the roofing had been removed and thrown into a large dumpster on the lawn. Next would come the joists, and then the floorboards and foundation would be ripped away to make room for the new porch.

The floorboards still creaked and groaned as she stepped onto the porch, but she knew it was stable enough to hold her for the time being. Shoving the key into the lock, Poppy unlocked the door and turned the knob, but nothing happened. She turned the knob harder, throwing her weight against the door. It wouldn't budge.

It hadn't rained and wasn't humid, yet somehow, the door had warped. Poppy frowned and walked around the side of the house to the back door that came in through the kitchen. Once upon a time, this was the delivery man's door where groceries were delivered. Milkman's stairs rose alongside the door, now obsolete and leading to nothing.

Poppy unlocked the back door, but that door won't open either. "Shit," she groaned, touching her forehead to the smooth wood. She pulled her phone out of her pocket and called James.

"Peters Construction," James answered on the third ring.

"James," Poppy said, thankful she reached him. "It's Poppy Isles. I have a quick question. Did any of your guys have any issues with the front door when they were here this morning? I just got home from work and can't seem to get the front or back door to open. It's almost as if they're warped from moisture."

"No," James drew the word out. "As far as I know, my guys

haven't even gone in the house yet. I told them to get started on the porch first, and later in the week, we'll move inside and start looking at the furnace and water heater. You're sure it's not something with the lock?"

"No, the knob turns, so I can tell the mechanism has unlocked, but the door won't physically open."

James sighed. "I can have my guys look at it tomorrow. Can you get into the house a different way?"

"I can go through the window that is boarded up," Poppy suggests.

"That's not ideal," James said, "but I don't have another suggestion at this point. I don't want you to have to break another window. Once you get inside, see if you can open the door from the inside, and then let me know."

"I will," Poppy said, then hung up.

Back at the front of the house, Poppy tried tugging at the plywood, testing how secure it was to the wall. The nails didn't budge.

After a quick trip to the garage, Poppy retrieved a hammer to pry the nails away. It was a slow, tedious job. James's men really secured the wood to the wall, which worked fine to keep the elements out, but didn't help Poppy in her attempts to get into the house.

She yanked the nails out one by one until she could pull the plywood back enough to slip inside. One leg at a time, she stepped in. As she pushed inside, something sharp scraped against the back of her right arm. Poppy bit down on her lip to keep from crying out, as she threw herself inside the house. She landed on the floor with a thud, and when she twisted around to see what grasped onto her like a groping hand, she saw a jagged piece of broken window dripping crimson onto the windowsill.

Poppy stood, turning her arm over to examine the wound. A long, narrow cut, maybe a quarter of an inch deep and half an inch wide, ran down the length of her right forearm. Keeping her arm elevated, she crossed to the bathroom and washed the cut with antibacterial soap. She hissed. The pain was sharper than she anticipated. Patting the wound dry with a clean towel, Poppy rummaged around in a box of unpacked bathroom supplies for gauze or a bandage. All she could find was a roll of white sports tape that she couldn't remember buying. She wrapped it around her forearm, but blood immediately began to soak through. She needed stitches.

Remembering that she saw a clinic on her walk home from work, Poppy headed back into the entryway. Taking a couple of measured, determined breaths, Poppy stalked toward the door, insistent that, one way or another, she'd get that door unjammed.

Poppy turned the knob and yanked on the door viciously. The door swung open easily, like the hinges were recently worked over with WD-40. Poppy groaned and stomped out onto the porch. She shut the door behind her, then tested it again to see if she could enter from the outside, and once again, the door opened without any resistance.

"Bastard," Poppy muttered as she spun and started down the porch steps.

CHAPTER FIVE

POPPY

Poppy made it to the clinic in exactly eight minutes. The windows of the small family clinic were dark. She checked her watch and frowned when she noticed it was barely past 4:30 PM. Stepping closer to the door, she read the hours on the door. *Monday - Friday, 8:00 AM to 4:00 PM. Saturdays, 9:00 AM to 12:00 PM.*

"Damnit." Poppy groaned as she leaned her exertion-warmed face against the cool glass of the door. "Now, what am I going to do?" Poppy could feel blood soaking through the sports wrap, droplets running down her arm to collect at her elbow. She forced back a wave of nausea and swore.

She couldn't call for an ambulance because of a simple cut, and she was sure the nearest hospital was in Marinette. The slightly larger city where she bought the mattress. Without her car, and with night creeping in on the horizon, Poppy didn't want to chance walking that far. She had only one option; to stitch up her arm herself. She hoped she had the stomach for it.

Poppy's arm throbbed intensely as she walked back to the house. She glared at the door again as the lock clicked and the door swung inward invitingly.

Gathering her tablet from the living room and the box of bathroom supplies, Poppy went to the kitchen and looked up how to stitch a wound. She knew she'd have to sterilize the needle in boiling water. For once, she was grateful for the small sewing kit her grandmother gifted her on her thirteenth birthday; which she never had the heart to throw out. Filling a pot with water, she set it on to boil and peeled the sports wrap off her arm. She nearly gagged at the dark blood soaking through the material as she threw it into the garbage. As she waited for the water to boil, she ran to the bathroom to wash the cut.

Back in the kitchen, she bit her lip, contemplating whether the instructions meant a full, rolling boil or just the beginning of the boil. Better to be safe than sorry, she decided and waited for the angry, churning boil to cast giant bubbles bursting in the pot.

First, Poppy sterilized a set of metal tongs that she'd need to dunk the needle and thread in and out of the pot. It took more than a half hour to sterilize the needle, thread, and tongs. All the while the cut on her arm continued to bleed. Poppy second-guessed her decision not to walk to the hospital more times than she'd care to admit.

Finally, the needle was ready. She scooped it out with the tongs and threaded the needle with the sopping thread, thankful that it threaded easily.

"You can do this," Poppy told herself, trying to psych herself up. "It's just like home economics from middle school. It'll be easy, like riding a bike; you don't forget a skill like that." Poppy's stomach roiled, and she had to close her eyes until the nausea passed. "This is ridiculous," she scolded herself. "You're just making it worse. Grow the fuck up and get started."

After a few centering breaths, Poppy opened her eyes and forced the needle through her skin. The pain was absolute. She had to grit her teeth to keep from screaming. "This is nothing," Poppy told herself as she forced herself to keep going; to pull the thread all the way through until she reached the knot at the end. "Remember the time Jack threw you through the glass coffee table, and you cut up your face? That was way worse than this. Or how about the time he threw you on the floor and stomped on your arm until your wrist snapped? Boy, you screamed that time."

She kept going, drawing her mind away with memories of the injuries Jack gave her in the years they were together. It bruised her spirit and threatened to rip away all the confidence she'd gained since leaving Jack, but soon enough, she reached the end of the cut.

The crooked, winding row of black stitches from the back of her wrist to the crook of her arm made her look like Sally from A Nightmare Before Christmas or Frankenstein's monster's Irish cousin. As Poppy wrapped her arm in fresh sports wrap, she couldn't believe she had done it and hadn't passed out along the way. Others would have - normal people.

Poppy felt strangely detached now. Arm sore and mind blank, she cleaned up the kitchen, plugged her phone into the charger, and plodded upstairs. She fell into bed, and subsequently, a dreamless sleep.

"What happened to your arm, honey?" Della asked as Poppy tugged off her sweatshirt and hung it on the hook in Della's office. Poppy considered wearing long sleeves, but she got so warm during her shift that she opted for her usual short-sleeved t-shirt.

Poppy looked down at the sports wrap covering her arm, thankful that the stitches seemed to be holding and there wasn't any more blood seeping through the wrap. "I had a little bit of an incident with my door last night and had to go through the window to get into the house," Poppy said, pretending it was no big deal. "I cut myself a little."

"A little?" Della echoed dubiously, staring at the wrap. "Did you have a doctor look at it, at least?"

Poppy shrugged, "The clinic was already closed by the time I walked back to it, and I didn't want to call an ambulance over a silly cut, so I stitched it up myself at home."

"Excuse me," Della recoiled, "I thought I just heard you say you stitched up your arm at home. But I know that can't be what I heard because that's just crazy."

Poppy winced. "I didn't really have any other option since my car isn't running yet."

"Didn't have any other option!" Della cried, drawing the curious stares of Alfred, Everett, and Father Edgar, who looked up from the newspaper they huddled over. Poppy stared at her with wide eyes. She didn't want to cause a scene. Sensing Poppy's distress, Della lowered her voice, sounding hurt. "Didn't have any other option? Honey, you know you can always call me, no matter what. I would have driven you to the hospital and waited with you. Even if you didn't want to call me, you could have called Nova, Trixie, or one of the boys," Della gestured to the men sitting at the counter, pretending not to listen "Anyone of us would have dropped everything to help."

"I'm sorry," Poppy hung her head, feeling like a small child being scolded. Another reminder that she was just as stupid as Jack always told her she was. And here she thought she was so brave for doing the stitches all on her own.

"Don't be sorry," Della's voice softened as she reached out and touched Poppy's shoulder. "I'm not mad at you, honey. It's just, sometimes I swear you never had anyone to look out for you in your entire life, and that makes me really sad for you."

Poppy wasn't sure what to say to that. She could still hear Jack's voice echoing in her ears, repeating the word "stupid" over and over again.

"Alright," Della finally sighed, "go on, wait on your tables."

"Thanks," Poppy murmured as she scooted past Della and walked along the counter, tying her apron on as she went.

She slipped her order pad into her apron pocket as the bell over the door jingled. Just as she looked up, Colton entered the diner. His face lit up as he looked at her. That's just what she needed — more trouble. Falling into his new habit, Colton ignored Nova's section and sat in the booth closest to the door in Poppy's section.

"Morning, Colton." Poppy greeted him weakly as she pulled the pad from her apron. "What can I get you?"

"Are you ever going to start calling me Fox?" Colton teased as he leaned back in the booth, stretching his arms across the top. "Everyone else does."

Poppy shrugged. "I've never been one for nicknames."

Concern creased his rugged face. "Hey, you okay, Poppy?" His gaze washed over Poppy, making her fidget under his scrutiny, then cringe when his stare landed on her bandaged arm. "What happened to your arm?"

"I cut myself," she said curtly. "It's no big deal. Can I take your order, or do you need more time?"

"Nope." Colton shook his head, forcing Poppy's attention to his face. "You don't get to change the subject like that. Now maybe you don't consider us friends yet, but that doesn't mean I'm not going to be concerned when I see a huge ass wrapping covering your entire arm. Are you all right? Did you see a doctor?"

"Not you, too," Poppy sighed. "Look, I've already had this argument with Della, and I'm not interested in getting into it again. I took care of it, and I'm fine. If it will get everyone off my back, I'll go to the doctor and get it checked out as soon as I can get my car in to be fixed."

"And when will that be?" Colton fixed her with a determined stare.

"I don't know. Soon, hopefully."

"Never mind." Colton shook his head, aggravated. "I'll come over and fix it myself this afternoon."

"That's ridiculous," Poppy scoffed. "You don't even know what's wrong with it."

Colton cocked an eyebrow, challenging her. "And you do?"

"No," Poppy admitted. "But seriously, you probably don't even have the parts to fix whatever's wrong with it."

"You don't know that, It could be a simple fix."

"And if it's not?"

"Then I'll check the shop, and if we don't have the part in stock, I'll order it, then bring it over and fix the car once it comes in," Colton said as if it should be obvious. "In the meantime, I'll give you a ride to and from work."

"No."

"Yes." Colton's tone was firm. "It's that, or I make sure Della does. And you're going to the doctor to make sure your arm is okay."

"You're not the boss of me." As soon as the words left her mouth, she mentally kicked herself. *You're not the boss of me. What am I? Four years old?*

Colton laughed, but the sound was bitter. "It's me or Della, Poppy. Make up your mind."

"Fine," Poppy growled. "But you're only giving me a ride until my car is fixed, so hopefully, it's an easy fix."

CHAPTER SIX

POPPY

"See, I told you I would get you on my motorcycle one of these days," Colton teased as he pulled up in front of the diner on a shiny, dark red Harley Davidson motorcycle at the end of Poppy's shift.

"I'm not getting on that thing," Poppy crossed her arms over her chest as she looked at the beastly machine. The engine idled noisily, taunting her.

"Come on. There's nothing more freeing than riding on a motorcycle."

Poppy shivered. "Until we crash and the hospital is picking pieces of gravel out of my skin and treating me for road burns and broken bones."

"That's just a horror story parents tell their kids to keep them from having any fun as teenagers, then turn into hypocrites when they buy one when they go through their midlife crisis phase around age fifty." Colton rolled his eyes. "Besides, we're not going that far, and I won't drive that fast. I promise, Poppy. You're always safe with me."

"I don't know," Poppy hesitated, inspecting the motorcycle cautiously.

"All right, if you're really that scared to try it, I'll go home and swap out for my truck and come back for you," Colton said.

"No," Poppy blurted. Colton glanced over at her, surprised. "No, it's okay. I'll get on."

"You sure?"

Poppy nodded, "I'm sure. Do you have a helmet?"

Colton retrieved a black helmet from his saddlebag and then got back on the bike. "Put your right foot on the peg and just swing your leg over. You can grab my shoulder for balance if you need to."

"Okay," Poppy pursed her lips as she followed his directions. Stepping onto the back foot peg and grabbing Colton's shoulder in a white-knuckle grip, she swung her left leg over, foot grasping for the foot peg on the other side. Once she found it, she stood strad- dling the bike, hands gripping Colton's shoulders like a trick rider on a horse.

"You okay?" Colton asked as Poppy sat behind him, wiggling into a comfortable position on the seat.

"So far, so good," Poppy replied with a paper-thin confidence.

Colton nodded. "Good,"

"Don't you need a helmet too?"

Colton shook his head and glanced over his shoulder at her. "I don't usually wear one since Wisconsin doesn't have a law requiring them. Where am I headed?"

"Oh, right." Poppy exhaled, breathing in the sharp scent of sandalwood and cinnamon as she leaned closer to Colton to be heard over the engine. "I'm the last house on the left at the end of North Splake Court."

"Gotcha," Colton nodded. "Now you can either lean back against the backrest or hold onto me, whatever you're more comfortable with. Just remember to lean how I lean when I make turns."

"Okay," Poppy agreed, the apprehension creeping back in.

Poppy was startled slightly as Colton shifted gears with his foot, and they pulled away from the curb onto French Street. She was grateful the roar of the engine muffled the surprised squeak she made as she leaned forward, holding on to Colton's side.

Heading across town, Colton yells something to her over his shoulder, but his words were lost beneath the noise of the engine and the rushing wind, so all she could do is nod as if she understood. Whatever he asked, Colton took her nod for agreement. He nodded back at her and picked up speed, though not enough to break the speed limit.

Poppy quickly learned to look off to the side over Colton's shoulder as the wind tore bits of her hair from her ponytail and slapped her in the face. They crossed the bridge over the Peshtigo River, and Poppy watched the river flow lazily by as the sound of the water rushing over the dam beneath the bridge thundered in her ears.

At the last second, Poppy remembered to lean into the first turn when Colton leaned, just past the bridge toward her house. Her grip tightened on his sides as she squeezed her eyes shut, hoping not to fall off. She kept her eyes closed until she felt Colton complete the turn, surprised that it wasn't as scary as she had anticipated. Colton was right. Riding on a motorcycle is the closest thing to freedom Poppy had felt in years.

When they reached her driveway a few minutes later, Poppy was almost sad the ride was over.

Colton pulled up the drive and parked the bike behind Poppy's car, kicking down the kickstand as he turned off the engine. He got off the bike first as Poppy reached up to unclip the helmet and hand it back to Colton, who set it on his seat before reaching out his hand to help her off the bike.

Colton's gaze was open and curious. "So what did you think?"

Poppy masked the smile she felt creeping onto her face as she felt her cheeks, flushed a glowing pink from the wind, hair wildly tangled about her face. "It was okay."

Colton snorted, giving her a once-over. His stare saw right through her. "Just okay, huh?"

Poppy allowed her smile to escape as she unsuccessfully tried to finger-comb some of her hair back. "So you got me on your motorcycle and drove me home, but don't you need some sort of tools to figure out what's wrong with my car?"

"I've got them right here." He patted the other saddlebag storage cubicle and unlatched it, pulling out a condensed toolbox. "Pop the hood for me, and I'll get to work."

Poppy unlocked her car and popped the hood, then stood back and watched him get to work, tinkering around and tugging on things she wouldn't even be able to begin to name.

"The problem's not just going to jump out at me right away," Colton's laugh echoes from under the hood. "You can go inside if there's something you need to get done. I'll let you know when I figure something out."

Poppy shifted her weight from one foot to the other awkwardly. "Are you sure?"

"Yeah," Colton poked his head out from the hood, nodding. "There's a breeze kicking up; there's no sense in staying standing out here in the cold."

"Okay," Poppy said. "Just come on in whenever you're ready."

"Will do," Colton replied, disappearing under the hood. The strong line of his back bending over, his back muscles and spine pronounced through the fabric of his black Henley.

Poppy jogged up the front porch stairs. She noticed that James's crew had started to remove some of the joists from around the porch and there was a brand new, unblemished window where the plywood had been this morning. It wasn't until she saw a torn piece of paper from a yellow legal pad that Poppy remembered in all the chaos and bloodshed the night before, she never called James back.

> *Poppy,*
> *You never called back last night, and I wanted to make sure everything was all right. I expedited the window installation so you wouldn't have to worry about air leaking in as it gets cooler. My guys also checked out the front and back doors. They couldn't see any signs of water damage or warping, but we'll keep an eye on it. Give me a call right away if you have any more problems.*
> *- James*

Poppy pulled her phone out as she unlocked the door, relieved as it opened easily today. She pulled up James's number and cradled the phone between her shoulder and her ear as she stepped into the entryway. She put her keys on the table by the door before wandering to the kitchen.

"Poppy, finally," James sounded relieved as he answered the call.

"Hey," Poppy said sheepishly, "I'm sorry I didn't call back last night. I encountered a bit of an emergency after I climbed through the window that I had to take care of and forgot all about calling you back."

"Are you all right?" James asked, concern etching his tone. "My guys saw some blood on the window, and my dad said you were all bandaged up when he saw you at the diner this morning."

"It's just a little cut," Poppy lied. "Don't worry, I've had my tetanus shot."

"That's the last thing I was concerned about," James sighed. "But don't worry. We removed the rest of the shards of glass when we installed the new window. We also got the other windows delivered to us for the first floor. We'll have to wait for the ones on the second floor until we have the porch completely removed, but they came in with the rest of the order, and I have them stored with our supplies."

"That sounds good," Poppy nodded even though James couldn't see her. "I really appreciate how quickly you're moving on everything."

"All part of the job," James said gruffly. "I want as many of the major issues taken care of before winter sets in. The winds can get brutal off the river there, and the snow tends to drift pretty deep. And don't even get me started on the ice shoves. I'll be coming in to look at your furnace and water heater personally tomorrow while my guys get the rest of the porch demoed."

"Great! It's still like a sweatbox in here, especially at night. And the water when I shower still fluctuates so rapidly. I was going to get started removing some of the wallpaper in the bathroom this afternoon."

"Have at it," James told her. "We'll get the heating issue figured out, don't you worry."

"Thanks, James," Poppy said as she hung up.

Rolling up her sleeves, Poppy headed into the first-floor bathroom with her scraper tool and a spray bottle of water and set to work.

It felt like barely any time had passed, but Poppy noticed the light from the doorway dimming as the sky darkened through the windows on the west side of the house. Frowning, Poppy dropped the scraping tool into a bucket and washed her hands before stepping out into the hallway, bracing one arm against the doorway as she squinted into the quickening dark.

Padding back toward the front of the house, Poppy could make out thick, angry storm clouds moving in as lightning flickered in the distance. Picking up the pace, Poppy stepped onto the porch as a clap of thunder rattled her bones.

"Hey!" Poppy shouted to be heard over the gathering storm.

"Looks like a storm's coming in. You better come inside, or you're going to get soaked."

"Be right there." Colton slammed the hood of Poppy's car and jogged over to his motorcycle.

"Crap," Poppy muttered. She shot a quick look up at the sky.

Colton kicks back the kickstand and pushes on the handlebars. Poppy rushes to help him. "You can put it in the garage," Poppy nodded ahead of them to the path leading alongside the house. "It will stay dry there." Poppy ran ahead and shoved the garage door open. They got the motorcycle pulled inside just as the first fat drops of rain began to hit the ground.

Once they secured the garage door, Colton yelled, "On the count of three, we run for the house. "

"Okay."

"One! Two!" He grabbed Poppy's hand and tugged her along."Three!"

They crossed the short distance between the garage and the house in less than a minute, but they were already soaked through; chests heaving as Poppy threw open the door, and they stumbled inside.

"I'll get us some towels," Poppy laughed breathlessly as she kicked her shoes off under the table in the entryway. Colton stayed there waiting as Poppy dashed to the bathroom and came back with two big, fluffy towels.

"Thanks," Colton said as she handed him the towel.

"Of course." Poppy towel dries her hair and then wraps the towel around her shoulders. "It looks like we might be stuck in here for a while."

"Why don't you let me make you dinner." Colton offered. Seeing Poppy's expression, he held his hands up, "just as a thank you for letting me wait out the storm."

"You can cook?" Poppy found herself teasing him, then instantly regretted it.

"I'm a grown man who lives alone; of course, I can cook," Colton said as he followed Poppy to the kitchen.

"Yet you come to the diner every morning for breakfast or, if not breakfast, every afternoon for lunch," Poppy pointed out as she flicked the light on in the kitchen. She pulled out one of the counter barstools she salvaged from the local thrift shop a few days before.

"That's more for the company than for actual necessity," Colton admitted as he rolled his sleeves up and washed his oil-stained hands in the pale pink kitchen sink. Gesturing to the matching pink refrigerator, Colton asked, "May I?"

"Of course," Poppy nodded, watching him as she slid onto the stool and rested her chin on her laced hands, elbows perched on the counter.

Colton surveyed the offerings in Poppy's refrigerator. She managed to pick up the staples: bread, milk, juice, lemonade, cheese, fresh fruit and vegetables, some ground Italian sausage, turkey, and beef, as well as some other meat she had placed in the freezer. Her pantry was half stocked with dry goods, baking supplies, and a bottle of Wisconsin-made and bottled rum that she first tried as a mixer at a bar on Clark Street, back home in Chicago.

Colton retrieved some bowtie noodles and a jar of pasta sauce from the pantry, whose door stood slightly ajar next to the basement stairs, before pulling the package of Italian sausage, a bag of baby spinach, a package of mushrooms, and some parmesan cheese out of the refrigerator.

"Italian okay?" Colton asked, turning back to Poppy.

"Sure." She watched as he added some dried garlic, Italian seasoning, and red pepper flakes to his growing pile of ingredients.

Colton began opening cabinets. "Pots and pans?"

"The two between the refrigerator and the stove."

Colton pulled out a big stock pot and a cheap skillet Poppy had also found at the thrift store. As he filled the pot with water for the pasta, the storm rolled in earnestly. Thunder boomed and lightning flashed through blackening clouds. Over it all, the wind ripped through the trees on the property line, nearly doubling the pruned bushes in the backyard in half. The wind was so loud it rivaled the thunder, and Poppy shivered. The wind sounded like the terrified screams of women and the anguished groans of men.

Colton winced, shooting a nervous glance out the back window toward the winding sliver of the river peeking through the trees. When he caught Poppy staring, his expression went blank. He turned on the lights and lit the gas stove before placing the heavy stock pot on the burner. Pulling the cutting board on the counter towards himself and setting it down on the counter where Poppy sat, he ripped open the package of mushrooms and started cutting them into slices.

"What do you know about Peshtigo's history?" Colton asked hesitantly, his gaze focused on the mushrooms. "And about this property's history?"

"What? Is this ghost story time just because it's raining? Well, it won't work. I don't believe in ghosts," Poppy laughed as she leaned back on the barstool, crossing her arms over her chest. Colton looked up at her sharply at the mention of ghosts, and Poppy's grin slowly faded. "James Peters, my contractor, told me this house had been abandoned for years and that kids used to dare themselves to come inside. Kids are kids, always attracted to old houses that fall into disrepair. They tell themselves and their friends all kinds of fantastical stories about horrific things that happen inside. Usually, they're not true."

This wasn't the first "neighborhood ghost house" Poppy had worked on restoring. It was just the first one she had actually lived in.

"They call Peshtigo the city that rose from the ashes," Colton told her as he picked up the cutting board and dumped the mushrooms into the skillet with a drizzle of olive oil. "You're from Chicago, aren't you?"

Poppy nodded, watching Colton stir the mushrooms as they

sautéed. She realized he couldn't see her nodding, so she replied, "Yes."

"Well, on the same night as the Chicago fire, October 8, 1871, the whole city of Peshtigo burned to the ground - all of it - houses, businesses, churches, trees - everything. Not just the town, but some of the surrounding counties and up into Northern Michigan. 1.2 million acres of land burned, and an estimated twenty-five hundred people died. People in town ran for that river out there, thinking it would save them. Not that it did any good."

Poppy shivered, drawing her zip-up sweatshirt closer around herself. "That's awful, but what does that have to do with this house? Obviously, if the whole town burned, this house was built after 1871."

"It was." Colton nodded as he removed the mushrooms from the skillet and placed them in a bowl. He put the Italian sausage in the same skillet and broke it up with his spoon, only pausing long enough to dump the box of bowtie noodles into the now boiling stock pot of water. "This house was built in 1872, a mere six months after the fire, on the property of what had been the most expensive house in town, owned by wealthy businessman Zachariah Sorenson."

"And?"

"And they never found Zachariah or his family after the fire," Colton shrugged, his back turned towards Poppy. Outside, the wind's screams increased in volume as a loud crash of thunder rattled the house. "True, they didn't find a lot of people after the fire. Most of the remains they did find were charred beyond recognition. There's a mass grave in town, down by the fire museum, for that reason. People even say they see the spirits of those who burned, wandering through town, their flesh burned, hair singed away, unaware that they're dead. But according to one written witness account from a survivor, someone saw a man staring up at the Sorenson house that night. Just watching it burn."

"Shit." Poppy jumped at another roar of thunder, sounding as if the storm was situated right above the house. "Fine, you got me. Good story."

"I didn't say I was done." Colton finally turned around as he spooned the browned sausage into the same bowl as the mushrooms and wiped the grease from the skillet.

"Oh?" Poppy questioned as Colton dumped the sausage back into the skillet with the seasonings and garlic, mixing it all together before reaching for the pasta sauce and spinach.

"As I said, this house was rebuilt in 1872. And in the one-hundred-and-fifty-odd years since, this house has caught fire three times. Never enough to bring it fully to the ground, of course, but people have a way of talking in small towns, as I'm sure you know by now. They said the house was cursed. Nobody in town would step foot in it for years and years. Buyers came from out of town, promising to fix it up. And they did, and they'd live in it for a time. But some tragedy or another would always befall them eventually. One hundred years after this house was first built and one hundred and one years to the date of the Peshtigo Fire in 1972, the last owner died, and after that, no one wanted to come near it. Except for stupid kids playing tricks on their friends. The house has sat vacant ever since."

Poppy suddenly felt like someone had walked across her grave. "What happened to the last owner? The one in 1972?"

The sauce boiled away on the stovetop, and Colton attended to it diligently. Finally, he shrugged, "he had lung cancer, I think. A neighbor found him sitting in a chair on the front porch, and he was all skin and bones. Not a lot of people had seen him in the months leading up to his death, but they figured he was busy getting treatments. But the way I heard it, the way that urban legends always go, passed down by word-of-mouth year after year until all the rough edges are buffed away and the story is more myth than fact, an autopsy was done on that last owner. And when they opened him up, his lungs were filled with smoke, and his throat was scorched."

"You're making that up," Poppy accused, leaning forward over the counter, unconsciously gripping the edges with white knuckles.

"I'm not." Colton shook his head as he strained the pasta and added it and the mushrooms to the skillet. "But as I said, it's probably nothing more than an urban legend, a scary story told at sleepovers to this day."

Poppy groaned as she slid off the stool and rounded the counter. "I think I need a drink."

"Dinner is ready, anyway." Colton stirred the pasta again, then turned off the burner.

Poppy reached around him, standing on her tiptoes to reach two Sicilian-printed bowls she'd bought at a fancy cookware store back in Chicago. She had salvaged them when she'd fled the city. Colton saw her struggling and grabbed the bowls, placing them on the counter in front of her.

"Thanks," she muttered as she reached for two tall glasses on the lower shelf.

Colton dished up the pasta, using the remaining spinach and mushrooms to make a small salad, which he placed in bowls. Poppy grabbed a tray of ice from the freezer, the lemonade from the refrigerator, and the rum from the pantry and made herself a drink.

"Numbskul, huh?" Colton watched as she made her drink. "I didn't know that had made it into Illinois yet."

"You a fan?" Poppy asked, offering him the bottle.

"Drink of choice for anyone who loves to create a little mischief," Colton teased, lightening the mood. Just like that, all the tension in the air vanished. They were just two people riding out a storm, about to sit down to a meal together again. "I've only had it as a shot, though."

"Try it with the lemonade," Poppy gestured to the bottle on the counter. "You don't even taste the alcohol. It's also delicious as a Numbskul and lemonade slushy."

"I trust you," he said as he made himself a drink. He set his drink and their dinner out on the counter. Colton and Poppy sat down on the barstools, legs pressed against each other, elbow to elbow, as they took their first bites. It was nice. Calming.

Until the lights went out.

CHAPTER SEVEN

The storm outside seemed to be ramping up. Or maybe it was Poppy's nerves. The vestiges of Colton's story came back to her. She felt like a noodle was wedged in her throat, and her breath turned ragged and labored. The kitchen was plunged into a certain darkness, periodically cut by the lightning and its negative white light. Poppy felt panic seizing her, phantom hands closing in on her throat.

Suddenly, there was a thin column of white light. Colton turned on the flashlight of his smartphone and laid it flat on the counter. The beam shined up to the ceiling, encasing them in a tiny dome of light in the otherwise dark room.

"Do you have any candles?" Colton asked. "Or a camping lantern or anything?"

"Candles, no," Poppy shook her head. "Not with the construction going on in the house. But there should be a small lantern in the living room in a box by the couch."

"I'll go get it. Will you be okay here for a minute?"

"I think so," Poppy said, although she wasn't sure. She felt ten years old again, afraid of the dark. She gulped her mixer, trying not to think about it as Colton took his phone and walked through the dining room and into the living room to get the lantern. Poppy heard his footsteps echoing across the hardwood floors, both a comfort and a nightmare in the dark.

"Got it," Colton said, bringing the lantern into the kitchen and pulling the top up to light it. He placed it on the kitchen counter by where they ate. "Are you okay?"

"I'm fine," Poppy said tartly and resumed eating.

Colton watched her in the sepia-tinted light, then turned back to his dinner. They ate in mostly silence as the wind howled

After dinner, they piled the dishes into the sink and took their drinks and the lantern into the living room. Colton sat on the couch, and Poppy took up the opposite end, curling one leg underneath her. She sat sideways on the sofa, facing Colton. Their shadows cast eerie, distorted silhouettes against the wall in the lantern light.

"Did you ever figure out what was wrong with my car?" Poppy asked finally, holding her drink in both hands. "Before the storm, I mean."

"Yeah, the starter took a shit." Colton turned to face her. "It's not a huge problem, but I'll have to get a new one from the shop. You could use an oil change, too, by the way."

"Okay. Will it take long to fix?"

"No," Colton shook his head. "I can get what I need from the shop in the morning and fix it tomorrow. Are you working tomorrow?"

"No, it's my day off. The contractor and some of his guys will be here tomorrow working on a few different projects, and I'll probably be working on getting rid of more of the wallpaper."

"Okay." Colton nodded, rubbing his beard. "What time should I come over? Is nine too early?"

Poppy laughed. "I'll probably be up earlier than that, but nine is fine."

"Sounds like a plan." Looking around the room, he asked,

"What are you planning to do furniture-wise for the house? Are you going to fill it up with fragile antiques no one can use or sit on? Or will you go more for a comfortable, usable feel?"

Poppy glanced around, too, picturing the room finished and furnished. "I want the house to be a home, not a museum piece. Throw a big rag rug on the floor in the middle of the room, get a couple of oversized chairs that invite people to sink into them with a blanket and a book, and eventually a television over the fireplace, some end tables or decorative trucks, and some bookcases probably."

"I can see that in here." Colton nodded as if he were seeing the vision of the finished product directly from Poppy's mind.

"It will be a process, getting the house fully furnished," Poppy explained. "There were a few pieces of furniture left behind by the last owner, but not much. I've been picking up a few pieces here and there from the thrift store in town and saving to do a bigger shopping for some bigger items. I'm starting over from scratch right now. Other than some tools, a few pieces of kitchenware, my clothes, and a few other things, I didn't have much when I moved here, and what I did have fit into the trunk and backseat of my car."

"That's rough. What brought you to Peshtigo? Why did you have to leave everything behind?"

Poppy looked away, watching the rain streaking down the south-facing windows like tear tracks down a cheek. "I just needed a fresh start, that's all."

Colton didn't say anything for a few long moments, waiting for Poppy to say more, but when she didn't, he didn't press her, and for that, Poppy was thankful.

They sat in silence for a spell, sipping their mixers and listening to the storm as it slowly trickled off, moving to the east. Colton waited a little longer, giving the roads time to dry before he tried to ride his motorcycle home.

Poppy yawned and discreetly checked the time on her watch as she covered her mouth to swallow the sound. It was already nearing ten o'clock.

"I should let you get to bed." Colton picked up on Poppy's unspoken cue as he set his glass down on top of a closed box next to the couch and stood to stretch.

"I'll walk you out," Poppy stood, rubbing her leg from where she sat with it curled under her for so long. She zipped up her sweatshirt and followed Colton onto the porch, flicking the light on as they stepped outside.

Tree branches were thrown everywhere as if a giant child threw a tantrum and scattered them across the yard like broken toys. The dumpster James's crew has been using had the cover thrown back. Poppy hurried over, wanting to put the lid back into place in case the rain started back up. Colton rushed over to help her, and together, they replaced the lid. Colton grabbed a stick from the yard and shoved it through the opening in the lid and the metal hook the garbage company uses to hook the dumpster up to the truck, creating a makeshift latch.

"Hopefully, that holds until morning," Colton said, wiping his hands on his jeans as he followed Poppy to the garage.

"Thanks," Poppy tilts her head toward the dumpster. "For helping, and well, for everything tonight. I appreciate it."

"Anytime." Colton grinned as they lifted the garage door. He walks his motorcycle out before climbing on.

"Are you going to be okay getting home?" Poppy asked, turning to squint at the road at the end of her driveway.

"I'll be fine." Colton put his helmet on - the helmet he told her he never wore. "It's not ideal, but I've ridden after storms like this before."

"If you're sure," Poppy drifted off. "I guess I'll see you in the morning."

"See you then."

Poppy watched as Colton eased the motorcycle down the driveway and disappeared down the road.

Poppy went inside, locked the door, and used the lantern to guide the way upstairs to her bedroom. Upstairs, she set the lantern on the side table next to her bed and undressed for bed. Slipping between the crisp sheets, she stared at the ceiling, rubbing the edge of her blankets between her thumb and index finger as she tried to clear her mind. She almost wished it were still raining. She loved letting the comforting sound of rain lull her to sleep.

Poppy was on the bridge that connected French Street to Front Street. The visage before her, behind her, and all around her was flickering orange and black with flame. Blood-curdling screams filled the air along with pained groans as flame-encrusted figures streaked by, comets in the night. Some slumped to their knees and died where they fell. Some threw themselves into the river and were extinguished. She rushed to the side of the bridge, peering over the railing. Hundreds of figures bobbed in the river, boiling alive.

She ran from the bridge, her lungs burning. It felt like it was a thousand degrees out as her skin bubbled and pricked, peeling from her bones as she ran between the river and the tree line. Something inside her told her she had to get to the house.

A woman knocked smack into her from the side, knocking her off-kilter a few feet, but the woman didn't stop; she just kept running for the river, screaming for her baby. Poppy cut through the trees, ash from the burning pines landing on her shoulders, scorching through the fabric of her nightgown.

There, maybe five hundred feet up ahead, was the house, already engulfed in flames. She skidded to a stop at the property line. She saw someone standing in the yard. At first, she felt relieved; perhaps he had made it out safely. And then the figure, cloaked in darkness, turned his head and looked right at her. She screamed.

CHAPTER EIGHT

POPPY

Poppy hadn't been able to get back to sleep. She'd tossed and turned, sweating through her sheets, so much so, that she got up and checked her temperature; just to make sure she didn't have a fever.

At four in the morning, she threw back her sheets, giving up on counting sheep, deep breathing, and visualizing the relaxing flow of a waterfall. She stood at her window, staring at the vacant lots north of the house. Leaning her forehead against the cool glass, Poppy peered out into the dark. Perhaps a quarter mile away, she could see lights flickering, and she squinted, trying to figure out what lay in that direction. A small park, maybe? That would explain the lights in the middle of the night. She never paid any attention during the day. Whatever was out there was on a different street entirely, separated from Poppy's street by an empty field that had yet to be developed.

She closed her eyes and took measured breaths, still feeling the blanket of unease from her nightmare. When she opened her eyes again, the lights in the distance had been extinguished altogether.

"Must be on a timer," Poppy mumbled as she turned from the window and rubbed her eyes.

Stretching, she crossed the room, peeling off her sweat-slicked nightshirt and panties, letting them fall discarded to the floor as she wandered naked to the bathroom. Poppy was relieved to see the electricity came back on during the night. She pulled the shower curtain back, turned the water on cool and wiggled her fingers beneath the faucet. Sighing at the glorious, cool relief, Poppy climbed into the tub, pulled the curtain closed, and turned on the shower head.

Poppy lathered and rinsed her hair, then poured a generous dollop of body wash onto her loofah and scrubbed the salty, sticky sweat from her skin. She stood beneath the spray, letting the water comfort and cool her until it turned to ice.

Dressed in a clean pair of jeans and a t-shirt, Poppy went downstairs and washed the dishes from the night before; leaving them to dry on the wooden rack on the counter. She pulled an energy drink from the refrigerator and sat down at the counter with her notebook full of plans for the house. James and his crew would arrive by eight to get started on the furnace and hot water heater, while the others finished hauling off the back of the porch. Poppy suspected she'd have to clear the storm debris from the yard first.

And then there was Colton, who promised he'd be over at nine to work on the starter. Poppy hoped it was a quick fix. The sooner he fixed it, the sooner he would be out of her hair.

She refused to admit that she had enjoyed his company last night; watching him methodically prepare dinner for her, taking care of her after the lights went out, making sure she was okay. Even if it was his fault that she was uneasy to begin with. First with his proximity, and then with his ghost story.

Pushing thoughts of Colton away, Poppy meticulously went

over her accounts again. Estimating how long it would take for her to save up and buy smaller pieces of furniture so that the house didn't look so empty, while still paying the utilities and buying food. She checked and rechecked James's timeline for the renovation, hoping the coming winter wouldn't stall them. She knew that part of James's company was working on the hospital expansion in the next town over, and soon, with that complete, there would be more men and women coming in and out of the house.

Poppy opted for a rustic kitchen look, far removed from the house's original style, with barn board floors and rich brown cabinets, stained to give a marbled effect. A huge farmhouse sink, marble countertops, a black glass-top stove, a massive French-door refrigerator, and glass fronted-upper cabinets. She wanted a wood-fired oven on one wall and a bigger island that would leave room for an informal dinner table and chairs by the window overlooking the new front porch. She'd picked out all the materials with James earlier that week and knew it would be beautiful when finished.

She'd taken that rustic look from the kitchen to the upstairs bathroom. The spacious shower stall would have a rustic, sauna-like look with a river-rock floor, one shower head on each end and a frosted glass door. The tile floor would be heated, and there would be a narrow row of built-in cubbies for towels and other storage next to the shower. The cabinets beneath the sink would have the same barn board aesthetic as the kitchen; a big bowl sink would rest on the granite countertop, and a row of Edison bulbs would hang overhead.

Poppy and James had gone back and forth on the merits of turning the full bath on the first floor into a half-bath, but in the end, James had convinced her that if she had the space, she might as well use it. The main floor bathroom would take an entirely different approach. Bright white cabinets, a huge soaking tub, light blue woodwork, and tile that would lend a nautical feel to the room. The rest she would make up for in decor. Poppy took the samples and brochures that she and James had gone over and sketched it all out in her sketchpad. Like a director creating storyboards for an upcoming shoot, sketching out the rooms always kept Poppy grounded in the renovation.

She was so lost in her work that she hadn't noticed that the morning sunlight drove away the eerie dark until she heard the sound of tires in the driveway, truck doors opening, and workers splitting off to prepare for their assigned tasks. Poppy yawned, feeling the effects of the few hours of sleep she'd had before the nightmare. She checked the time on her watch and was shocked to see it was just past seven.

The crew couldn't start until eight to avoid disturbing her neighbors, but they always arrived an hour early to unpack their supplies and draw up the plan for the day. Once the outside crew finished demolishing the old porch, they'd begin work on the new foundation for the new one. Inside the house, James and a smaller team would spend most of the morning in the basement; checking on the plumbing and heating, checking parts, and considering the best replacement so James could get the order in.

Poppy set aside her sketchbook and her ledgers. Slipping on a sweatshirt as she went and braved the morning, she took in a deep whiff of fresh, crisp morning air. She waved to James, who was talking to his crew as they shared thermoses of coffee and several boxes of treats from the bakery in town.

The yard was even more of a mess in the daylight.

The lawn was spongy, and her feet sunk into the soft ground with every step she took. Holes and divots that weren't there the day before covered the yard. There were branches scattered every-where, and the leaves Poppy raked into a neat pile were now all over the yard again, so soaking wet she feared there would be no moving them. Some of the ornamental shrubs in the backyard had ripped from the dirt, dangling a half foot from the ground; held back only by their stringy roots.

With no other choice, Poppy sighed, rolled up her sleeves, and gathered her gardening and yard tools from the garage.

Poppy felt the icy tendrils of the cold ground reaching through the heavy denim of her jeans chilling her to the bone. Her jeans were soaked from kneeling in the yard, trying to gather the sopping wet leaves into oversized black garbage bags. Soon she realized shoveling them up would be an easier solution. Her lower back ached from bending over, and her face was red and chapped from the wind. She had filled three bags already, and pursuing the wet leaves seemed like a losing battle.

She leaned on her shovel, hands covered in thick yellow work gloves, crossed at the wrist, and propped her chin up. She stared at the yard, miserable and wondering why she ever wanted a house with such a sizable yard in the first place. She weighed the merits of giving up and going into the house to make a fresh pot of coffee when the hair on the back of her neck rose. Her skin prickled as she sensed someone standing behind her.

She turned, startled by the sudden appearance of Colton, shifting his weight and holding two small to-go cups of coffee.

"Figured you might need a pick me up." Colton offered her one cup as he surveyed the yard. "Fuck. It looks like a damn tornado blew through back here."

"Or something," Poppy agreed as she accepted the cup and took a long drink, scalding her tongue on the hot liquid. "Thanks for the coffee."

"Don't mention it." Colton shrugs as he drinks from his cup.

Poppy turned to face the driveway. "I didn't hear the bike."

"I thought the truck was a better option." Colton smiles wryly. "Plus, I needed more space for the parts."

"That makes sense." Poppy mentally kicked herself. She hated that she could be so dense; or that she allowed herself to make stupid comments before thinking them through. *Jack would have -* Poppy stopped herself right there, reminding herself that it wasn't a healthy path of thinking.

"Do you want some help before I get started on the car?" Colton asked, squinting at all the work to be done in the yard.

"No," Poppy said abruptly. Colton looked startled by her tone. Lowering her voice and softening her tone, she said, "No, it's fine. Really. You do your thing, and I'll do mine."

Colton frowned. "All right." After one last sip of his coffee, he headed to the front of the house, discarding the empty cup in the dumpster by the garage.

Poppy pushed up the sleeves of her sweatshirt and got back to work.

Poppy looked up and saw Colton's boots sticking out from the undercarriage of her car. He had pushed it up by the garage and out of the way of the construction crew. Through the cacophony of sounds - guys working, talking, birds and other animals around the yard - Poppy hadn't noticed that she was hyper-focused on the clanging of tools as Colton worked on the starter. Occasionally, she heard a muffled grunt as Colton swore to himself.

She smiled a little and turned back after hauling the last bag of leaves to the upper part of the yard. Next, she set to removing the branches scattered in the yard and clearing up the shrubs all but ripped from the earth. She'd have to plant new ones come spring, but had winter to decide what she wanted to plant and where.

She went to work on a particularly stubborn shrub on the southwestern corner of the property, whose roots had grown thick and branched out in an unusual manner. The more she tugged, the more resistance the shrub seemed to give, even though it was split down the middle and scorched by lightning. She was lucky the whole yard didn't start on fire and spread to the house, but she supposed the rain took care of that. Grabbing the pruning shears, Poppy aggressively cut away at the roots, tossing the broken bits aside. She had almost one section cleared when her shears hit something solid. Reaching down, Poppy ran her fingers along the ground where she'd created a line between root and lawn. Her fingers caught on something sharp and metallic.

"Ouch," Poppy mumbled, pulling her fingers back and seeing that the tips had all been scored from a metal cut. "Shit."

Poppy kneeled again, her knees protesting. The yard had dried out some, free of its soaking wet, leafy blanket, but it didn't lessen the cold. She grabbed what she could of the base of the shrub and yanked as hard as she could muster, tearing it entirely to one side. Poppy sat back, confused at the sight that greeted her.

Beneath the shrub, as if it were planted in a thin layer of dirt above, was a square metal cover. It was nearly as big as the space the shrub occupied, roughly four feet by four feet.

The metal was rusted and pocked from age and the elements. Poppy carefully ran her fingers along the edges of the thin piece, trying to pull it from the earth. It was stuck firmly to the ground and wouldn't budge. The raw edge sliced at Poppy's fingers through her gloves and the little fingernail nubs she'd been able to grow bent backward and snapped off.

Giving up, Poppy pulled off the ruined gloves and wiped her bloodied, broken fingertips on her jeans and pushed to her feet. She crossed the yard, passing Colton taking a smoke break against his truck, scrolling through something on his phone.

Colton glanced up sharply, catching sight of her dirty, bloodied fingers and disheveled appearance. "What's wrong?"

Poppy ignored him, slipping into the garage and digging through her toolbox until she found a flat pry bar and walked back into the yard. Crossing back to the hatch, Poppy wedged the sharp edge of the pry bar into the gap where she'd initially cut her fingers and kicked it in until she was sure it was secure. Slamming the sole of her shoe down on the other end of the tool, she used all her weight to force the pry bar to unearth the hatch.

Poppy could feel Colton watching her curiously from across the yard, but he made no move to come closer. Finally, the hatch gave way with an audible *pop* as it swung upward with a metallic screech. It took her a minute to realize what she was looking at.

The rainwater from the storm had leaked into the cracks around the hatch, filling what was unmistakably the remnant shaft of an old well, now mostly filled with water. And there, bobbing up and down, no more than a foot below ground level, was a skull.

A tiny human skull.

CHAPTER NINE

POPPY

Poppy's scream cut through the morning like a blade across the throat: sharp, cleaving, irreversible. She heard footsteps thundering across the yard, a vibration felt from the ground up, but all she could focus on was the skull as she stumbled back a few steps.

"Poppy!" Colton called for her. Paralyzed, she didn't notice that he was standing beside her, shaking her shoulder to get her attention. The outdoor crew stood a few feet away, and she could feel their fear and apprehension.

James pushed through his workers, coming up beside Colton and Poppy. "What? What is it?"

Poppy shook her head, nausea blazing a path up her throat like lava. Colton saw it, too, and then James, who blanched and stepped back. She and Colton stare at the skull in macabre silence; unable to look away.

Finally, Colton cleared his throat. "We have to call the police, Poppy."

"Why?" Her tone bordered on hysterical as she forced another hot wave of nausea down. "What good can they do? That hatch was sealed, Colton. The roots have been growing over it for decades, maybe even over a century. Whoever that was, whatever happened to them, it happened so long ago the police won't be able to do anything about it anymore."

"They have resources," Colton reasoned. "They can call in people to figure out how long the skull has been in there, to find the rest of the remains."

"The rest?" Poppy echoed, her voice going shrill. Her eyes widened as she collapsed backward, sitting firmly on the grass, legs bent at the knee. Poppy stuck her head between her knees, hyperventilating. *Of course, the rest,* she realized numbly. *You don't just find a head without an arm, leg, and rib bones not far behind.*

"You got her?" Poppy heard James ask as Colton crouched beside her. James's voice sounded like it was filtering in from the distance, or trying to be heard underwater.

"Yeah." She heard Colton reply as he tugged her gently toward him. She buried her face in his shoulder as he rubbed the back of her head like he was comforting a small child instead of a grown woman.

Poppy noticed what came next in bits and pieces. James sent his crew home for the day, none of whom protested too much as they ambled toward their vehicles. He called the Peshtigo Police Department, who were on the scene in minutes. Poppy recognized the red-bearded Officer Michelson and another officer, who must have been the Chief of Police. They spoke in hushed tones with several other officers, peering into the well with their hands on their hips as if they were unsure exactly what to do.

Poppy found it comical and stifled a giggle as Colton and James looked at her with concern. She sobers, realizing she's in shock, and bites down hard on her tongue. The pain grounded her.

Two officers - a short-haired African American woman and a pale man with a shaved head, large ears, and small eyes who reminded her of Wallace from Wallace and Gromit - moved the trio to the side of the house. They promised to take their statements shortly as the Chief radioed dispatch, requesting the Sheriff's Department, and a forensic team.

Before long, the yard was swarming with deputies and forensic investigators; taking photographs, collecting the metal hatch, and other things Poppy couldn't see from over the officer's shoulders. The entire road at the bottom of her driveway was clogged with law enforcement vehicles. Down the road, she could see a deputy setting barriers to cordon off her end of the street.

Finally, a deputy wandered over to where Poppy waited. A tall, lanky guy with dark hair and what he believed was a charming, disarming smile. He pulls a small notepad out of his pocket and looks at Poppy first.

"Miss Isles, is it?" He asked, squinting at his notes.

Poppy nodded. The deputy looked up from his notes. "Yes."

"Okay, Miss Isles, do you mind stepping over here so I can get your statement?"

Poppy shrugged. "Sure."

"Are you sure you're okay?" Colton asked her quietly, rubbing a pattern into her shoulder to soothe her.

"I'm fine." By now, the shock had worn away, and she felt numb. She followed the deputy a few feet away as he flipped to a new page in his notepad.

"Tell me, Miss Isles, were you aware there was a well on this property when you bought it?" The deputy began.

Poppy shook her head, "No, it didn't show up on the survey or the title documents or anything."

"And you happened upon it by accident today?"

Poppy narrowed her eyes, speaking as clearly and concisely as possible. "There was quite a bit of yard debris from last night's storm. I've been working in the yard all morning. There was a huge shrub on top of where the well apparently was, and it had split down the middle after being hit by lightning. I was trying to cut the roots away to dispose of the bush. I couldn't have known there was a metal hatch concealing an old well underneath it."

"Of course not, miss." The deputy glanced up from his notepad. "That wasn't what I was suggesting."

"What *were* you suggesting?" Poppy asked, finally gathering confidence from somewhere. She hoped she sounded believable, even though she could feel her heart hammering.

The deputy's eyes twitched as he began mentally backpedaling. After several false starts, the deputy tucked away his notepad and said, "I think that's all I'll need for now, miss."

Poppy watched him silently, appraising him. She could see her stare get under his skin as he fidgeted, scratching the back of his neck and glancing over his shoulder at the sheriff and the forensic crew. People had always commented about Poppy's eyes, even before she started wearing colored contacts to conceal her identity. How she seemed to look right through someone. It was yet another thing that sent Jack into a rage, his fists flying as he tried to conceal his fear of her, of what she might find out.

"What happens now?" Poppy asked. "This isn't a recent death, obviously."

"The forensic team has sealed off the area and will have to come back with some specialized infrared equipment to make sure there aren't any other human remains buried in the yard." The deputy explained.

"Can they tell how old the remains from the well are?"

"That's not my area of expertise," the deputy said, suddenly adopting an 'aw shucks' tone as he scratched his neck again. "It's hard to say. That's for the forensic team to determine."

"Will we need to stop work on the house?"

"You shouldn't need to." He shook his head. "The house should be fine; just the yard area will be taped off."

"All right." Poppy nodded, frowning that she wouldn't have the yard cleared up anytime soon.

"If you have any questions, here is my card with the case number for your reference." The deputy reached into his vest pocket and retrieved his business card before scribbling an eight-digit case number at the bottom and handing it to her. Poppy glanced at the name - Deputy Jared Mulligan - before sticking the card in her pocket.

Once the deputy was finished speaking with her, Poppy went into the house and watched the forensic team scuttle around as the deputies secured police tape around a large portion of the back-yard. Outside the living room window, Deputy Mulligan spoke with Colton, who gestured around the yard. A lit cigarette hung loosely between the middle and index finger of his right hand, dropping ash onto the ground.

Poppy noticed a thick silver ring on his middle finger. It shone dully in the muted light breaking through the clouds, and Poppy could faintly see a design etched into the metal. It was odd to notice, especially now, but she suddenly couldn't look away from his hands. She wondered if they were work-roughened and how they'd feel on her bare skin.

Poppy shivered and averted her eyes, chastising herself for such thoughts, especially after human remains were just unearthed in her yard. She shivered again, unease unfurling in her stomach as she wondered what other secrets were waiting to be disinterred.

Turning away from the window, Poppy walked toward the kitchen to make a pot of coffee. As she passed by the staircase, she heard a faint thud upstairs, as if something had fallen off a shelf. She paused, cocking her head to the side; debating whether to go upstairs and look.

The scent of coffee brewing comforted Poppy as she pulled a

mug out of the clean dish rack and leaned against the counter, closing her eyes and meditating on the fragrant brew. She threw her eyes open as she heard the front door open and then close again. Booted footsteps came clomping through the house. She held her breath in anticipation until Colton appeared in the doorway, followed closely by James.

"Sit down, Poppy," Colton insisted, pulling out one of the bar stools on the island. "I'll get the coffee."

"And you know how I like it now?" Poppy cocked an eyebrow as she set her mug on the counter where the last dregs of coffee were sputtering into the carafe.

Colton's eyes darkened at Poppy's unfortunate turn of phrase. "Just sit down, woman; you've had a shock."

"I don't do well with being told what to do." *Not anymore, never again.*

"For fuck's sake, I'll get the coffee," James growled, glancing between them with barely concealed frustration. He pushed past Poppy and slid her mug, along with two more he found in the cabinet above the coffeemaker, next to the machine. As he yanked the carafe away, a few droplets of hot coffee hit the burner, hissing and steaming. He poured the coffee into the mugs, his wrist flicking as effortlessly as a bartender serving drinks. Spinning on his heels, he went digging around in the pantry before returning triumphantly with a bottle of Bailey's Irish Cream, which he poured generously into each mug. James passed out the coffees before rounding the island and settling onto a barstool.

Poppy sighed, taking a deep sip of the spiked coffee before settling next to James. "I'm sorry you had to send your guys home early because of my mess." Poppy couldn't help but think that this description could encompass a significant portion of her life.

James shrugged. "Can't be helped. The weather's been shit anyway, all muddy and damp. We'll be able to pick up again tomorrow."

"I just about had the starter finished in the car before everything happened." Colton leaned against the island, sipping from his mug. "But it's no rush." Poppy thought of riding alone with Colton in his truck and swallowed hard.

"How long do you think the remains have been there?" James asked, staring out the back window at the swath of dark evergreens. The sky had already started to darken again, threatening another fall thunderstorm.

"Hard to say." Colton absentmindedly scratched at a bee sting on his elbow. "This house has been abandoned for years. It could have been there fifty years or even one hundred."

"It could have been leftover from the fire all those years ago." Poppy's pupils dilate as she thinks of what could have caused, what was obviously a child, to end up in a well so long ago. Her stomach sours. She pushed the coffee away as a headache began to throb in her temple.

"Might be." James nodded, oblivious to Poppy's discomfort. "So much of the area was nothing but charred ruins. It would have been easy to overlook a well that collapsed in the destruction and confusion that followed."

Poppy thought of all those frightened people running from their burning homes, then imagined a small child, cut off from their parents in the middle of it all. Her heart breaks.

James and Colton changed the subject to the local fall festival and her attention drifted. She stared out the window, gaze unfocused, when a dark figure darted past the back door in a blur. Poppy yelped and skittered back onto her barstool.

"What's wrong?" Colton asked; concern etching his face as he and James approached.

"There is someone outside the window," Poppy raised a shaky finger toward the window.

"Where?" James leaned toward her to get a better view. He turned toward her, narrowing his eyes. "I don't see anyone. Are you sure there was someone there?"

Colton crossed the kitchen in two strides, threw the door open, and looked around the backyard. He stepped back, shut the door, and shook his head. He turned to face Poppy and James. "I don't see anyone in the backyard."

"I'm telling you, there was someone there," Poppy insisted. "A man, I think. I'm not sure. I saw a dark figure tall enough to be a human adult pass by the window."

"And you couldn't make out any of their features?" James asked.

"I'm not making this up!" Poppy yelled as she rubbed her fists over her eyes and fisted her hair.

"Hey." Colton puts his hands out in a soothing gesture. "No one is saying you are. It was probably a member of the sheriff's department or the forensic team doubling back to get something. You could have seen a flash of one of their dark coats or something."

"Yeah, Colton's probably right," James nodded quickly, adopting the same tone, "There's no reason to get all worked up about it."

Poppy shook her head, gazing down at the counter. She was in no mood for placating or gaslighting right now. "I think I just want to be alone right now."

"Alright, we'll head out," James patted the countertop and shot a look at Colton.

Colton ignored it, his gaze solely on Poppy. "Are you sure you'll be all right?"

Poppy smirked. "I've been fine on my own this far. What makes you think I won't be now?"

Colton stared at her a beat longer, his frustration a palpable thing sucking all the air from the room. Finally, he nodded and followed James out, but not before saying, "Call me if you need company. No matter what time."

"I'll be fine," Poppy frowned as she got up and gathered the empty mugs from the counter, busying herself by placing them in the sink and clearing things up. She didn't turn around until she heard the front door snick shut. Then she slunk down into a crouch against the cabinet, covering her face with her hands as all the adrenaline flowed out of her, and she began to cry from sensory overload and the stress of the day.

CHAPTER TEN

COLTON

Colton needed to blow off some steam. He'd never met a woman as frustrating, or closed off as Poppy Isles. It seemed whenever she let someone see a crack in the door, she slammed it again, going on total lockdown to keep anyone from so much as being her friend. He tried. Everyone had tried. Della and the girls at the diner, the three old coots that sat up at the counter morning after morning, the guys from Burning Blood he'd occasionally met for breakfast, and James, the contractor. She had warmed up to him more than the others, though, while mutually oohing and ahhing over bathroom tiles and kitchen cabinets. It seemed any time Poppy warmed up to someone, even in the slightest, a shadow passed over her, and she'd crawl back into herself again, becoming glacial, disinterested.

Colton watched Poppy fall apart when the tiny skull was unearthed from the well. It was the most open and untethered he'd seen her. But the minute he'd tried to comfort her, she'd shut him out again.

He wasn't going to chase after her forever. He'd seen interest in her eyes the first day at the diner, and yes, he'd been curious about her, too. There was longing in her eyes. He saw it as he watched her with the customers, a longing for connection. Still, she held herself away from others despite it. He wanted to be the one to unravel her, make her smile, laugh, run his fingers through her hair, and just be near her. But there was a fear in Poppy greater than her need for connection. So he'd give her space.

It was almost seven, and Colton threw his toolbox in the back-seat of his truck, in case the moody storm clouds decided to give way. He needed to get to the clubhouse. The Burning Blood Riders Motorcycle Club met once a week in Della and Len Just's old garage. Vlad had called a vote for accepting a new probationary member into the Burning Blood Riders.

The breezy morning slipped into a humid afternoon. Colton shucked off his leather jacket and rolled up the sleeves of his flannel shirt before climbing behind the wheel. He cast one last glance at the house on the hill before pulling down the driveway and towards town.

When he arrived, a few of the older members were outside the garage; they converted it into the MC's clubhouse after Len built a new garage and workshop behind the house ten years ago. The older members were smoking, waiting to help Della carry in the giant vat of chili she prepared for every fall and winter meeting. It was a welcome meal after the bite in the air that morning, but the evening was growing oddly warmer. They greeted Colton with a nod, murmuring his club name as he passed and pulled open the side door to the garage.

Vlad and Hunter "Igor" Lewis were standing around the bar at the back end of the clubhouse; Igor, as usual, was trying to jockey for more influence. Gomez "Spike" Romero, Lazarus, and the current probationary member, Corbin Edwards, were congregating around the pool table in front of the no-longer-in-use garage doors, talking shit. After nodding to Vlad; Colton strode over to join them.

"What's the word?" Colton asked as he slapped Spike and Lazarus on the back. Corbin lined up a shot and scratched instead.

"No wonder you don't have a girlfriend, Probie," Spike teased, "you couldn't find the hole if it had a flashing neon arrow pointing the way.

"That ain't what your mom said last night," Corbin retorts without looking up.

"That the best you got?" Lazarus snorted. "What are you, twelve?"

Corbin shook his head and moved away from the table.

"Hey, I heard over the scanner about the remains being found at your girl's house, Fox." Lazarus clapped him on the shoulder. "Is that why she moved up here? To hide bodies?"

"She's not my girl." Colton glowered as he tugged at his beard, studying the game in progress. "There's no thawing that girl out, no matter what I do."

"Ah, the old man's losing his touch," Spike teased again. "Maybe I should give her a try. She may prefer a little lovin' south of the border."

Colton bit back a reply and went over to grab a beer from the bar.

"Fox," Vlad said, as he handed over a bottle from a local micro-brewery.

"We waiting on Wolf yet?" Colton asked, referring to Freddy Collins as he cracked the cap off the beer.

"Yeah," Vlad nodded, surveying the room. "He got off work at seven, so he should be here soon."

Freddy "Wolf" Collins and his wife had relocated from Boulder when he got a job at the local shipbuilder, Marinette Marine. He fit in like he'd been with the club for a decade instead of just two years. "Where's the new prospect?" Colton asked.

Vlad handed Igor a few bottles to set on the table for the meeting. "I told him to come at 8:30 after we have some time to discuss things."

Vlad brought the gavel down to start the meeting. "This meeting is called to order." Lazarus sat to Vlad's right and Colton to his left, with Igor, Spike, and Wolf filling the rest of the active seats. Igor, as club secretary, sat taking minutes. Once everyone quieted, Vlad continued. "We are here to discuss the possibility of a new prospect joining the club and finalize details for the club's involvement in the Peshtigo Fall Festival."

Igor had placed a folder in front of each seat before the meeting and a bucket of ice filled with bottles of local microbrew in the center of the table. Colton reached for the folder and flipped it open as Vlad reviewed the request from the prospective member.

"The potential prospect's name is Damien Dogoode. He just moved here from Indiana and is looking to patch over from our sister chapter there. He'd been a member with them for five years." Vlad read the information off the cover sheet.

"In good standing?" Lazarus asked. "Were there any issues? Did he get along with the other members?"

"He paid his dues on time." Vlad pursed his lips. "I've got a call in for the president of that chapter, but I haven't gotten a call back yet."

"What else do we know about this guy?" Colton asked, parsing the sparse information on the single sheet. "What is his temperament like? Was he involved in any specific events that they held?"

"This is all I have on him," Vlad lifted the folder. "That is why I wanted to discuss things before meeting with him. I met with him briefly the day before yesterday, and he seems like he'd fit in. A bit quiet, but he's interested in the charitable work we've been doing with our chapter."

Spike asked the only question that really mattered to him. "What does he ride?"

Vlad smirked. "He rode up on a Heritage Classic,"

The new prospect was a curious man. Colton had trouble pinpointing his age. He could be fifty or twenty-five. It was impossible to tell.

Damien Dogoode was a slim man, maybe five-foot-eight and a buck twenty-five. His dull black hair was neither long nor short, and his skin was sallow; his flesh sunken unto bone like it had been ages since he'd last eaten. He wore a well-loved long-sleeve black shirt and a holey pair of black jeans over black boots that had seen better days. There was something off-putting about the guy, more than his appearance, but Colton couldn't put his finger on what it was.

Colton glanced over at Vlad, giving him a 'what the fuck were you thinking' look. Unsure of why he entertained the idea of letting this guy join the chapter. Vlad had a bland, somewhat bored expression on his face. He clearly wasn't seeing what was so glaringly obvious to Colton.

The other members had the same unconcerned look.

Colton listened as Damien gave a speech about the toy drives he had participated in and the disaster relief they organized after a 3.8 magnitude earthquake leveled half of their town. He had everyone eating out of the palm of his hand; if the nodding and smiles on their faces were any indication. He had to admit, Damien was convincing, but it was overshadowed by the sense of *otherness* that Colton couldn't shake.

"Thank you for your time, Damien," Vlad said once Damien was done. "Could you step outside while we take our vote?"

"No problem," Damien said amiably as he backed out of the clubhouse. His gaze seemed to land on Colton, and he could have sworn he saw Damien smirk in satisfaction. Colton blinked, and Damien was already turning away.

"Alright," Vlad steepled his fingers once Damien left the room. "All those in favor of Damien becoming a probationary member, raise your hand." Everyone in the room raised their hand except for Colton. "And those opposed." Vlad looked at Colton, who reluctantly raised his hand. "What is concerning you?"

"I'm not sure," Colton said carefully. "I can't explain it. There's just something about that guy that doesn't sit right with me. I mean, did you see how he looks?" Colton knew then that he should have kept his mouth shut.

Everyone laughed. Spike banged his fist against the table, unable to control himself. "I didn't know that fashion sense was part of the criteria of who could join and who couldn't."

"So the guy could use a little weight on him," Wolf shrugged. "I'm sure Della can fix that problem quickly."

"Well, the majority has it." Vlad closed the folder before him. "If you don't have any more concrete reason why he should be excluded, we will let him patch over on a probationary basis."

Colton nodded, remaining silent as Damien was invited back into the clubhouse to be welcomed to the club. He stayed in his seat, staring down at the table. Vlad shook Damien's hand and welcomed him, giving him a quick rundown on upcoming meetings and events before ushering him out so they could finish their meeting and finalize the details of the fall festival plans. Colton barely heard what was said the rest of the meeting and bowed out early when Spike and Igor asked him to hang around for another drink.

CHAPTER ELEVEN

POPPY

The small display screen on Poppy's phone read 3:15 AM when she awoke to something crashing and thrashing about on the main floor. She traced the sound, moving from one end of the first floor to the other in a maze-like pursuit. Someone was in the house, clumsily crashing into boxes and building supplies as they wandered through the house in the dark.

Panic clawed its way up Poppy's throat as her pupils dilated and her breath struggled from between her lips. It was Jack. He found her. No, if it were Jack - if he had traced her down, he wouldn't be silently knocking things about downstairs. He'd be on her, hands closing around her throat, screaming at her, calling her names. *Perhaps kids, then?* Colton and James admitted local kids had a history of breaking into this house to prove they were brave enough to spend the night.

The panic was washed away by a new feeling, anger. *Couldn't the kids see that someone was restoring this house? That it was no longer unoccupied?* Poppy shoved the blankets away and tiptoed out of the room in the dark. She didn't dare turn on a light, lest it announced her presence to the intruder in case it was not children fulfilling a dare but a vagabond or a thief.

Avoiding the creaky board just outside her bedroom door, Poppy slowly slipped down the hall to look over the landing. The main floor was lighter than the upstairs, illuminated by the street-lights and moonlight filtering through the windows.

As she peered down and heard the clumsy footfalls again. Poppy darted behind the safety of the wall at the edge of the land-ing, just as a thin, dark figure passed in front of the entryway. The figure was stout, but tall enough to be an adult. It had a slouched posture and its steps were heavy, clumsy, and unsteady.

Poppy clapped her hand over her mouth, her breath amplified in her ears. Down below, the figure paused its pursuit back toward the dining room and looked up toward the landing where Poppy hid. The figure cocked its head to the side, curious, listening. Poppy scrunched her eyes shut, holding her breath as her stomach roiled with dread. She stumbled backward into the wall and lost control of her bladder in fright. Her heartbeat thundered in her ears as she waited, frozen in place, for the sound of footfalls on the stairs. But the sound didn't come. After a beat or two, Poppy heard the clumsy footfalls resume their unsteady path toward the dining room.

A minute passed, then five. Poppy counted the seconds in her head, until finally, the footfalls stopped, and the main floor fell silent.

Poppy dry heaved, then soundlessly stepped over the puddle left on the floor and started for the stairs. She descended them slowly, placing both feet on one step before continuing to the next. At the foot of the stairs, Poppy hesitated before first checking the front doors. Locked, just as Poppy left them after her meltdown in the kitchen.

Poppy moved to the dining room, finding the newly installed windows locked. Swallowing hard and grabbing for the fire extin-guisher James placed in the dining room, Poppy forced one foot in front of the other as she crossed into the kitchen. The kitchen was bereft, save her. Pale moonlight streamed in through the window by the sink, and the warm yellow glow of the streetlight in front of the house washed over Poppy's back.

The trees at the back of the property cloaked the backyard in shadowy darkness. Poppy flicked on the kitchen light, and dark shapes turned into bar stools, objects on the counter, and the refrigerator. Poppy crossed the room and checked the door handle with a shaky hand. Also locked.

Suddenly questioning her sanity, Poppy doubled back through the dining room, flicking more lights on as she went from room to room. She raced around, yanking on every window, but not a single one raised even an inch, each lock holding firm.

Poppy shook her head as tears welled up in her eyes. She tugged at her hair in frustration. "You're losing your mind, girl."

Poppy slunk out of the living room, defeated. She swore she saw someone in the entryway. She couldn't believe she'd imagined the clumsy, thrashing sounds of movement. After turning the lights off, Poppy tiredly dragged herself back upstairs, pausing to grab paper towels, a microfiber cleaning cloth, and wood floor cleaner.

Poppy kneeled, wiping up the mess she'd created. *That* she hadn't imagined. Poppy didn't scare easily, but tonight she saw something that scared her so badly that she pissed herself. She sprayed the cleaner on the floor and scrubbed at the spot with the microfiber cleaning cloth until the floor was dry. Shoving the soiled paper towels into the garbage bin in the bathroom, Poppy shucked off her nightshirt and turned on the shower.

Stepping under the spray, she soaped herself up and tried to wash away the bizarre events of the day: the remains found in her yard, the noise downstairs, and the figure that was there one minute and vanished the next. Poppy was just glad that she didn't call the police. What would they make of the crazy new woman in town, jumping at shadows?

Poppy noticed the suffocating change in the temperature the minute she stepped out of the shower. The humidity made her skin feel sticky and sensual as she dried herself off with a damp towel. Her hair began to frizz as she dried it, applied smoothing gel, and brushed it back. She stepped out of the bathroom naked; her soiled nightshirt balled in her hand with the towel, headed for the laundry hamper. Walking into the brick wall of unbearably hot air, Poppy flicked the hall light on. The light popped and hummed before casting the narrow hall in a buttery glow.

Squinting to look at the small numbers on the thermostat, Poppy mutters to herself, "That can't be right."

The little dial showed the temperature was set to 64 degrees, a standard setting for northeastern Wisconsin at this time of year. Caught between summer and fall, with no need for heat just yet. But the reading showed a temperature of 86 degrees. Impossible. James told her that he and his men had just replaced the coil on the furnace this afternoon. Everything should've worked smoothly. Instead, it felt like the house was preparing to cook her alive.

Then something odd caught Poppy's attention.

A set of narrow red footprints made a path out of her bedroom and down the stairs. *Had they been there before when I got up to investigate the noises downstairs? She* bit her lip as gooseflesh rose on her arms and the back of her neck. She crept slowly toward her bedroom, wishing she had something to protect herself, and shoved the bedroom door open in a flurry and threw the switch on the light, hoping that if anyone was in the room, she would startle them in the process.

But it was Poppy who was surprised.

She screamed as she took in the dripping red letters written in big, messy scrawl across the wall between the two windows on the far side of the room.

You don't belong here.

Embedded into the wall beside the dripping words was the exacto knife Poppy had misplaced over a week ago. Pinned beneath the exacto blade was a lock of Poppy's hair. Poppy gathered her wits; enough to scoop her cell phone off the bedside table before stumbling out of her room and racing down the stairs two at a time. She threw open the locks on the front door and ran barefoot out into the night, frantically stabbing 911 into the keypad on her phone.

The police arrived after what felt like hours and found Poppy standing naked on her front lawn, too shocked to be embarrassed by her state of undress. A female officer wrapped a fleece blanket around her that itched and faintly stank of gasoline. She ushered Poppy to sit in the back of her squad car as her partner called for backup and EMS personnel to check her over.

The night's events spilled out of Poppy in a torrent as she shivered, despite the muggy air. Two more squads arrived on the scene. The officers went into the house with the female officer's partner to make sure the house was clear. EMTs also arrived on the scene and checked Poppy over.

"Your blood pressure is slightly elevated." The male EMT took her vitals. "I believe you are experiencing a significant case of shock. We should get you to the hospital for a more thorough check-up, and they can monitor you overnight and give you some medication to calm down."

"No hospitals," Poppy said, suddenly sobering as she met the EMT's eyes for the first time.

The two EMTs exchanged looks with the female officer. "You'll have to fill out a form saying you're refusing treatment against medical advice." The female EMT informed her gently.

"I'll sign whatever you need," Poppy insisted, "just no hospitals."

The female EMT sighed and went to retrieve the form.

"What happened here?" The male EMT asked, motioning toward the puckered skin from where Poppy had pulled the sloppy stitches from her arm.

"I cut myself on a broken window when the house first started being remodeled," Poppy explained sheepishly. "It looks worse than it was."

The EMT exchanged another look with the female officer. She could practically hear their silent exchange and was sure at least one of them thought she should be put on an emergency mental hold. Jack tried to convince enough people she was crazy back in Chicago. She became far too familiar with that particular look.

"I'll be okay," Poppy insisted. "Really."

"Is there anyone we can call for you?" The female officer's gentle tone almost made Poppy tear up again. The officer looked slightly younger than Poppy. Her smooth, dark brown hair was pulled back in a tight ponytail, and her gray eyes studied her like a concerned mother hen.

Poppy hesitated, took her phone back from the officer, and scrolled through the few contacts until she got to Colton's name. The phone rang once before it went to voicemail. *I guess Colton finally took the hint.* Poppy was confused by the pang of sadness this knowledge brought her. *Isn't this what I wanted? For Colton to leave me be?*

Poppy shook her head. "I can call my boss, I guess." The female officer waited and listened as Poppy called Della, who picked up on the second ring and told Poppy she'd be right over.

After she hung up, Poppy signed the form that the EMTs held out to her. The other officers came out of the house and rejoined her and the female officer as the EMTs cleared the scene. The female officer stepped away from her for a few minutes to confer with her partner. Poppy waits, sitting in the back of the air-conditioned squad car.

"There's no one in the house right now; that's the good thing." The male officer explained as he approached Poppy. "Based on the size of the footprints and what you described to Officer Mullins, it sounds like you were the victim of vandalism caused by either one or a group of teenagers. We'll start a vandalism and trespassing complaint, but I suggest installing a security system soon. In the meantime, we can also do extra patrol of the house. We do not suggest staying here tonight, just to be on the safe side."

"My boss is coming to get me"

The officer nodded. "That's a good idea."

"Is there anything you need out of the house before your friend arrives?" The female officer asked. "Some changes of clothes or personal belongings?"

"Um, yeah," Poppy looked down at herself, clad only in the blanket the officer gave her. "I should get dressed and pack a bag."

"I'll go inside with you." The female officer said kindly. Poppy followed the officer into the house and up to her bedroom. The female officer goes ahead of her to show her that no one is inside before stepping outside to give her privacy.

After changing into jeans and a short-sleeved T-shirt, Poppy threw a few changes of clothes into a small duffle bag, along with her wallet, and a few toiletry items.

Della was waiting outside when Poppy reemerged from the house with Officer Mullins in tow. When Della saw her, she rushed forward and pulled her into a tight embrace.

"Oh, honey," Della cooed, treating Poppy like a small child. "I'm so glad you're all right. You must have been so frightened."

Poppy smiles weakly. "I'm just glad it's over with."

"We'll do some investigating and see if we can track down who is responsible," Officer Mullins assured Poppy, although she didn't hold out much hope. "Here is the case number, my work extension, and my email in case you have any questions."

Poppy took the card, sliding it into her pocket, where it would join Deputy Mulligan's in her wallet. "Thank you."

"Come on, let's get you home." When the officers released her from the scene, Della guided Poppy to her car. "I'll make you an omelet and some coffee, and it will make you feel all better."

"Thank you, Della," Poppy said. "I mean it. You've been so kind."

"Think nothing of it, honey," Della squeezed her shoulder. "Let's get some food in you and then get you some rest."

CHAPTER TWELVE

POPPY

"I tried to tell her to take the day off and get some rest, but she wouldn't hear of it," Poppy heard Della tell Alfred, Everett, and Edgar while refilling their coffees.

Poppy reached into her apron pocket for her ringing cell phone. Seeing that it was James calling, Poppy waved to Della, signaling that she was taking her break before heading back toward the bathrooms for privacy.

Alfred observed as he sipped his coffee. "That girl needs to learn to relax." Everett and Edgar grunt their agreement before the conversation moved on to complaints about the city government.

Poppy appreciated Della taking her in early this morning and her offer to take the day off. Still, she'd rather keep busy than spend all morning wondering who broke into her house. "Hey, James," she murmured, finally answering the phone before it went to voicemail.

"Hey, Poppy," James's voice was warm and comforting, and she was glad she'd found a friend in him. "I got your message, and

I'm so sorry to hear about the new development. How are you doing?"

"I'm a little shaken up," Poppy admitted. "I felt like I was going crazy there for a minute, but once I saw the message on the wall, I knew someone had been in the house."

"I'll personally scrub down the wall and paint over it," James said. "Can we resume work on the house, or do the police want us to stay out for a while?"

Poppy sighed. "It sounds like we can return to work immediately. They suggested installing a security system and said they could do some extra patrols of the house to make sure nobody was messing with things at night. I have a Ring camera on order from Amazon, and it should be delivered tomorrow. I'll just need to get it installed. I can give you the officer I spoke with's telephone number, though, if you want to call and check if it's okay to resume the remodel to be on the safe side."

"Sure, I can do that." Poppy retrieved the officer's card from her wallet in her apron pocket and rattled the number off to him. Then he asked. "Are you going to be staying at Della's yet, then?"

"Just for tonight and maybe tomorrow. I don't want whoever broke in to think they've won and driven me out of the house."

"That's understandable," James said. "It seems we've had a dramatic change in the weather with today's warm-up and sunshine, so my guys will finish the porch this morning. My heating guy is coming in to see what's going on with that furnace early this afternoon. Since the element didn't do the trick, we might have to replace the unit completely. Then this afternoon, while I'm fixing the wall in your bedroom, my guys will be moving into the house to tear up the kitchen, so it's probably better if you stay elsewhere for a couple of days, anyway."

"Sounds like we're really getting into the thick of things." Poppy smiled, relieved that the conversation had turned to the progress on the house. She could see the bits and pieces coming together in her head.

"I'm going to try to get you down to just the cosmetic work by the end of October so that by the first major snowfall, you'll be able to sit back and relax for the holidays."

"That sounds amazing! I can't wait to see the old place all decorated for Halloween and then Christmas, maybe a big tree in the living room window."

"Have I told you I'm happy you're breathing new life into the old place?"

"No, but I appreciate you saying so." Poppy laughed. "I have to get back to work. Call me if anything comes up."

"Will do." Poppy hung up and tucked her phone back into her apron before she headed back into the dining room.

"Look at this forecast. Have you ever seen anything like it this time of year?" Alfred pointed to the small television mounted to one corner of the wall as Poppy returned behind the counter.

She picked up the order for her table by the window where Della and Len's son Michael sat. He was going over accounts for the bar he owned down the street. Poppy glanced up to where Alfred was pointing and saw temperatures rising into the mid-80s for the upcoming week, a stark contrast to the cozy 60s Poppy had been enjoying since she arrived in town.

"Farmers can't catch a break," Everett said as Poppy whisked the breakfast platter to Michael. "First a dry, hot summer, and now this."

"Thanks," Michael smiled at Poppy as she set the platter of eggs, pancakes, bacon, sausage, toast, and ham in front of him. He nodded over at Alfred, Everett, and Edgar. "Those three are quite the group. They've been coming in here every day for as long as I can remember."

"They are entertaining." Poppy laughed. "But they're great guys."

"They are," Michael agreed. His gaze settled on her, his bright green eyes cautious but open as he studied her frankly. "You're friends with Fox, aren't you? Colton, I mean."

Poppy forces out a breath. "I'm not sure I'd go that far, but we're friendly enough."

"He's good people," Michael told her as his tone turned serious. "I think you'll find in small towns like these that people go out of their way to help their friends and neighbors and do it without an ulterior motive. They're just trying to be your friends if you'll let them."

"That's not as easy as it sounds." Poppy raised an eyebrow. "I don't trust very easily, anymore."

"And I'm sure you have a good reason for it." Michael nodded. "I'm just asking you to try. Ma and Pop, the girls that work here, Colton, they'll all be your biggest champions if you let them."

Poppy nodded and got back to work. He was the second person to tell her she needed to stop being so guarded. If only the memories that kept Poppy up at night would abate enough to allow it. But, if she could form a bond with James, maybe she could make room for others around her as well.

She moved on to Shirl and her gaggle of older ladies, bringing them their usual breakfast. As Poppy approached, she saw the other old ladies leaning in as Shirl told some story. Her glasses perched on top of her permed gray hair, her hazel eyes twinkling with mischief.

Shirl whisper-shouted something as Poppy approached the table, and the woman in the green sweater gasps next to Shirl. "She's sleeping with him! In the house Tom built for them? Their vacation home in Door County?"

Shirl nodded, wiggling in her chair; pleased to have the freshest bit of gossip.

"How dare she?" The woman in the green sweater continued. "You know she's been trying to keep him a secret. I wouldn't have even known it, but I saw them at the market the other day, and she flushed red when she saw me because she knew she'd been caught."

As the woman gesticulated, her arm swiped out. Her elbow

knocked into her glass of water, tipping it over and soaking the table. The water ran off the table and onto the woman and her unpleasant looking friend across from her.

The woman in the green sweater gasped, hopping up from the table. "Oh, my!" She began gathering all the napkins on the table and blotting at the wet spots.

"I've got it," Poppy told her as she set their meals on the vacant table beside them and grabbed a rag from behind the counter.

"Nova, can you grab a mop?" Poppy asked the brunette standing behind the counter, swiping through her phone and ignoring her tables.

"What?" Nova glanced up from her phone, popping a gum bubble between her teeth. When she saw the mess at Shirl's table, she wrinkled her nose and muttered, "Old people."

With a rag in hand and a Rubbermaid bucket in tow, Poppy returned to the table and began clearing it. Once it was cleared and dry, she gave the ladies new silverware rolls and set their meals before them.

Nova lazily rolled the mop cart over. "You cleaned it all before I got here."

"The ladies did most of the work; I just cleared the table." Poppy winked at the woman in the green sweater, who looked embarrassed by her snafu. The woman smiled back gratefully.

"Whatever," Nova rolled her eyes, did two swipes on the floor, then rolled the bucket back behind the counter.

"I'll bring you some more water and refills on coffee." Poppy clasped her hands together. "Is there anything else I can get you, ladies?"

"No more water." The woman in the green sweater blushes. "It already looks like I wet my pants."

Shirl and the other ladies titter. "None for me either." The severe-looking woman frowned. "My shirt is soaked."

The other woman's face fell. "I'm so sorry."

"It's just a good thing I have a ramble frock underneath." The woman lifts the wet shirt to reveal a black T-shirt underneath her gray and black designer sweater.

"Well, there you go." Poppy forced a smile. "It's too warm for a sweater today anyway, although yours is beautiful."

The woman sniffs. "Thank you."

Poppy walked away to retrieve their coffees as the women resumed their conversation, talking about the upcoming fall festival fundraiser, a dinner party Shirl was throwing and who she'd be inviting, and home renovations their husbands were embarking on.

The late-morning lull shifted into the lunch rush. Poppy tried to make conversation with some of her regulars between waiting tables. She heard many complaints about the unusual heat from the older customers, including Shirl and her friends, who still occupied the table in the middle of the diner. Shirl complained about her perm getting frizzy from the sudden warm spell and her gaggle of elderly ladies moaned about how they were *positively wilting* in the noontime sunshine. However, the two ladies with the wet clothes admitted that the weather meant their clothes dried faster.

Leah and Samantha, the high school girls who had swooned over Colton, came in around lunch to grab sandwiches. "Hey girls," Poppy greeted, setting menus in front of them. "Are you enjoying the nice summery day?"

"Sort of," Leah, the one who had been checking Colton out, replied. "Only half of the high school is air-conditioned, though."

Samantha narrowed her brown eyes at her friend. "At least you weren't made to change into your gym shorts."

"Shorts must be long enough to reach the tip of your middle fingers when laid flat against your legs," Leah teased in a sing-songy tone.

Samantha snorts. "Yeah, well, that's great when you have short arms like you, Lee."

"I sure don't miss those rules." Poppy smiled at them. "What can I get you girls to drink?"

"Diet Pepsi," Leah said quickly. "Homecoming is coming up." She smiled ruefully at Poppy.

"I want Dr. Pepper," Samantha added, always having to be contrary to Leah.

"I'll be right back with those."

The bell over the door chimed as Poppy filled the tall plastic cups with ice and soda. She looked up as Colton stalked through the door. His gaze was mutinous as he came behind the counter, ignoring Poppy's protests. "I need to talk to you."

"Oh, now you want to talk?" Poppy rolled her eyes, the sting from being sent to voicemail still nagging at her. "It will have to wait. I'm just about to take an order."

Colton pointed to the table where Michael was still sitting. "I'll be right over there."

Colton's demanding tone sent a spike of adrenaline through Poppy. She forced herself to pay attention as she brought the girls their drinks. After triple-checking the order, making sure she had it right, she put it into the system. Letting Colton stew for a while longer, Poppy took her time filling a few drinks and clearing a few plates. Finally, his burning stare became more than she could take. She passed by his table and said, "Come with me."

Colton followed her to the alcove by the bathrooms, where Poppy crossed her arms over her chest. "So what do you want?" Poppy's tone was sharp like a slap, despite shaking inside.

"How could you let me find out from James that your house was broken into last night?" Colton demanded without a preamble.

"I can't believe he told you!" Poppy glared at the floor. She'd deal with James later. Looking up at Colton, Poppy narrowed her eyes. "I tried calling you while I was out with the police, but you sent my call straight to voicemail."

"Did you ever think to leave a voicemail?"

"It was humiliating enough being sent to voicemail in front of the officers and EMTs who already thought I was crazy," Poppy said hotly, mentally kicking herself for the stinging in the corner of her eyes. "Did you ever consider that calling you at 3:30 in the morning wouldn't be some random social call?"

"You're so fucking independent it's infuriating." Colton sighed angrily. "Are you all right, at least?"

"I'm fine," Poppy bit out. "Della came to get me and took me to her house."

"You're getting a security system put in that house," Colton said. "I don't want you going back there until it's installed."

"Don't tell me what to do." Poppy lifted her chin. "Not that it's any of your business, but I'm already working on it, thank you very much."

Colton growled. "Good."

"Is there anything else?" Poppy placed her hands on her hips, losing patience with Colton's alpha male bullshit. "I have to get back to work."

"I'll be sitting with Vlad until your shift is up. I'm taking you back to Della's personally."

"No." The firmness in her tone startled her.

Glaring at him once more, she turned to go back to the dining area. Before she could get too far, Colton's large, calloused hand gripped her wrist. Fight or flight surged through her as he yanked her back and kissed her. Every ounce of frustration bled from her and into him and she whimpered, her eyes squeezed tight. Staggering backward, she blinked at him, her face an open book full of fear and hurt. Without a word, she darted away, barreling through the diner and back behind the counter.

∾

Colton

"Now, what did you do?" Vlad asked when Colton slumped into the booth across from him. "Your girl practically ran away from you, and now it looks like she's seen a ghost."

"She's not my girl. And I doubt she ever will be," Colton grumbled, scrubbing his hands over his face. He could feel Vlad waiting for him to explain further. "I don't know how to get through to her," Colton lowered his voice.

Vlad looked vaguely sympathetic. "I don't think storming in here like Rambo is the right approach."

"I was worried and wanted to see for myself that she was okay." Colton sighed.

He'd watched Poppy's demeanor go from angry to haunted in the blink of an eye. Instead of pushing her further, he let her go, shaken by the shift. He was still kicking himself for allowing her call to go to voicemail in the middle of the night. It was a dick move. He knew, even then, she wouldn't be calling him in the middle of the night for no reason.

Vlad sighed, closed the ledger, and saved something on his laptop. "I have a feeling there's something in her past that makes her clam up like that. I don't know what it is, but whatever it is? It haunts her. It is the deciding factor behind every choice she makes."

"She's guarded." Colton nodded. "I noticed that right away."

"It's more than that," Vlad mused as he watched her wait on tables. She purposefully ignored Vlad's table, letting Nova take over. "She's afraid of something, of someone. And she's terrified to let anyone else in."

"You think someone hurt her?" Colton asked, his tone darkening.

"I do." Vlad nodded. "But that right there, that intensity, that look on your face? If that woman has been physically abused, you going all *who hurt you, I'll burn down the world,* is going to scare her away instead of drawing her in."

"Who hurt you?" Colton huffed out a laugh. "Where do you get this shit?"

Vlad rolled his eyes. "Some book shit Trix left at my house. Apparently, it's something called a book trope."

Colton coughed, trying to cover his snicker. Vlad and Trixie Edwards had been dancing around each other since she started at the diner. It was one of the reasons Vlad had taken Trixie's brother Corbin into the Burning Blood. Colton didn't know what was currently going on with them, but he knew that they'd spent at least a few nights together in the past.

"Shut up," Vlad growled. "Worry about your own woman issues."

Colton raised an eyebrow. "And what do you suggest?"

"Give her some space." Vlad shrugged. "If she wants something from you or wants to spend time with you, let her come to you. Otherwise, you're just going to scare her off again. You're too fucking intense."

"I thought women liked it when you paid attention." Colton groaned.

Fuck. This was why he didn't do relationships. *Shit, this wasn't even a fucking relationship.* All he'd wanted to do was get to know her; take her out on a date and see where things went. Vlad gave him a pitying gaze. Flipping him off, Colton turned his mug over to signal Nova for another cup.

Colton watched Poppy at a distance for the rest of her shift. Her demeanor relaxed as she interacted with the two teenage girls he'd seen her wait on before. She'd smiled and laughed and waved them off. Poppy then listened patiently as the old nag, Shirl, lectured her on how to secure a man by adding a few highlights to her hair. But it was the three old coots at the counter that put

Poppy the most at ease. He could tell that she adored them as much as they worshipped her.

At the end of her shift, Poppy hung up her apron and exchanged a few words with Della. He was too far away to hear them, but he saw Della nod, and then old Alfred Upton, the retired police chief, rose from his stool. Colton stood, ready to give Poppy a ride as he'd promised, then sunk back down. He watched disappointedly as Alfred led Poppy out to his car.

"Like I said, my friend," Vlad said, grabbing Colton's attention. "You came on too strong; you need to give her space."

CHAPTER THIRTEEN

POPPY

"Everything should be good to go." James stepped back from Poppy's laptop, which was set up on the kitchen island. "The Ring system is all set up on your laptop. All you have to do is log in from anywhere, and you can see both cameras. You'll also get a text anytime there's an alert on the camera, so if there's a delivery or even if there's someone outside, that shouldn't be. There's an app for the system, too, but your phone isn't really set up for that."

Poppy bit her lip wryly. "I thought when I moved here, I could get away from all the high-tech stuff."

James laughed. "I think that's pretty impossible in this day and age unless you become Amish."

"Yeah, let's not go that far." Poppy shook her head. "So, I should be good to move back in tonight?"

"Yep." James nodded. "Whenever you're ready. Are the police still doing extra patrols in the neighborhood?"

"I guess so." Poppy shut her laptop down and tucked it back

into her laptop case. "I haven't gotten any updates, so it doesn't sound like they found out who broke in either. By the way, I can't thank you enough for telling Colton all about the break-in."

James ducked his head, looking remorseful. "I know, it wasn't my place. I'm sorry. He showed up that morning when my guys were getting set up, looking for you, and I told him I wasn't sure if you were at Della's house or work. When he asked why you would have been at Della's house, it all came out. I assumed you'd told him."

"I hadn't really had a chance." Poppy sighed, "Then he came storming into the diner and picked a fight with me."

James crossed the kitchen island and poured them both a glass of wine. "I'd say he was just concerned, and he means well, but I know that's not much of a comfort."

"Yeah," Poppy slumped onto the barstool as she reached for her wine goblet. "I've had enough possessive, controlling men in my life to last a lifetime."

"I can only guess what sent you running to our little town," James said as he placed a reassuring hand over hers. "But you have to know that not every man you'll meet is like that. Sometimes, the ones that look the toughest on the outside are the ones that would rip out their hearts for you, and the ones that look harmless are only there to rip yours out and stomp it to pieces. You may not be ready yet, but someday, you'll find someone worth taking a chance on."

Poppy hoped James was right.

She thought back to the incident in the diner. How Colton's intensity frightened her, but lit a flicker of interest that she hadn't felt in years, possibly ever. When he kissed her, before her anxiety rose, it was better than any kiss she'd been given; a scorching need burning them both alive from the inside out. Then reality set in, and she couldn't get away fast enough. Deep down, Poppy could feel that Colton meant her no actual harm. If only the PTSD that woke her in the dead of night, panting for breath, heart-racing, wild-eyed, and disoriented, would loosen the vise grip on her throat.

"Do you need a ride back to Della's to pick up your things?" James asked after they'd finished their wine, him a single goblet and Poppy nearly two.

Poppy shook her head. "Colton came and finished the car this afternoon. There was a note under the windshield wiper when Della dropped me off." She was thankful for the gesture and even more grateful not to have to rely so heavily on others anymore. She hated feeling beholden to people.

She panicked when she saw the note flapping in the muggy, halfhearted wind. As she pulled the sheet of loose-leaf paper free from her windshield wiper, careful not to snap it off, she saw the hasty scratchings of Colton's handwriting, telling her that he was sorry and that her car was fixed and should run fine. Her nerves settled. Jack would never be caught dead using inexpensive school-style notebook paper. Only the finest, most expensive monogrammed stationery on thick, creamy linen pages would suit him.

"I'll leave you to it, then." James pulled her from her thoughts. "Let me know if you need anything. Otherwise, I'll be around tomorrow."

"Thanks, James." Poppy placed her hand on his shoulder, the gesture foreign to her. "I appreciate all you've done for me. Truly."

Morning came after a long night plagued with nightmares: human remains, faceless strangers darting through the house, and unhappy memories that she'd rather stay buried. She rose early as usual, despite it being her day off, at Della's insistence.

Ambling into the kitchen to put on a pot of coffee, she found that she was completely out. She shook her head, suddenly remembering a logo on the to-go cup Colton had brought her the morning she found the skull in her yard. Fire Roasted Coffee Shop and Cafe. Grabbing her keys, she was off in search of coffee.

Poppy parked in front of the large storefront on the intersection of French Street, Oconto Avenue, and North Emery Avenue. She smiled as she walked around to the front door and stepped under the black-and-white striped awning with the coffee shop's name scrawled in a bright pink, elegant script.

A bell chimed over the door as she stepped inside the dimly lit coffee shop. The space boasted a massive section of tables and couches that could easily seat more than a hundred people off to one side, a main counter, and a large self-service candy bar taking up the smaller portion of the space.

A slim blonde in her late teens greeted her as she stepped up to the counter. "Welcome to Fire Roasted." She pushed a wisp of frizzy curls away from her face. "What can I get started for you?"

Poppy scanned the menu on the wall over the girl's shoulder. "I'll um, I'll have the creme brûlée latte."

"What size?" The girl asked as she looked down to type the order onto the iPad in front of her.

Poppy bit her lip. "Just a small."

"Hot or iced?" The girl prompted next as her pale blue eyes briefly darted up from the iPad to look at Poppy.

"Hot."

"Anything else I can get you?" The girl asked.

"A small black coffee, too," Poppy blurted spontaneously. "Both are to-go."

"Six-fifty-nine is your total."

Poppy handed over a ten-dollar bill.

"Alright from ten dollars," The girl typed the payment onto the iPad and the cash drawer popped open. "Three-forty-one is your change and your number is 24. We'll call out the number when your order is ready."

"Thanks." She dropped a dollar of the change into the tip jar and moved off the side.

Poppy found her gaze drifting around the room, taking in all the finer details. Across from where the drinks were prepared was a separate wine bar that Poppy pictured being busy later in the day and on weekends. Against the far wall was a small section of miniature tables for kids, along with some toys and coloring books. A young mother sat at an adult-sized table watching her toddler color at one of the kids' tables. Two middle-aged business women sat at a table on the opposite end from the children's section, discussing a spread of papers in front of them while sipping from steaming mugs. The whole coffee shop had a welcoming, cozy atmosphere, despite the vast space.

"Number 24!"

Poppy looked down at the matching card in her hand before wandering over to the counter. "Thanks." She smiled as she took the to-go cups from the girl.

"Have a nice day."

Once she was back in her car, Poppy navigated toward the body shop she knew Colton worked at.

Colton

"Hey Fox, there's someone here to see you," Colton's coworker, Frank, called as he stepped into the body shop. He could see Frank's small dusty brown boots from where he lay beneath a Jeep changing the oil.

Colton slid out on the creeper from beneath the SUV and sat up, wiping the sweat from his face with the dirty rag he'd shoved in his pocket. "Who is it?"

"Some broad." Frank shrugged his slim shoulders as he pulled a comb from his pocket and fixed his already unmovable, slicked-back head of thick black hair. "A pretty one."

He sighed warily as he got up from the creeper, standing almost a foot taller than Frank, who blamed his shortness on his

Italian American heritage almost as much as he blessed it for his ability to "charm" women.

Reluctantly, Colton made his way toward the lobby. It wasn't the first time a club hang-around had stopped by the body shop, trying to get his attention. They'd show up in their tight white Harley Davidson tanks and even tighter jeans, hair over-processed and crispy, and faces full of makeup, no matter the time of day. Enough women paraded around the club trying to bag the status of *old lady*, wanting to be the one to say they tamed a wild biker, that he knew to steer clear of them.

His last relationship was with a nurse friend of Lazarus's, who had broken up with him because she thought the club life was too dangerous. Colton braced himself before passing through the door from the body shop into the air-conditioned lobby, then came up short.

Poppy stood to one side of the counter, shifting from one foot to the other nervously as she juggled a to-go cup in each hand. Her light brown hair was slicked back into a ponytail that swished as she moved, her gray eyes widening when she took him in.

"Hi," Colton said dumbly. "What are you doing here?"

"Hi," Poppy said meekly. "I wanted to say I'm sorry about how I acted the other day." She bit her lip, a nervous habit. "At the diner, I mean."

"You have nothing to be sorry for." He could see the dark circles under her eyes and the haunted look shining out from them. "I overreacted big time, and I was an asshole. I'm the one that's sorry."

"You were an asshole." The side of Poppy's mouth quirked up in a half-grin. "But I brought you coffee, anyway." Poppy extended a cup to Colton, and he caught the fire logo from Fire Roasted on the sleeve.

"Thanks." He accepted the cup and took a long sip that scorched his tongue.

"It's not the most practical drink when it's not even nine in the

morning, and it's already climbing into the upper eighties, I know."
Poppy shrugged. "But I can't start the day without caffeine."

"I'm with you there," Colton said, watching the blush creep up
Poppy's neck. "Is everything going all right with your car? No more
issues?"

"Everything is working great." Poppy nodded. "Thanks for that.
I owe you way more than a two-dollar cup of coffee."

"Don't worry about it." Then he had an idea, an idea he hoped
wasn't being too forward. Poppy was here, after all. She had sought
him out. "What are you up to today?"

Poppy shrugged. "It's my day off, and James and his crew are
working on my kitchen today. I'm just trying to stay out of their
way."

"Want to go for a ride with me?" Colton asked, holding his
breath as he watched her reaction.

Poppy considered it for a second. "Where?"

Colton tried to remain nonchalant. "Anywhere. The sun is out,
the weather is warm, it's the perfect day for a ride. We won't have
many more of these before the weather turns colder. We could
drive over to Door County."

"I've never been there." Poppy bit her lip.

"You'll love it," Colton grinned. "What do you say?"

Colton watched Poppy mull it over as she tried to draw things
out by finishing up her coffee. Finally, he saw something shift and
soften inside her. "Okay."

CHAPTER FOURTEEN

POPPY

"Are you nervous about taking the motorcycle to Door County?" Colton asked as he led her out of the body shop. "It's okay if you are; we can take my truck instead."

"No, it's okay," Poppy shook her head.

For some odd reason, the idea of Jack on a motorcycle popped into her head, as unimaginable as it was. Jack always looked down on bikers and called them criminals, thugs, and trash. *But what did Jack know, really?* Jack and his hedge fund friends were always oohing and ahhing over luxury vehicles that, in her mind, would be obnoxious to actually own. If Jack and his friends were really that good at the Stock Market, they'd be in New York, not Chicago.

Simone, her old friend, used to call them spoiled little boys trapped in men's bodies.

Colton nodded, probably figuring that would be her answer. Already, he seemed to be able to tell when she was unwilling to back down. He looked her up and down, an appraisal that sent a shiver down her spine, despite the unbearable humidity.

"You're going to need a sweatshirt," Colton said finally. "There's one in my locker. Let me run back and grab it."

"What? Why?" Her eyes crinkled with confusion. "It's like one hundred degrees out."

"Just to be on the safe side," Colton explained. "I've never been in an accident before, and I don't intend to today, but if we crash, you won't want to hit the road with bare arms; trust me. It's a good thing you're not wearing shorts."

"Oh!" Poppy paled at the thought. She managed to block out the stories she'd heard about motorcycle accidents and what kind of injuries she'd endure if they were to crash - if she survived at all.

"Don't worry." Colton hesitated before putting a gentle hand on her shoulder. Poppy held her breath for a second, willing herself to stay calm. *This is a good touch. He's not trying to hurt me.* "It's perfectly safe. I'm a good rider. And I have the helmet too. Wait here, I'll go grab a sweatshirt for you."

Colton jogged back into the shop as Poppy watched his retreating form. Turning, Poppy eyed the motorcycle warily. It had been fun on the short ride home from the diner, but now she was nervous to ride it on a busy highway. The cherry red paint glistened in the sunlight. From what little Poppy could tell, it looks sturdy enough and well-maintained.

The gravel behind her crunched, and she turned to see Colton with a heavy gray hoodie in one hand and his leather jacket in the other. "Here." He held the hoodie out to her. "It's clean, I swear; it just might smell a little like motor oil from being in my locker."

"Thanks," Poppy smiled shyly as she grabbed the hoodie and slid it over her head as Colton shrugged into his jacket. The hoodie's sleeves were too long, sliding down over her hands, and the hem fell nearly to her knees, making her look like a child playing dress-up. She wasn't even that short.

"You're welcome." Colton shrugged, but his eyes appraised

Poppy as if he liked the look of her in his hoodie. He handed her the helmet next and helped her put it on.

"You're still not wearing one?" Poppy asked when she noticed him about to get onto the motorcycle.

"I don't usually wear it," Colton insisted, shaking his head. "It's okay; I am more concerned about your safety since this is only your second time on a motorcycle, and we're going much further this time."

Poppy was more than doubtful. "Okay."

Colton climbed on the motorcycle first, and she automatically stepped onto the footrest and swung her left leg over the seat, bracing herself on Colton's shoulders. Once seated behind him, she hesitated for a minute.

"Scoot forward a little and put your hands around my waist." Poppy did as he said as he continued, "If you get nervous or need to stop, just tap me on the shoulder. It will be pretty windy and loud, so I might not hear you otherwise."

Poppy nodded, even though Colton couldn't see it. "Okay."

He starts the motorcycle with a loud roar that sent a rush of adrenaline through her. He shifted the bike into gear and accelerated forward, startling Poppy. She tightened her grip on his waist, having forgotten the feeling of riding.

"You okay?"

"Fine," Poppy shouted breathlessly.

Once they got through town, and onto the interstate, they began to pick up speed. Poppy was grateful for the hoodie as the wind whipped at her clothes. The end of her ponytail lifted and slapped against her back. Colton's hair, braided down his back, and swung like a pendulum.

Colton didn't speak much; when he did, Poppy could only make out bits and pieces. She hoped if he heard her responses, they made sense. They passed farm fields and forests in a blur, though not so fast that she didn't notice the crops had dried out and the grass was dead and brown. Some of the evergreen trees were tinged brown from the heat and lack of nutrients in the soil.

Poppy knew from experience that there was no bouncing back once the trees were stricken; they just wither and die. Other trees were already losing their leaves, too early for the fall. Alfred's worries suddenly make a lot more sense.

Once they passed Green Bay, Colton motioned to a small park area, indicating that he was pulling over for a minute.

They came to a stop, and Colton guided Poppy through dismounting on the non-muffler side so she wouldn't burn her leg. Her legs were shaking and sore as she stood beside the bike, her inner thighs aching like they'd taken a good pounding. Poppy blushed, thinking of what other activities could cause that kind of pleasant soreness. She turned away, removing the helmet and shaking her hair out.

"How do you feel?" Colton asked. "Are you doing all right so far?"

Poppy turned and smiled. "I love it. It's terrifying, but it's so freeing at the same time."

"I thought you might like it." Colton smiled wryly. "I figured you might like to stretch your legs a little bit and take a break."

"Thanks," Poppy nodded appreciatively. After the coffee she drank before they left and the continuous vibration against her core, she immediately excused herself to the bathroom. When she comes out, she spots Colton leaning against a picnic bench, scrolling through his phone.

"How far are we from Door County?" Poppy asked as she rejoined him.

"We're about twenty-eight miles from Sturgeon Bay," Colton said. "It's the first major city we'll hit once we're into Door County, as well as the county seat. We can decide from there what you want to do. There are wineries, cherry and apple orchards, lighthouses, state parks, all those little kitschy shops that rich tourists flock to, not to mention some amazing restaurants."

Poppy tingles with excitement as he lists things off.

"I can't wait." Poppy bounced on the balls of her feet. "Definitely the lighthouses. And I wouldn't mind checking out some of the shops."

Colton grinned, handing her the helmet. "You got it."

When they reached Door County and began heading towards Bailey's Harbor, Poppy understood why this is known as the Cape Cod of the Midwest.

All the towns had a cozy coastal charm that reminded her of coastal New England in movies. They passed a farmer's market where tourists and locals were storing up on vegetables, homemade crafts, and baked goods. Cute shops lined the main roads through the little towns and villages, as well as funky little bars and restaurants that bled into bed and breakfasts and resorts that overlooked Lake Michigan.

They continued toward the lighthouse that Colton said she'd really love, just north of Bailey's Harbor. Bailey's Harbor gave way to a heavily forested area, still unaffected by the unseasonably hot weather. He signaled toward a gravel parking lot where a man with a wide-brimmed hat sat on a green tractor hitched to a long, tall wagon that was partially filled with people.

Poppy was brimming with curiosity as they got off the motorcycle, and Colton hooked the helmet to the handlebar. "Where are we?"

"We're just off Cana Island. The wagon can take us across, or we can walk. There's a rocky path across that is accessible when the tide is low enough."

Poppy's eyes widened with excitement. "Seriously?"

"Walking it is." Colton laughed. He waved to the man on the tractor as they headed down the dirt road toward the path.

After a bend in the road, the trees flanking them opened up to blue skies overhead and a wide white-rock pathway. The tide lapped lazily, no more than an inch or two deep, through the cracks in the pathway. Ahead, she saw the island where the path disappeared again into the forest.

"This is so cool!" Poppy's smile was broad. She couldn't remember the last time she was this carefree and honestly happy.

"It is," Colton agreed with her. He paused, his hand swinging toward Poppy's. She allowed him to take her hand in his, which seemed to relax him. "Cana Island Lighthouse is one of the most photographed and most popular lighthouses in Door County."

"How many lighthouses are there?" Poppy asked, looking up at him. The lake spanned out behind him, the fanning of trees peeking out behind his shoulder. *It would make a beautiful photo.*

"Eleven in all." He sobered momentarily. "Even so, there have been a lot of shipwrecks around Door County over the years."

"I know it's kind of morbid, but I've always been fascinated by shipwrecks," Poppy confessed. "I'm sure you'll think that sounds weird. I don't think I ever grew out of my Titanic phase."

"I think we all had one of those." Colton laughed, lightening the mood. "And you don't grow up somewhere like Peshtigo, with its tragic history, without having at least a slight interest in morbid things."

"I bet." Poppy nodded as they reached the end of the path and stepped onto Cana Island.

Uphill through the forest, a small, modern building appeared, followed by bathrooms. Further up the path, Poppy could see the side of the lighthouse. They stopped at the first building, the gift shop and admissions counter. Poppy pulled her wallet out of her pocket to pay her admission, but Colton's light touch on her wrist stopped her. "I've got this."

"Okay." Poppy bit her lip. "Thanks."

Colton pulled his wallet out and paid the woman at the counter, who handed him two bright pink wristbands. Colton fastened the wristband loosely around Poppy's right wrist, and she returned the favor with his.

Back outside, they rounded a curve, and the lighthouse came entirely into view at the far end of the island. A few other buildings scattered the island, and they stopped and checked those out, reading the plaques inside that explained what each building was used for when the lighthouse was still in operation.

"This is so cool," Poppy kept murmuring like a giddy kid, which made Colton laugh. She took a few photos of the exterior with Colton's phone before they went inside. A guide told them about a couple keepers who worked the lighthouse and lived in the residential quarters below with their families.

Poppy stared up the stairs leading up to the top of the lighthouse, imagining a keeper climbing them all multiple times a day. Poppy passed a sign that read, *Shh, the ghosts are sleeping*, and a chill ran down her spine. The hair on the back of her neck rose. Poppy may have loved morbid history, but deep down, she was a big scaredy cat about certain things. Ghosts were one of them. Though, if asked, she would insist she didn't believe in them.

They finished touring the parts of the lighthouse open to visitors, then headed back outside, where the temperature rose dramatically compared to the unnatural cold and stillness inside.

"Where to next?" Colton asks once they visited all they could on the island.

"Surprise me!"

Colton took Poppy to a candy store in the middle of nowhere between Ellison Bay and Gill's Rock. The owner satisfied their sweet tooth with large s'mores-filled candy bars and chocolate-covered nut brittle samples. Afterwards, they went north to the

Death's Door Maritime Museum, where a guide told them about the ships that had foundered in the waters surrounding the Door County Peninsula, specifically a corridor called Porte des Morte. After browsing a couple of boutiques in Fish Creek, whose clothing had price tags that were completely out of her budget, they ended the day with burgers and beers in an atmospheric restaurant in Egg Harbor, which tied the lighthouse and maritime museum together.

⌇

The skies were darkening as Colton pulled up alongside Poppy's car in the body shop parking lot. Her legs were stiff and sore from the round-trip motorcycle ride and all the walking. She couldn't wait to get home, take a hot shower, and rest.

"Do you mind if I follow you home to make sure you get in safe?" Colton asked as she handed him his motorcycle helmet and his hoodie.

Poppy shrugged. "I don't mind. I haven't gotten any alerts on my phone from the security cameras, but it's still coming home to a dark house. I didn't know I was going to be out this long."

"Did you have a good time?" Colton asked, sounding almost afraid that she didn't.

"I loved it." Poppy grinned as she slid her hands into her back pockets. "I didn't realize how badly I needed a day like today."

Colton relaxed at her reassurance. "I'm glad."

Poppy went around to her driver's side door. "I'll see you at the house."

The drive from the body shop to the house took no time at all. The traffic was light, and most of the storefronts were closed for the night. Poppy passed a squad car on her street, and she waved, thankful the officers were keeping up their patrol. She saw the lights on in a few of her neighbor's houses, dimmed to cut down on excessive heat.

Poppy turned into her driveway. The headlight of Colton's motorcycle flashed in her rearview mirror as he turned in behind her and made the climb up the driveway, and they came to a stop alongside the porch. Colton got off the bike and opened Poppy's door. She slid out and Colton slammed the door before Poppy beeped the locks twice. As they walked up the porch steps Poppy sighed. She felt the rush of the oppressive heat cling to her. It refused to break or cool off even though the sun had long set. Colton trailed her onto the porch and leaned against the house as he shoved his hands in his pockets.

Poppy groaned, turning to Colton. "I didn't think I'd have to worry about air conditioning until next spring."

"You can almost forget it's this hot out when you're riding until you come to a stop, and it all comes rushing back." Colton watched as Poppy pulled out her house key.

"Do you want to come in?"

Colton shook his head. "No, I just wanted to make sure you get in okay."

Poppy saw a folded note tucked into the glass. Turning slightly away from Colton, she unfolded the note written in blocky caps in red Sharpie.

FOUND YOU.

Her stomach plummeted. She doesn't have to guess who the note is from.

Colton tried to get a peek at the note. "What is it?"

"Nothing." Poppy stammered, trying to calm her thundering heart. She forced a carefree smile as she refolded the note and shoved it into her pocket. "Just a note from James explaining they're still having trouble figuring out what's wrong with the furnace."

"You sure you're okay?" Colton studied her. "You look nervous all of a sudden."

"I'm fine," Poppy choked out.

She reached out, checking to see if the door was locked, feigning using it for balance. "I really did have a good time today."

"I'm glad." Colton relaxed, leaning into her a little, taking her sudden mood change for nervousness over something else.

Poppy exhaled, realizing the opportunity that had fallen in her lap. Colton believed her, and she was going to make sure he didn't suspect anything was amiss. She smiled, trying to muster a nervous, flirty smile as she moved closer. Standing on her tiptoes, she closed the distance between him and pressed a chaste kiss on his lips.

Colton groaned, placing his hands lightly on her waist as he deepened the kiss. Poppy gave in to him, forcing herself to calm. He pulled back, smiling and unaware of her underlying anxiety. "I shouldn't push my luck. I'll let you go in and get some rest."

"I'll see you soon," Poppy said as she traced his jawline.

Colton watched as she inserted the key in her door and disappeared inside, flipping on lights.

Poppy waited until she heard Colton's motorcycle cut through the stillness of the night, listening until the roar faded. Spinning around, she made a turn into the dining room where she'd left her laptop. She woke it up, fingers flying over the keyboard as she logged into the security camera program.

Pulling up the footage from this afternoon, Poppy watched James and his crew come and go from the house, hauling old cabinets out and new cabinets and appliances in. She fast-forwarded until James and his crew were leaving for the day. She watched the workers leave, and then, coming around the side of the house, a familiar figure ran up onto the porch like he'd forgotten something. Oblivious to the camera pointed directly at him.

Dressed more casually than Poppy thought he was capable of, Jack stalked up onto the porch, looking around to make sure nobody noticed him. He tucked the note into the glass pane in the door. The look on his face was murderous. His cheeks had hollowed out since she left and his blond hair looked like he had just ran his hands angrily through the strands. He wore a black, nondescript shirt. It looks like any ordinary t-shirt, but she figured it has some sort of designer label.

She couldn't tell where Jack disappeared after he left the note and walked out of shot. *What if he's still here on the property?* Blind panic overwhelmed Poppy until she remembered that the police just drove by the house. If Jack was lurking around outside, they would have found him. The front door was locked, and none of the windows were broken, so he couldn't have gotten inside. She relaxed slightly before entering the kitchen. She walked past the island and the new cabinets and appliances, not even sparing them a glance as she moved to the back door and checked the locks.

Letting out a deep exhale, Poppy relaxed a little more, finding the door secured as she left it. Then she turned, moving back through the dining room and up the stairs, taking them two at a time in her haste to get to her bedroom.

She threw her duffle bag on the bed and started throwing clothing inside. The police could only protect Poppy so much. Now that Jack had found her, there was no telling what he'd do. But one thing Poppy knew was, she wasn't going to stick around to find out.

CHAPTER FIFTEEN

POPPY

As Poppy entered the Michigan unincorporated township of Watersmeet, the vintage telephone ringtone shattered the calm inside the vehicle. She jolted, slamming on the brakes and receiving several angry honks from the drivers behind her. She waved her hand apologetically and pulled off into Ottawa National Forest Visitor Center.

Trixie's name lit up the small square display in blocky digitized letters. Poppy inhaled deeply to steady herself. Playing it cool until she was far enough away to be able to switch numbers again, she had to answer.

Poppy answered the phone on the final ring, trying to sound normal and infuse a little perkiness into her tone. "Hey. If this is about covering a shift, I'm out of town today and won't get back in until late."

"No." Trixie's breathless tone made her pause. "Did you hear?"

"Hear what?" Poppy felt her walls sliding up, snapping into place.

"Fox's motorcycle was trashed," Trixie sputtered, as though she had to say it to believe it.

Poppy's eyes narrow. "What do you mean trashed?"

"I mean, it looks like someone tried to compact it in a machine," Trixie says slowly. "It's awful. It's all dented, parts are broken off, and the wheels are contorted at weird angles. Fox is freaking out. It's pretty much a total loss."

"Shit," Poppy muttered, her stomach sinking with suspicion.

"Definitely," Trixie commiserates, though Poppy hadn't intended for her to hear her. "Didn't Fox call you? Where are you, anyway?"

"Uh, no, he didn't." Poppy bit her lip. Honestly, she wasn't sure if Colton had tried to reach her or not. She'd lost signal about an hour ago going into the heavily forested area. The surprise call from Trixie was the only indicator that she was near a cell tower. Coming up with an excuse on the fly, she added, "I wanted to see the fall colors, so I'm taking a drive up into Michigan."

"Kind of a bust, right?" Trixie's tone suggests she's wrinkling her button nose. "Everything is pretty much dead, and the leaves are just dropping instead of changing. I can't wait for winter. This heat is murder."

"Yeah." Poppy allowed her to rant briefly as she put together a timeline. Jack must have been lurking when she came home with Colton the night before. He'd probably lingered long enough to see her reaction to his note, then followed Colton home. *But how would Jack have done that much damage to Colton's motorcycle?* The way Trixie described it, it sounded like he would have had to have some sort of heavy machinery to do the extensive damage. *Or a huge luxury SUV used as a battering ram.*

"Anyway." Trixie's tone brightened. "A bunch of us are getting together at the clubhouse tonight. You know, in Della and Len's spare garage, to see what can be done. I'm sure Fox would like it if you came. So hurry your butt up and get back to town, girl!"

"I'll try to make it," Poppy said vaguely. She let her vision soften and stared out at the sea of evergreens swimming in and out of focus ahead of her.

"Later," Trixie chirped before hanging up.

Poppy snaps the phone shut on autopilot and drops it into the cupholder. Crossing her arms over the steering wheel, she lowered her head and let out a heavy exhale. She tried to ground herself, breathing in for four seconds, holding for seven counts, then exhaling for eight seconds. When that didn't calm her racing heart or the nausea churning up her stomach, she moved to her *three things* exercises.

"Evergreens, red car, visitor's center." Poppy named the first three things her eyes landed on. "Traffic, wind, birds." She continued, naming three things she could hear. Then she tried the calming breaths again. Five minutes passed, and then ten. Finally, she felt her heart rate return to normal. She looked at her hands, noticing the tremors she'd thought stopped. Taking another deep breath, Poppy shifted the car into drive and turned around. Returning in the direction she came from.

Colton

"It's hard to tell what caused this." Officer Benjamin Michelson circled Colton's bike. "My best bet would be a big SUV or a truck. There isn't any debris from another vehicle, so I'm thinking they have a cowcatcher on their grill."

"Thinking a drunk driver?" Colton scratched the stubble on his chin as they surveyed the damage. No matter what hit the motorcycle in the night, it was total loss. His insurance agent had poked around earlier, making tutting noises like he knew how much the company would have to pay out to replace the motorcycle if the person responsible couldn't be found— or worse, if they were uninsured.

"Most likely." Officer Michelson nodded thoughtfully. "I can't see why they wouldn't have stuck around or reported the accident otherwise. They may even have damage to their vehicle as well. They couldn't have caused this kind of damage without a scratch. We'll check the Flock cameras coming in and out of town and see if we can spot anything; hopefully, we'll get a license plate. You said you didn't hear anything?"

"No." Colton shook his head. "My bedroom is upstairs and faces the back of the house. I knew I should have put it back in the garage when I got home last night, but it had been a long day."

"That's understandable." Officer Michelson finished filling out a packet of paperwork. "Nobody expects when they leave their vehicle in their driveway that someone's going to come along and total it overnight."

Colton laughed dryly. "Right."

"Here's your victim information packet, which includes the case number. We also gave Don at your insurance agency the case number, and he asked us to forward him the report when it's ready."

"I appreciate that." Colton took the packet from Ben. Considering all the contact he'd had with him lately, he'd be on a first-name basis with the red-bearded officer.

"You take care, and we'll be in touch when we know more," he told him. "If you have any questions, you have my card."

"Thanks." Colton rolled the packet into a tube as Officer Michelson got into his squad and pulled away from the curb.

Two deep ruts gouged across his lawn where the vehicle had come off the road and cut across the grass towards Colton's motorcycle. He followed the track toward the heap of metal that had been his Harley, and winced. Frank would be able to haul the scrap away once he got the okay from the insurance company.

By now, everyone knew his motorcycle was wrecked. He knew the lines of gossip from the biker wives had crossed with the biddies at the diner and the old coots that competed for first dibs on the latest juicy tidbit of scandal. But so far, if someone knew who had done it, they weren't talking.

Vlad was organizing an impromptu meetup at the clubhouse tonight to take Colton's mind off things, but right now, all he wanted were answers.

~

Poppy

The clubhouse was already hopping when Poppy arrived, just after eight. She'd only made it about two and a half hours away from home when Trixie called and she returned home. She drove past the body shop on her way into Peshtigo, and sure enough, there was his once beautiful motorcycle, now twisted into an unrecognizable heap of chrome and chipped red paint. Pulling up to the curb, she stared at the wrecked motorcycle. Her stomach twisted in knots.

90s grunge music thumped from inside the garage, and Poppy could make out people loitering around outside. Motorcycles and cars littered both sides of the otherwise quiet street. Hesitantly, she got out of her car and leaned against the driver's side door. It wasn't too late. No one had seen her. *I could get back in the car and go home, and no one would have to know.*

Lit cigarettes flickered in the dark like fireflies. Poppy watched the silhouettes tilt their heads. They were looking in her direction. Poppy took a deep, fortifying breath and pushed off from the car. Her steps crunched on the pavement, each step a screaming stomp announcing her arrival.

Walking up the driveway, Poppy nodded to the bikers milling around outside.. They were all older, probably in their late fifties or early-to-mid sixties. She didn't recognize any of them, though the jackets and vests with sewn-on patches announced them to be members of the Burning Blood Riders Motorcycle Club.

The men watched her open the door and step into the clubhouse. It wasn't at all what she had pictured. There were no signs of the garage that it used to be. The walls had been painted black and were adorned with posters and signs for different types of alcohol, as well as big-busted, scantily clad women. A long bar sat along one wall, and behind it was a young woman taking orders. Behind her was a shelving unit full of bottles, from top-shelf brands and rare-to-find labels to everyday run-of-the-mill fare. Black padded, backless stools lined the front of the bar, some occupied by men and women, most wearing leather jackets or Harley Davidson attire.

Poppy wove through the bar area, her gaze searching for someone familiar. Della, Len, Colton, Michael, or even Trixie. The partygoers looked at her curiously, but their gazes didn't linger, instead turning back to their hands of cards or bottles of beer. A biker pulled a buxom blonde into his lap, who giggled like a schoolgirl. A large, carved wooden table sat against the far wall, but all the chairs around it were empty, as if they were being reserved for something or someone special.

Finally, she located Colton, leaning on a pool cue on the right side of the room near the garage doors, now painted black and secured to the cement floor so they could not be reopened.

As though sensing her presence, Colton looked up from the game and their eyes locked. All the air was sucked from the room, and time seemed to slow ever so slightly as Poppy watched Colton's gaze transform from sharp and moody to soft and relieved.

An invisible lasso wrapped around her, pulling her toward him, her feet moving before she realized it. The crowd seemed to part, letting her pass as Colton watched her approach.

Poppy rounded the table and sidled up to Colton. "Hey," she said, sounding slightly out of breath.

"Hey." Colton grinned. "I'm glad you're here. Today has been such a fucking mess."

"I'm so sorry about your motorcycle," Poppy rushed to say. Her stomach twisted again when she thought of the ruins in the parking lot of the body shop.

"Yeah, it's a shame." Colton shook his head. He didn't realize that she felt responsible for it. "The police seem to think it was a drunk driver. Hit and run."

"Actually—" Poppy says, just as Michael and the shorter Hispanic biker she had seen him with at the diner approached.

"Poppy, you know Vlad—Michael, Della and Len's son." Colton tipped his head towards Michael. Gesturing to the other man, he added, "and this is Spike."

"My real name's Gomez." He winked at her as he shook her hand. "So you're Fox's girl? We've heard a lot about you."

Michael elbowed him sharply in the side. "Don't scare her off." He gave his friend a chagrined look. "He means we've heard from Mom since you started working at the diner. She adores you. Fox has explained, you're just friends."

Michael gave Gomez a look, as though to dare him to contradict. Colton scratched the back of his neck.

"It's okay." Poppy shrugged. Her grin took on a slightly wicked tilt. "I know how guys like to exaggerate things."

Gomez guffaws, almost spewing the beer he's sipping. He slaps Colton on the shoulder. "I like this one. She's feisty."

They all laugh, even Poppy, before Michael practically drags Gomez away. Colton studied her face, frowning at something he saw there. "Are you okay? You're not overwhelmed, are you? I know the club can be a bit like a big, noisy family at times."

She shook her head, suddenly wishing she hadn't come. "I'm okay. Don't worry about me. I just feel bad about what happened to your motorcycle."

"Don't sweat it. The insurance company will cover it."

"I just feel like it's all my fault," Poppy murmured, but her words were lost as someone shouted from the bar area, where a couple of guys were playing bar dice with the bartender.

"What's that?" Colton leaned toward her.

Poppy raised her voice to be heard over the din. "I think I'm going to head out. I don't want to keep you from your friends. I just wanted to make sure you were all right after what happened."

"Hey, don't go," Colton shouted as Poppy started to turn away. He reached out his hand, then remembered what happened the last time and thought better of it. Poppy felt him at her heel as she skirted through the throng of people and stepped out into the night.

Crickets chirped in the distance, and the heat of the night enveloped Poppy in a stifling embrace as she gasped for air. She didn't stop as she crossed the street, reaching into her pocket for her car keys. Colton was no more than a step behind.

"Hey," Colton said, softer now. "Don't go. I like spending time with you. Stay, and I'll introduce you to some of the guys. Trust me, they're not as scary as they look."

Poppy shook her head, facing the car. She fidgeted with her key fob. "I shouldn't have come. This is all my fault."

"What do you mean?" Colton gently turned her to face him. His brow furrowed in confusion and concern.

"What happened to your motorcycle wasn't an accident." Poppy frowned, avoiding eye contact.

Colton's attention burned a hole in her chest. "What makes you think that?"

Poppy hesitates, gulping in air. Finally, she raised her gaze to meet Colton's. "My name isn't really Poppy Isles."

CHAPTER SIXTEEN

COLTON

"What are you talking about?" Colton asked as he watched Poppy's face drop into her open palms. His concern carved a tight look onto his face, and all he wanted was to reach out and hold her, but he didn't think she'd allow it. She was torturing herself enough already.

Colton had a shitty day all around. He already had to squabble with the insurance company about what they would pay out. Officer Michelson had also informed him that they hadn't found any vehicles with front-end damage and would have to investigate further. The gathering had been the last thing he wanted tonight, but Michael insisted, and Della and Len had gone all out. Everyone was there, showing him support.

Colton had been trying to hide his frustration and desire to disappear when Poppy walked through the door. He'd immediately felt lighter, like some love-sick fool from a romance novel.

"I said my name isn't really Poppy Isles," she repeated quietly, her tone shaky as if each word cost her.

"Okay, well, what is it?" Colton crossed his arms over his chest to keep from touching her. Then realized it made him look angry and defensive and let his arms drop to his sides.

"My real name is Fallon Boseman." Poppy sniffled as she wiped away the tears forming at the corner of her eyes.

"Okay, so you changed your name?" Colton knew he sounded ignorant. He thought it best to let her draw it out.

"I had to," Poppy murmured. "I had to leave Fallon behind. Let her die."

Suddenly, fear for her stole the breath from his lungs; a thousand possibilities racing through his mind. "Why?"

Poppy shook her head, looking toward the end of the street. She was quiet for a while, the crickets and the fainter sounds from the party behind them filling the silence.

Colton watched as Poppy seemed to fold in on herself; one minute, she was standing, and the next, she was crouched down in front of the driver's door of her car. She covered her face again as her shoulders began to shake. Colton watched helplessly. Finally, she scrubbed her eyes and looked up at him. He crouched next to her.

"I was in an abusive relationship for six years." Her tone was bitter, resigned, and more than a little embarrassed. "I worked in historic home restoration back in Chicago. I loved bringing old, forgotten, and unloved spaces back to their former glory. I had just finished leading a project restoring a three-story Victorian home on Michigan Avenue, the biggest and most successful project of my career so far, when I met Jack. He was a friend of the homeowner, and he worked in stocks."

"He knew all the right things to say to get women to fall under his spell. Things progressed fast. A whirlwind relationship. Then we moved in together. It was like fate or something. Fancy parties and referrals to other wealthy, powerful friends of his at parties. He loved showing me off; his fiery girlfriend with a talent for making old things new. But what he was really interested in was the increased business and connections it brought him. Until he began to resent it."

"Go on," Colton said, watching as Poppy looked past him, her gaze lost somewhere in the past.

"It started slowly at first," Poppy explains. "Little outbursts, grabbing onto my wrist a little too hard. Then came the jealousy. He claimed I was paying too much attention to his friends. He said I dressed like a slut; that his friends would think I was up for anything. He'd say I was stupid and that my job was stupid and useless. You have those things told to you often enough that you start to believe them. Then he started getting more violent. A back-hand here, a dislocated shoulder there. I avoided the emergency room until one day, when he was so enraged, he threw me through a glass coffee table, cutting my face to ribbons before stomping on my wrist until it broke and kicking my ribs until they broke too. By that time, I'd been through so much and was covering up fading and new bruises on a daily basis. I hated him touching me, but he took my free will over that away, too."

"That fucker!" Colton swore, his tone venomous. Poppy glanced at him, but her gaze wasn't fearful this time. All Colton saw was resignation.

"My friend Simone took me to the emergency room when I didn't show up for work for a big project I had just taken on." Poppy curled in on herself. "She was livid. I thought she'd kill Jack herself. The emergency room doctor called the police, but I told them I wouldn't press charges. Not then, anyway. They worked with me for hours as the doctors ran tests and tried to patch me up. Finally, the police and my friend Simone convinced me to file a report and a restraining order. I told them I just wanted out."

Poppy sighed, and Colton's heart hurt for her. He thought of his mother, or Della, or the girls who hung around the club going through what Poppy has just described. Colton suspected there was more that she wasn't ready to disclose, and the thought was unbearable. He wanted to hunt down her ex and rip him apart.

"I won't discuss how, but it took some time and some maneuvering. I was able to secure a new identity and a restraining order. On the day Jack was arrested, I fled town and left behind everything that made me Fallon Boseman. I had some money hidden away from the last project I had completed and bought the house here, sight unseen. Once I entered Wisconsin, I bought a disposable cell phone and threw my old one in Lake Michigan. A plan had been in the works to make it look like I had died in a car crash back in Chicago. I was supposed to have a fresh start and a new life. Small town Wisconsin, in a place I'd never heard of before fleeing Chicago, a place I never thought Jack would find me."

"And now you think he has," Colton said, filling in the blank.

"About a week after I moved to town, I got a threatening voicemail from Jack." Poppy closed her eyes, leaning her head against the car door. "I went to the police immediately and showed them the restraining order and gave them the telephone number for the detective I had worked with back in Chicago. They said since it was just a call and there was no proof Jack had tracked me down to Peshtigo, there wasn't much they could do. They told me to change my number, a number that I have no idea how Jack would have gotten ahold of in the first place."

Something dawned on him. "Was he the one that broke into your house?"

Poppy shook her head. "No, I have no clue who that was. Kids, maybe, like the police believe."

Colton watched her. "I'm sensing there's more, though."

"Last night, when we got back from Door County, there was a note on my door," Poppy said slowly.

Colton thought back. "You said it was from James. Something to do with the remodel."

"I lied." Poppy looked down. "It was from Jack. He found me.

The security cameras caught him sneaking up to the door as James's crew was leaving for the day."

"I'll hunt him down," Colton vowed. "I'll get the club to help me. They don't stand for men hitting on women."

"Colton." Poppy sighed, her tone plaintive. "Aren't you getting it? Jack must have been waiting around for me to get home and saw us together. Then he must have followed you home and waited until you went to bed, then trashed your motorcycle. He always drives luxury SUVs, even when he travels. For Jack, it's like a status symbol."

"Poppy." She refused to make eye contact, so Colton gently placed a finger under her chin, tilting her face up toward his. He kissed her forehead. "The motorcycle is the least of my worries right now. It's replaceable. You're not."

"I tried to leave." Poppy's eyes filled with tears, threatening to cascade down her cheeks. "In the middle of the night, I packed up. When Trixie called me this morning, I was halfway to Duluth, Minnesota. I was going to just vanish. I wasn't going to say goodbye to anyone."

"I know you're scared." Colton's thumb traced her trembling jaw. "It's understandable with all you've been through. But you have me now. You have Della, Vlad, and those three old coots at the diner. And more than that, you'll have the backing of the club. I won't let anything happen to you. If that fucker is still in town, we'll find him."

Poppy

Colton disappeared into the clubhouse after making sure Poppy wasn't going to take off before he returned. He asked Michael to take his truck back to Poppy's house. He told him that he was going to be staying with her, and that would explain everything later. Now he was taking her car back to his house to pick up a few things.

Colton took charge seamlessly, but not in a frightening way. Not in the way Jack had swooped in and taken away her free will.

His jaw ticked as he drove, and she wanted to ask him what he was thinking, but thought it would be better if she didn't know. Instead, she fiddled with the air conditioning and leaned back in her seat.

Colton lived in a two-story farmhouse on the edge of the city. A hundred years ago, after the fire leveled everything for miles, it was probably surrounded by farm fields. Now, sometime in the last forty years, a subdivision sprung up, and his house sat sandwiched between one-story prefab ranch-style homes.

He parked the car on the curb and hopped out, ducking down to look at her through the open door. "Do you want to come in? I'll only be a few minutes."

"Sure." Poppy shrugged, unbuckling her seatbelt. She trailed after him up to the door and watched as he unlocked it and flicked on a light in the entryway.

"I'll be right back," Colton said as he jogged up the stairs.

Poppy eyed the metal motorcycle and mechanic-style signs hanging on the white walls. There was one framed photo of Colton and an older woman, his mother, most likely. Poppy could see the resemblance in their warm brown eyes and the way they both smiled.

The living room branched off the entryway, and through the sparse leather furniture, she saw the open layout give way to the kitchen. Poppy drifted into the living room, where the leather couch and armchair faced a 50-inch television with some kind of gaming system set up beneath. Video game cases sat in a haphazard stack on the console, spilling over onto the floor. An empty pizza box and a couple of empty packs of cigarettes were scattered on the rough wooden coffee table.

Glancing off toward the kitchen, Poppy noticed a small stack of dishes ready to be washed in the kitchen sink, and on the wall behind the sink were dozens of shot glasses lined up on shelves.

Poppy leaned against the arm of the leather couch, tossing a flannel shirt onto the seat. Something brushed up against her ankle, startling her. She glanced down to find an enormous tabby cat blinking up at her. It purred steadily as it rubbed against her leg, leaving its scent all over her. Reaching down, she scratched the cat behind the ears, and it turned its head into her palm, soaking up the attention.

Colton's footsteps echoed as he bounded down the stairs and rounded the corner into the dark living room. "Marge, stop being such an attention seeker." Colton shook his head at the cat.

Poppy laughs as she looks between the cat and Colton. "Marge?"

"Short for Large Marge." Colton snorted. "My mom named her and gave her to me as a present. She thought having a pet would make me want to settle down. Unfortunately for her, Marge is a failed vet's office cat who was left alone with her last owner's corpse for three weeks and had to resort to eating her owner. The only thing Marge makes me want to do is sleep with one eye open."

"That's fucked up." Poppy raised her eyebrow. She moved her ankle away from Marge, who is still looking up at her serenely, probably sizing up her next meal.

Colton laughed. "She's a good cat, though."

"Do you need to bring her with you?" Poppy asked hesitantly.

"Nah," Colton shook his head. "Cats are pretty self-reliant as long as they've got food and a clean litter box. With all the people coming and going from your house with the remodel, it's probably best that she stays here."

"Okay." Poppy nodded, relieved to be leaving the man-eating feline behind.

He filled the cat's bowls with water and kibble, then grabbed his duffle bag as Poppy trailed him back to the car.

Michael and Trixie were waiting in the driveway when they arrived at Poppy's house. Michael tosses Colton his truck keys as they approached, while Trixie leaned against the door of a small silver sedan. Poppy didn't realize that Michael and Trixie were together. She figured Trixie had to be one of the biker's girlfriends, since she was so familiar with them when they came into the diner.

"I'm not sure what's going on," Trixie said, a conspiratorial look in her eyes. "But I want all the details later."

Poppy smiled wanly and said, "It's a long story."

"All the best ones are." Trixie wagged her eyebrows.

"Now, don't be getting ideas, Trix," Michael slung an arm over Trixie's shoulder after exchanging a brief, hushed conversation with Colton. "You're as bad of a gossip as Old Shirl and those old coots at the diner."

"I never!" Trixie batted her eyelashes in mock outrage. "I'll have you know I am the soul of discretion."

"Sure you are, Bunny." Michael laughed as he tugged at her long blonde hair. "Let's leave these two to get some rest. It's been a rough day all around. What do you say? Your place or mine?"

Trixie snorted. "You wish. At this rate, I may off you and dump your body in the river before taking off with your cash and your bike."

"Won't get too far with twenty-five dollars and a quarter tank of gas."

Trixie swatted Michael's firm stomach before they got into Trixie's car. Michael looked like he was getting into a child's toy car as he slid into the passenger seat. Standing side by side on the newly stained porch, Poppy and Colton watch as they drive off.

Poppy crinkled her nose. "Did he just call her Bunny?"

"Yeah." Colton snorted. "Because her name is Trixie, like Trix, the rabbit from the cereal."

"Okay, that is kind of cute," Poppy admitted.

Colton watched her with a pitying sort of look that made her squirm. She didn't tell him her truth because she wanted his pity, or his protection. She meant to warn him that Jack was out there; violent and unpredictable.

Poppy shook her head and unlocked the door, letting Colton inside before locking up behind them. Now that they were inside, she wondered why she went along with this crazy plan. She didn't need him staying here with her for about a dozen reasons. It would make Jack angrier, and it could give Colton the wrong idea.

Her feelings toward Colton were already conflicting enough; caught somewhere between wanting him and wanting to let him into her life fully, and wanting to push him as far away as possible. But she promised herself on the long drive back to Peshtigo, that she would try.

Then she promptly talked herself in and out of it several hundred times.

"What's going on in that beautiful mind of yours?" Colton asked as he set his duffel bag on the floor.

Heat flushed her cheeks. "I wish you wouldn't say things like that."

"I don't think people have said things like that to you enough," he countered. "I think for too long you've let someone tear you down when they should have been building you up. You're an amazing woman—smart, talented, sexy. You deserved someone that would tell you that every day. And I'm going to make sure from now on you know your value."

"Colton—" Poppy began, but Colton shook his head.

"No. Whatever you were going to say, whatever wall you're already bricking up to keep me and everyone else out, just stop. I'm not going to push you. We've both had a long, hard day. It's not the right time. But you better believe that this is going to happen. It's already happening, and this thing, this chemistry brewing between us, is inevitable. But for now, I'll give you your space. Just tell me where you want me to get set up."

Poppy bit her lip. "I don't have another bedroom set up or any furniture. There are two rooms across the landing from mine on the second floor. But I haven't had a chance to buy beds for them. There's the couch, which isn't very comfortable, believe me. I also have a sleeping bag and an air mattress that leaks slightly."

Colton laughed. "It's okay. I can rough it in the sleeping bag."

"Are you sure?" Poppy flushed again. "I fully plan to get the spare bedrooms furnished and decorated, but I've been waiting for the remodel to be closer to completion so I can get a vibe for whether I want to go with more of an antique look or a more modern, clean look, and it's a bit of a work-in-progress."

Colton grinned, cutting Poppy off mid-ramble. "It's no big deal."

Poppy took a gulping breath, embarrassed that she rambled on about her vision. Most people's eyes would glaze over when she talked about her restoration projects, except the coworkers she'd left behind in Chicago and, lately, James.

"It's fine." Colton touched her shoulder gently. "I love that you're so passionate about bringing this place back to life. It's nothing to be embarrassed about."

Poppy nodded. "Well, I guess I should show you the guest room. I need to get to bed. I work the opening shift at the diner in the morning."

She showed him up the stairs, branching off to the left after pointing out the bathroom. She opened the door to the bedroom on the opposite side of the house from hers and flipped on the light. It hummed to life.

Colton surveyed the room, studying the intricate crown molding and the cracked slate-gray paint on the wall. The hardwood floors were dull and needed to be re-finished and a stack of boxes sat in the corner for the bathroom remodel.

"I can't wait to see what you do with the room," Colton said. "I assume you're keeping the crown molding, right? They don't do it like that anymore."

"I wouldn't dream of ripping it out." Poppy cleared her throat as she pointed to the sleeping bag rolled up in the corner. "The sleeping bag is there, and there should be a pillow behind those boxes. Do you want some extra blankets?"

"On an eighty-degree night?" Colton quirked an eyebrow teasingly. "I think I'll be fine without it."

"Well, I'll leave you to it." Poppy wiped her sweaty palms on her jeans and forced a smile. Leaving Colton in the spare bedroom, she darted into the bathroom, washed up, and brushed her teeth quickly before disappearing into her bedroom.

CHAPTER SEVENTEEN

POPPY

Poppy wasn't able to sleep a wink, restlessly tossing and turning, unable to clear her mind with Colton just down the hall. Sometime around three-thirty in the morning, she gave up the fight and got out of bed. She dressed quietly, then tip-toed around the creaky floorboards and went down to the kitchen. Preparing a pot of coffee before she left for work, Poppy poured herself a travel mug and then made sure the rest of the pot stayed warm until Colton woke up.

Walking out the front door and letting it snick shut behind her, activating the lock, Poppy stopped dead in her tracks. Her trees, all the marvelous trees lining her driveway, were wrapped in what looked like toilet paper. Not only the trees, she realized, but the columns on her porch as well.

"What the fuck?" Poppy exclaims, torn between bewilderment and annoyance.

After taking an angry sip from her travel mug, the hot coffee scalding her tongue, Poppy pulled out her phone and texted James.

I'm leaving for work, and I noticed
someone toilet-papered my house. Should
I call the police?

She didn't expect James to answer until he got up in a few
hours, but his answer came immediately.

It's homecoming week. The high schoolers
go around doing that. My guys will clean it
up when we come in. Don't worry about it.

Poppy burned with indignation. *First, someone broke into my
house while I was sleeping, and now kids were toilet-papering it as
part of some dare? What's next? Dead animals on my porch? A bomb
in my mailbox?* Given the developments surrounding Jack's threatening note and what Poppy could all but confirm he did to
Colton's motorcycle, Poppy had to visit the police department,
regardless.

Before heading into work, Poppy swung by the police department,
still fuming over the prank played on her house. That, mingled
with the lingering guilt about what Jack did to the motorcycle,
made for an exhausting morning. She wished she could have
gotten some sleep last night before taking this on.

As she approached the counter, she noticed Office Michelson
was manning the dispatch desk. "Ms. Isles," he greeted her
warmly, recognizing her right away. Which was no surprise, given
how often she had to speak to the police lately. "What can I do for
you today?"

Poppy clutched her purse tightly, the leather crinkling beneath
her grip. "I have information about the damage to Colton Sterling's
motorcycle."

"Oh?" Officer Michelson raised his eyebrows, his tone chilling as he surveyed her. "Why don't you step inside, and we'll chat somewhere a little more private?"

Poppy nodded and waited for him to meet her at the door. He turned to say something to someone inside the office; another officer came and took his place at the desk. An unfriendly looking woman with her brown hair pulled aggressively into a bun.

Officer Michelson opened the door and said, "Right this way."

He led her into the same interview room where she had previously spoken with him. Once she sat across from him, he set a notepad in front of himself and said, "Why don't you start at the beginning?"

"Well, as we discussed last time I was here, my situation is a bit unusual."

"Yes, I remember." Officer Michelson nodded as he sat back in his seat, studying her. "I did get in touch with Detective Milbauer in Chicago, and he was able to confirm your story and your identity —that your real name is Fallon Boseman, and you're living under an assumed identity for your protection against your ex-boyfriend. Is that what you're hinting at today, that your ex somehow found you and damaged Mr. Sterling's motorcycle, because, and this is just the local rumor mill talking, but because you and Mr. Sterling have been seen getting close in recent days?"

Poppy didn't appreciate the flippant tone Officer Michelson gave her. "I'm not hinting, I know." She opened her purse and retrieved the note Jack left for her, tossing it across the table. "I found this on my door the night Colton's motorcycle was destroyed."

Officer Michelson read the note, then glanced up at her skeptically. "This could be from anyone."

"Really?" Poppy met his gaze, matching its intensity.. "Could it?"

"Fine." Officer Michelson rubbed his beard absently. "I admit, it's unlikely to have come from someone from town. Is there a reason you didn't come forward with this yesterday?"

"Yesterday, I was halfway to Minnesota trying to run again until I got the call about Colton's motorcycle." Poppy sat back in her seat, crossing her arms, even though she knew the officer would read into her body language. "I felt awful because it's all my fault. I knew I shouldn't have let myself get close to Colton, or to anyone in town, for that matter, and I was right. Now look what happened."

Poppy's breathing was choppy, and her chest contracted like a large stone had settled on it. She rubbed her collarbone as she forced herself to breathe in and out slowly, counting until the pain lessened.

"Relax now, Fallon. Can I call you Fallon?" Officer Michelson's expression softened as he regarded her like a wounded animal in need of soothing. He waited until she nodded before he said, "This is not your fault, not what you went through back in Chicago, and not your ex tracking you down here. Detective Milbauer sent over the case files regarding you and Mr. Richards. I haven't had a chance to look it over much yet, but I will make it a priority now. If Mr. Richards is still in town, and if he is, in fact, responsible for Mr. Sterling's motorcycle being damaged, we'll find him and bring him in. Now, is there anything else I should know?"

Poppy sighed, the stress cascading off of her. "How much do you already know?"

She spent an hour at the police department going over details with Officer Michelson. She told him that Jack was likely to be driving some sort of luxury SUV, something large enough to turn Colton's motorcycle into little more than a heap of scrap metal in the yard. Officer Michelson promised to be in touch and told her not to stay alone and to call immediately if she got any further messages from Jack.

∾

That afternoon, when Poppy returned from work, James and his crew had fully moved into the house. The landscaping in the back-yard was still off-limits until the anthropology team from UW-Milwaukee could come and assure the Marinette County Sheriff's Department that there were no other human remains.

Poppy had been chomping at the bit to meet with James all afternoon. Anything to get her mind off of Jack and where he could be lurking. Once she'd arrived home, she slid her shoes off, leaving them by the front door. She'd paused to rub her sore feet before wandering into the kitchen to find James, pouring over notes and blueprints at the kitchen island.

"We'll do the living room first, since you're not really using that room right now, it shouldn't be a problem." James pointed at the room with his pen as she came to huddle over the blueprints. "From there, we'll do the dining room, leaving a section for you to get to the kitchen. Then, when the first portion dries, we'll do the remainder, and you'll have to walk on the other side. Does that make sense?"

Over the next three days, James and his crew would be painting the first floor and refinishing the hardwood floors, leaving a maze for Poppy and Colton to navigate as the wood was cured and left to dry. James explained the plan to Poppy as they sat at the island, where they swapped coffee for ice-cold iced tea to stave off the furnace-like heat.

"Up until you want me to hop a foot and a half to get to the kitchen." Poppy pointed out wryly.

James cocked his head. "I could make you walk outside and come back in through the back door."

"Charming." Poppy smirked at him. "Hire a contractor and get a comedian thrown in for free."

James chuckled as he tilted his glass, sweating ice twirling around the bottom like skaters on an ice rink.

The HVAC guy James contracted had been fretting over the furnace all afternoon. Swearing and clanging echoed from the basement as he tossed and replaced parts, only for the house to stay stiflingly hot. Finally, the HVAC guy gives up for the day, and stomps his way upstairs.

"I don't know what else to do with the fucking thing." He marches into the kitchen, hovering in the doorway with his hands fisted at his waist.

"We know you're trying your best." James tried to calm the man.

"I really do appreciate what you've been trying," Poppy added.

"And I appreciate your understanding, Missy, but that's not going to solve the conundrum." The HVAC guy sighed. "I think we're going to have to replace the whole system, just rip the whole thing out and put in something else, perhaps a hybrid system. And I would definitely suggest getting central air installed sooner rather than later if these temperatures don't drop soon. A house feeling like it's in the tropics when it's twenty below zero out isn't so bad; however, when it's nearing one hundred degrees out, you're just lucky you haven't been hospitalized for heat stroke."

Poppy shot James a concerned look as she tried to move figures around in her head to estimate the cost of putting in a whole new heating system after they just replaced the furnace.

James patted her hand. "We'll get it all figured out. Arnie, why don't you and I go discuss options downstairs and let Poppy get started on fixing herself something to eat? Look at her! The girl is all skin and bones."

Poppy watched James usher Arnie out of the room. Her stomach growled on cue, and she glanced at the clock on the stove, calculating how long it would be before Colton arrived from work.

CHAPTER EIGHTEEN

POPPY

Poppy with a start, like an alarm had sounded. Flipping the pillow to the cooler side, she punched it, wishing, just once, she could sleep through the night. She didn't know what pulled her from sleep this time. The house was silent. Glancing at her phone, she saw it was just after one in the morning.

The thin quilt on Poppy's bed had been kicked to the foot of the bed and the ceiling fan clicked as its blades carved through the air. They only distributed hot air through the room, bringing no relief from the oppressive temperature. The water bottle on her nightstand was empty, and her throat was scorched. Grabbing the bottle, Poppy yawned and got out of bed, leading herself blindly down the stairs and to the kitchen.

Pulling a pitcher of filtered water from the refrigerator, she refilled the bottle. From the corner of her eye, movement outside the window overlooking the front porch startled her.

Poppy gasped, dropping the pitcher onto the marble countertop with a clunk. Thoughts of Jack lurking outside in the dark flitted through her mind. Grabbing a kitchen knife from the block, she crept to the entryway and flicked on the porch light. Nothing appeared out of place as she glanced through the windows, but that didn't mean anything. *Would Jack really be standing in plain view, ready to be seen?* She didn't think so. Something in her gut told her he was waiting for the right moment to show his hand.

Flipping the locks, Poppy raised the knife to eye level and yanked the door open, hoping to catch Jack, or whoever was creeping around in the dark, by surprise.

"Whoa there." Colton's voice startled and soothed her at once. "Are you all right?"

Poppy stepped onto the porch, the new boards smooth beneath her feet. "I'm sorry." She slowly lowered the knife. "I came down to refill my water bottle and saw something moving on the porch."

Colton chuckled, raising his hands in surrender. "Just me. Don't stab me; I'm innocent, I swear."

Poppy's gaze traveled down his form. Knots snarled his long hair, making him look like a wild man with eyes hooded from fatigue. His chest was bare, glistening beads of sweat dripping slowly down his defined abs. A thick patch of hair covered his pecs, trailing down his stomach and disappearing into a black pair of boxer briefs that hugged his muscular thighs.

Lines of black ink and colorful shading covered his arms, his ribs, and his legs. There were so many designs that Poppy couldn't tell where one tattoo began and another ended, nor could she make out what they were in the dim light. She gulps, her gaze snapping back to Colton's, his stare molten and intense with want.

"I, um," Poppy swallowed again, her throat like sandpaper. She cursed herself for running outside before she had a chance to quench her thirst. She wet her lips. "I should get back to bed."

Colton's gaze locked on her lips. "You should."

Poppy backed up against the door, which had snicked shut behind her. Her hand wrapped sweatily around the cool brass doorknob, but she made no move to open the door and slip inside. Instead, she watched Colton.

Keeping eye contact, Colton dropped and snubbed out the cigarette he'd been smoking. She should have scolded him for putting it out on her new porch, but she couldn't form words. Closing the distance between them, Colton stood before her.

She inhaled sharply, his tobacco, sandalwood, and cinnamon scent overwhelming her. "What are you doing?" she whispered as she tilted her face up toward his. She could feel his body heat seeping into hers, making her flush all over. The warmth was unbearable.

"Tell me to stop." Colton's breath whispered against her mouth.

"What?" She couldn't think straight. All she could see, all she could think about, was him.

"Tell me to step away, and I will," Colton continued as if she hadn't spoken. "Tell me you don't want me."

"I—" Poppy's pupils dilated as she stared into Colton's hungry gaze.

Suddenly, she'd never wanted anything more than she wanted him right now. It wasn't like it was with Jack. She wasn't afraid. Not anymore..

Colton waited a beat, then two, and then his lips crashed down on hers, pressing her back against the door. Colton's hands bracketed either side of her head, as if he feared touching her would shatter the moment and send Poppy running away.

Poppy placed her hands on his ribs, running up and down the ink covering his sides. Colton groaned, his tongue gliding against hers. He removed one hand from the door and cupped the back of her head, his long fingers splaying from the top of her head to the nape of her neck as his other hand snaked around her waist.

"We should," Poppy pulled away from his kiss, "go inside."

Colton nodded, placing a kiss on the pulse point on her neck.

Catching her breath, she turned the knob and backed inside.

She led him upstairs as the door slammed shut behind them. Unable to keep their hands or mouths off of each other, they struggled up the steps until Colton couldn't wait any longer. Scooping her up into his arms, he carried her the rest of the way up the stairs and into her bedroom. Pushing the door open with his foot, he tossed her onto the bed, crawling up the mattress after her.

She sat up, panting as he captured her mouth again, sliding his hands up the oversized cotton t-shirt covering her body. He broke away, only long enough to strip the shirt off and toss it to the floor. His lips traveled from her neck down to her collarbone before capturing her right nipple. His tongue swirled around the stiff peak. Poppy gasped, gathering him to her chest as he sucked and nibbled before moving the left nipple and giving it the same treatment.

Kissing down her stomach, Colton's fiery gaze found hers as he slid his hand between her spread legs, slipping one long finger into her wet heat.

"So fucking wet for me." Colton's rough voice sent a shiver through her as he thrust his finger in and out of her. "I knew you would be. I can't wait to taste you."

"Colton," Poppy moaned, lifting her hips greedily.

Colton chuckled, blowing cool air over her sensitive flesh, and then his mouth was on her, making her back arch with pleasure as he tasted her.

"Look at me," he told her. "I want to see your face when you come undone for me."

His words made her soaking wet with arousal as he continued to lick and suck her clit. His finger, quickly joined by two more, continued to pump in and out of her.

Clutching the sheets, Poppy tilted her head up. Her eyes locked with Colton's as he hit just the right spot to have her spiraling out of control; screaming his name as she came.

She was almost embarrassed by how quickly she came under his ministrations. It had been so long since anyone tended to her needs or cared about giving her pleasure, all she could do was bask in the sensations she'd long forgotten.

Colton kissed her, his mouth hot on hers, as she let go of the sheets and rubbed the back of his neck. He groaned, pulling away. "I'll be right back."

Poppy sat up, confused, as Colton swaggered out of the room. She couldn't help staring at his tight ass as he crossed into the hall. A minute later, he was back and tossed a condom onto the bed. Poppy sighed with relief; she hadn't even been thinking about protection.

Colton stole her breath as he stood at the end of the bed, shucking off his boxer briefs. He fisted his thick, long length as Poppy stared hungrily. He tore open the condom wrapper with his teeth and covered himself before covering her body with his. "Tell me you want me," Colton ordered.

"I do," Poppy half moaned. "I want you."

Kissing her neck, Colton fit himself between Poppy's thighs. She gasped as she felt the head of his cock at her entrance, steadily thrusting inside her, her pussy stretching to accommodate his thick cock as she clung to him.

"Fuck baby, you feel so good. Even better than I imagined." Colton groaned as he thrust into her. " I've imagined it a lot since I first saw you at the diner. How your tight pussy would feel around my cock. How sweet you would taste. The look on your face when you come apart. But even my wildest dreams don't live up to the reality of you."

Colton's thrusts increased as Poppy's hips rose up to meet him, unable to get enough as they developed a rhythm all their own. Her hands roamed over his back as she bit down gently on his shoulder. They both moaned as her pussy clamped down around his cock; their mouths joined and Colton's tongue imitated his cock, moving in and out of her.

Poppy felt him become frenzied as her orgasm rose as well.

"That's it, baby." Colton's voice was husky, barely above a

whisper, as he nipped at her earlobe. "Come all over my cock, baby. Let yourself fall over the edge with me."

"Colton!" Poppy screamed as her orgasm ripped through her. Colton groaned, burying his face in her neck as he followed her over the edge.

Bodies slick with sweat, Colton rolled her so that they were lying side by side. His hot breath stirred a few strands of hair that had fallen into her face. He kissed her, withdrawing from her slowly as he got up to dispose of the condom.

Sliding back into bed, Colton collected Poppy into his arms. "Are you okay?" Colton kissed her gently. "I wasn't too rough with you?"

"It was perfect." Poppy snuggled against his chest. His chest hair tickled her sensitive nipples.

Colton smiled lazily as his thumb stroked over her hip bone. "You're perfect." Poppy blushed. "Uh-uh." Colton's hand moved to cup her chin. "None of that. You're beautiful and smart and sexy as fucking hell, and I don't want you to ever think anything less of yourself."

"I'll try," Poppy murmured, burrowing into his chest as his arms tightened around her. She yawned, throwing one leg over his. Sleepily, she wondered why she was trying to push this gorgeous, sexy, caring man away in the first place. "There is so much I don't know about you yet."

"What do you want to know?" Colton asked as he let the silky strands of her hair slide through his fingers.

"You grew up here, right?" Colton's beard scratched against her forehead as he nodded. "Do you still have family in the area?"

"My mom lives just outside town in the house I grew up in. My dad died in a car crash when I was in my senior year of high school, and my brother was in basic training. My older brother Jaeger is a career Air Force man and is currently stationed in Alaska. His wife and their kids live on base with him."

"I'm sorry to hear about your dad." Poppy bit her lip as she ran her hand across Colton's chest. "Are you close with your mother and brother?"

"Yeah." Colton nodded. "I try to help my mom out as much as I can. She's been a nurse at St. Mary's Hospital in Green Bay for thirty-eight years and is getting ready to retire soon. Mom is also close friends with Della, and Della checks in on her when I can't. Jaeger and I get along well—better than we did as kids. It's been hard on Mom, with him being stationed all over the world for so many years."

"I can't imagine." Poppy gazed into Colton's eyes. His lips were a whisper-light touch on her skin as he kissed her forehead. "So you haven't had any recent relationships?"

Colton snorted., "Is that your backward way of asking if I was seeing anyone before you moved to town?"

"Maybe." Poppy felt pink from her head to her toes.

"No." Colton's fingers traced along Poppy's spine. "My last relationship ended a while ago."

"I doubt you've been a monk since, though," Poppy teased.

"Not exactly," Colton admitted. "But not as bad as you're imagining."

"Oh?" Poppy propped herself up on one elbow to look at him clearly.

"When you're in a motorcycle club, there are always women around trying to get with the members." Colton stared up at the ceiling. "I'm not saying I never took one home for the night, but they were always temporary, shallow, looking for something I wasn't going to give. Nothing worth pursuing anything serious with."

"Why?"

"They couldn't see past the prestige of the motorcycle and the club vest." Colton frowned, but then his expression smoothed. "Not like you."

CHAPTER NINETEEN

POPPY

When Poppy closed her eyes and laid her head on Colton's chest, it seemed like only ten minutes had passed. His reassuring aroma filled her nostrils, soothing her to sleep as his fingers—the same ones that had given her her first orgasm of the night—stroked her hair slowly. They'd stayed up talking for a while. He told her whatever she wanted to know and, in turn, she talked freely about her childhood and parents but stayed vague about her relationships.

Now, her obnoxious alarm was beeping as her phone vibrated towards the edge of her nightstand, about to clatter to the floor. Jolting awake, she reluctantly left the comfort of Colton's arms to flop over and silence the alarm.

"Mmmm." Colton groaned, half asleep, as he turned onto his side.

"It's okay," Poppy whispered. "Stay, go back to sleep. I need to hop in the shower and get ready for work."

"Stay." His arms reached out for her, but Poppy chuckled and moved off the bed, out of his reach.

"I can't." Poppy sighed regretfully. "I have to work, especially since it looks like the heating in the house has to be completely redone."

"Sucks," Colton mumbled, still half asleep.

"That it does." Poppy snorted, her hair fluttering as she shook her head. She leaned in to kiss Colton's forehead, but at the last second, he moved his head, kissing her, his hand splaying around the back of her head. She sank into him for a moment before pulling away. "Enough of that, or I'll get back into this bed, and I'll never get to work."

"That's the idea." Colton laughed as Poppy darted around the bed and toward the bathroom, giggling as she grabbed the clothes she'd set out for work the night before.

Showered and dressed, Poppy practically skipped down the stairs to the smell of coffee brewing from the delayed brew function. For the first time in longer than Poppy cared to admit, she felt good, relaxed even. She wouldn't let thoughts of Jack pull her down anymore. The police are looking out for her, and with the security system and Colton staying with her, Jack would have to be completely insane to come around again. No, she's going to show him, *if he's watching*, that he can't get to her anymore.

Poppy poured a travel mug full of coffee, breathing deep as the nutty, smoky, slightly vanilla-y scent tickled her nostrils. She left the rest of the pot for Colton, or James and his crew if they wanted, and headed out. She locked the door behind her, her hips swaying to the beat of an unfamiliar melody stuck in her head.

The streets were mostly deserted as Poppy went to work. The only other cars on the road were the factory workers heading to or from work and the one squad car patrolling her street. She waved at the unfamiliar officer who was driving. Flipping on the radio, she turned to the pop station out of Green Bay and sang along to an upbeat love song, missing half the words and singing loudly out of tune.

At the diner, Della filled the salt and pepper shakers ahead of the morning's opening while Len organized the kitchen. He hummed a tune loud enough to be heard over the clattering of pots and pans.

"Morning, honey." Della looked up at her, a slow smile spreading across her face. "You look happy this morning."

Poppy blushed, ducking her head as she set her coffee down behind the counter and hung her bag and hoodie on the hook toward the back of the diner. "Morning, Della, Len." Len paused his humming long enough to grunt a greeting.

Fastening her apron on and sliding an order pad into the pocket, Poppy took a long sip of coffee, letting the caffeine perk her up.

"You know you can have free coffee here any time you want," Della smirked

Poppy shrugged. "It's just part of my morning routine to make a pot at home."

"What she means is your coffee is so strong it could put hair on your chest, Della Darling." Len teased his wife with an infectious laugh. "And she'd rather make it home, especially when she has a young man staying with her now to take care of."

Poppy sputtered, nearly spitting out her elixir of the gods, as Len winked at her. Shaking her head, she changed the subject. "What do you need me to do?"

"Why don't you refill the tables with the jelly and jam packets? I swear those things sprout legs and walk off on their own," Della grumbled, shaking her head. "And there's nothing wrong with my coffee. I haven't had a complaint yet."

The morning went along smoothly. Poppy found herself getting sucked into Alfred, Everett, and Edgar's lively debate on whether Michael and Trixie will admit they are together or not. She discreetly said that she didn't know if anything was going on between them or not.

Alfred humphs, pointing at her. "You know more than you're saying, girly."

"James tells me you have a gentleman caller staying with you," Everett added, his eyes alight with mischief. A few tables back, old Shirl leaned forward, straining for the latest juicy worm of gossip.

Poppy flushed, preparing to excuse Colton's presence, when a loud bang shocked the dining room into silence. A plume of black smoke and orange flames licked up the wall from the pass-thru as Len rushed from the kitchen. "Fire! Everyone out!"

Colton

Colton was struggling with a particularly difficult transmission on a Dodge Journey when his phone pinged. Hands coated in transmission fluid, he ignores it. Then a second ping came in, then a third.

"Are you going to get that, bud?" Frank rolled out from under an older model Ford Escort, which was holding on with a whisper and a prayer.

"I wasn't planning on it." Colton wiped the sweat from his brow with the back of his arm.

"Sounds like someone is trying to get ahold of you mighty urgently," Frank teased.

Colton thought of Poppy, and his blood ran cold. If her ex found her, he'd kill the fucker. Grabbing a rag, Colton hastily wiped the oil from his hands and reached over to the toolbox for his phone.

Lazarus

Just got the call. Fire at the diner. Don't know how bad yet.

Lazarus

Vlad's on the way. Can't get his parents on the phone.

Lazarus

You might want to check on your girl.

"Shit," Colton growled as he shoved his phone in his pocket and stalked across the garage for the row of lockers.

"What's up?" Frank sat up. His white wife-beater was stained with oil and grease, and his black hair stuck up at all angles, making him look like an extra from Jersey Shore.

"There's a fire at Della's Diner," Colton called over his shoulder. "I have to go check on Poppy."

Frank whistles. "Boss ain't going to like you skipping out on work like this all the time."

Colton rolled his eyes. George, his boss, was a retired member of the Burning Blood Riders and served in Desert Storm with Len. He'd understand.

"Damn," Frank added quietly, "Della's can't burn. Where the hell else am I going to find a cheap Friday Fish Fry in this town?"

"Yeah." Colton shook his head. "that's really the most pressing issue right now. Your Friday Fish Fry fix."

"Damn, man." Frank clutched his chest dramatically. "Why do you have to be so heartless?"

Colton shook his head again as he grabbed his jacket and punched his arms into the sleeves. "I'll be back as soon as I can."

The fire department was already racing into the building as the ambulance crew staged down the block. Patrons lined up and down the block, and several squad cars arrived to block off that section of the street and redirect the traffic. Shirl was holding court in front of the Curl and Cut, fanning herself with a napkin, playing up the ordeal to a flock of ladies from the hair salon.

Colton scanned the crowd, looking for Poppy. He saw Vlad rush up to his parents, who were standing by the door, looking twenty years older and exceedingly shaken as Della shivered in her husband's embrace.

His erratic heartbeat didn't calm until his gaze fell on Poppy, helping an overwhelmed-looking older gentleman out of the restaurant. The man's arm was slung over her shoulder, and he looks more frail than Colton has ever seen him. He wasn't sure of the man's name, but he knew he was one of the three old coots that sat at the counter every morning, soaking up Poppy's attention.

Colton crossed the street before he was even conscious of his movement. An officer rushed over, yelling for him to stay back. He ignores him, his footsteps quickening until he reached Poppy. Pulling her from the old man's support, he tugged Poppy into his arms and embraced her. His grip on her was tight as he inhaled the citrus scent of her shampoo.

"I'm okay," Poppy whispered in his ear as she tapped on his back, trying to get him to release his hold.

Reluctantly, Colton loosened his grip and took a step back, clearing his throat. "What happened?"

Poppy glanced over her shoulder at the firemen already retreating from the diner. "I think it was a grease fire. Len got everyone out right away after he tried to smother it out, but it was stubborn and wouldn't extinguish. I noticed Everett wasn't with his friends and went back in."

"I'm mighty glad you did," the older man wheezed as he extracted a handkerchief from his pocket and coughed into it. Pulling the cotton away, Colton saw that the fabric was stained with soot.

"Everett twisted his ankle in the rush out the door," Poppy explained. Seeing the soot on the handkerchief, Poppy's face blanched. "I think you need to be checked out by the EMTs. Do you want me to call your son?"

"I'm fine." Everett's face turned stubborn and indignant. "There's no need to be worrying my boy over this. He's got his hands busy fixing up that eyesore of yours."

Poppy clucks her tongue. "You've got soot in your lungs. You might need oxygen."

"Nonsense." Everett shook his head as his two cohorts ambled over to make sure their friend was okay. As the three old men wandered a few feet away, Everett's attitude changed, and he launched into the story about Poppy's heroic rescue.

"I'm still going to call James." Poppy shook her head as she pulled her phone out of her apron pocket, muttering. "Stubborn old fool."

Colton chuckled as he watched Poppy call James Peters. He'd be jealous of their friendship, except that he saw that James had taken her under his wing like a fragile, younger sister. Colton appreciated James being there for her.

Vlad was heading in Colton's direction, so he caught Poppy's attention, tipping his head in Vlad's direction. Poppy nodded and turned away to make her call.

"Hey, how are your parents doing?"

"Shaken up, but they'll be okay." Vlad sighed, scrubbing his hand over his face. "Trixie was off this morning, thank fuck."

Colton chose to let that little bit of information, and Vlad's emotion over it, slip away into the ether. "Is the damage extensive?"

"The stove top is ruined and will need replacing." Vlad's attention disappeared down the street, somewhere off in the distance. "The wall around the pass-thru is all burnt, and will need to be ripped away to assess any damage behind it. It was a grease fire. The traps were overdue for cleaning. We're just hoping the insurance company will cover everything. Pops thinks the restaurant will have to be closed for a week, maybe two, while the insurance company goes over everything and repairs can hopefully be expedited."

"If your parents need anything, let me and the rest of the club know." Colton patted Vlad on the shoulder. "You know we have your back."

"Thanks, Fox." Vlad nodded gratefully. "How is your girl holding up?"

"She's stronger than she looks," Colton told him as their gaze shifted to where Poppy was pacing. Her bottom lip was between her left thumb and pointer finger, worrying it as she listened to something James was saying on the phone. "I should get back to her."

"No problem," Vlad nodded understandingly. "I'll catch up with you later."

~

Poppy

"I'll be there soon," Poppy told James as she hung up.

"Everything okay?" Poppy jumps, startled by Colton's sudden approach.

She sighed. "I thought for sure this was going to be a good day."

The left corner of Colton's mouth kicked up with a cocky half-grin. She shook her head, feigning annoyance. "Joking aside." Colton's face turned serious. "What is it?"

Poppy groaned, covering her face. "James had an electrician working on the breakers on the second floor, and apparently, the section he was working on was not controlled by the breaker that he turned off. He hit a live wire and shocked himself so badly that he fell backward off the ladder and halfway down the stairs. The ambulance is there with them right now, but it's a bad fracture. Bone sticking out of flesh at an odd angle, bad."

"Shit." Colton whistled. "Is the guy okay?"

"James says he's a little confused, but they think that was from the shock. I have to get over there. It doesn't look like I'll be going back to work today, anyway."

"I'll drive you. We can come back for your car later."

"Okay." Poppy nodded, her mind already five steps ahead to insurance claims and how James will proceed. She followed Colton back to his truck on autopilot. As she crossed the street, a flash of black clothing caught her eye.

Sitting on a black motorcycle was a curious figure. Dressed head-to-toe in black with a short-sleeved shirt and no jacket. The man was deathly pale. His black hair was on the shaggy side, hanging limply around his face. His cheeks were gaunt and so defined that the bones look like they could cut like a knife. Even his eyes looked black from this distance. But it was the look on his face as he stared at the still-smoldering diner that disturbed Poppy the most.

A look of unbridled glee.

The stranger's gaze swung towards her, and she shivered at the predatory look in his eyes. Colton noticed that Poppy had paused in the middle of French Street and turned to her.

"Are you okay?" Poppy tore her gaze away from the man and turned toward Colton. "Yeah, but look at that creepy guy over there."

Colton glanced over her shoulder. "What guy?"

"The one on the—" Poppy turned to point him out, but the stranger, and the motorcycle, were gone. "Never mind. It must be the stress making me see things."

Colton stared at her worriedly as she walked past him to the truck.

~

The back doors of the ambulance were open wide when Colton pulled up the driveway. Two EMTs worked on a shirtless, twenty-something-year-old guy sitting on a stretcher. The electrician was younger than Poppy expected, with brown military-style hair. His features were mostly obscured by an oxygen mask.

She hopped out of the truck the minute Colton parked. She power-walked across the driveway, first peering at the electrician, who gives her a lopsided thumbs up. Then over to where James was talking with his crew, a clipboard tucked under one armpit.

"How did this happen?" Poppy asked breathlessly. "I didn't think we had any issues with the electric."

"You don't." James sighed, rubbing the gray and brown stubble along his jawline. "Everything has tested out fine on the first floor, and you haven't mentioned any electrical shorts or outages, so we were just doing a cursory check of the second floor to make sure everything is up to code. The condition report was a little vague, and you and I both know how many of these houses are operating with copper wires wrapped in asbestos. Since you wanted to replace the light fixture in the upstairs hallway, I decided to have our electrician check it out. He thought he had turned off that breaker. He'd even checked it with a multimeter, and it was showing as cold. But once Derek got in there and started replacing the wires, he got zapped. Not just a little shock, a full-on electrocution. Threw him backward off the ladder. One of my guys who was painting the entryway said Derek stumbled backward, his foot caught on the edge of the landing, and he tumbled down the stairs. His leg smashed into the wall hard when he somersaulted and twisted under him, breaking just below the knee. From what my guy said, it's damn lucky he didn't break his neck."

"Fuck," Poppy muttered, running her hands over her head and tugging at her ponytail in frustration.

"This project is cursed," one of James's guys said, glaring at Poppy. "That's what the problem is. It's been one fucked up thing after another."

"Trey," James barked out a warning.

"What?" Trey narrowed his eyes in disgust. His gray-blue eyes were small, shrewdly sizing Poppy up. "Don't tell me you can't see it, James. Human remains in the backyard, a heating system that never cools off no matter what you do with it, and little 'accidents' here and there. Does she even know about that?" Trey tips his head in her direction.

"It's an old house that's been empty for far too long," James deflected as Poppy swung her gaze in his direction. "Little incidents are bound to happen."

"Whatever you say, boss," Trey said sarcastically as he shook his head and walked away. He started talking to two other guys in a hushed tone, but his gaze kept creeping back.

"It'll be okay," James tried to reassure her. "We're in the home stretch, anyway. I haven't been keeping anything from you. This is the first major accident we've had on the project."

"Promise?" Poppy asked as she felt Colton's strong, soothing presence at her back.

"I swear to you, Poppy. I know how much this means to you."

Colton cleared his throat, and she tilted her head back to look at him. "Your electrician will be fine. The broken leg is the worst of it. The EMTs say there are no signs of a concussion, no heart arrhythmia, and only minor burns on his hands. He'll most likely be sore for the next few days, and he'll need to keep the weight off that leg for at least eight weeks. They're taking him to the hospital to set the bone and cast him."

"Thank goodness." Poppy exhaled hard as she placed her hand over her racing heart. "It could have been so much worse."

"See." James patted her shoulder. "Derek's like a cat. Got nine lives that one. He'll be fine."

"He's got something." Colton snorted, pulling Poppy back into him. "He was asking the EMTs to patch him up here so he could get back to work."

"Damn fool." James smirked. "Sounds like he took a few too many volts to the brain."

"This is going to be all right, isn't it?" Poppy worried her lip between her teeth as she crossed her arms, rubbing them against an unnatural chill, despite the dry heat. "What if your crew doesn't want to come back to finish things up?"

Colton shot James a look. "Then James and I will finish things up."

James nodded. "Like I said, we're in the home stretch. Mostly cosmetic stuff now: painting and putting in the new fixtures. Arnie thinks he has an idea for fixing the heating issue for good. You said you wanted to help with the painting anyway, so it shouldn't be a problem. But my guys will come through. Trey's just an asshole. I only hired him because he's my ex-wife's baby cousin, and he can't hold down a job. My guys know that if they don't show up, they don't get a paycheck."

"Thanks, James." Poppy rocked out of Colton's embrace to hug him.. "You've been such a professional and a great friend throughout all the setbacks. I've worked with great crews before, but this surpasses it all. Now go check on your father. That's what you should be focusing on right now."

"I'm heading there now," James nodded. "My guys are going to call it for the night. I have the correct breaker shut off in the upstairs hall right now, so the light won't work until tomorrow, when I get the new light fixture put in. I'm going to have to sit on Derek to keep him from coming in to finish the job, cast and all."

Colton huffed out a laugh as Poppy shook her head, watching the ambulance pull down the driveway. "Come on." Colton grabbed her hand. "Let's go inside. I'll find something to make for dinner."

"You don't have to. We could order a pizza or something. You can help me figure out how to decorate the living room, or we could watch a movie."

"Alright," Colton conceded, "whatever you want."

Inside, Poppy excused herself to get changed while Colton ordered the pizza. There was a small, softball-sized dent in the drywall above the fourth step from the top of the stairs. Poppy crouched down, running her hand over the cracked plaster, and closed her eyes, picturing Derek's kneecap slamming into the wall right before his leg snapped beneath him. A wave of nausea fluttered in Poppy's stomach.

She knew the pain of a break like that. Jack had once twisted her right arm behind her in a way that snapped her radius bone right in half. She had nearly bitten her tongue off, trying not to scream, when the bone poked through her skin. She'd learned much earlier that crying or screaming at Jack's cruelty was the worst thing she could do. It was as if he got off on hurting her; he literally got aroused by it. She wouldn't let her mind go there. Shaking her head, she pushed the thoughts away.

Poppy went to her bedroom and changed into a pair of black yoga pants and a loose gray t-shirt before brushing her hair out of its ponytail and twisting it into a knot at the nape of her neck.

Back in the hallway, Poppy dared to look up. The porcelain shade had been removed, along with the lightbulb and the plate that covered the wires in the ceiling. All that remained were two wires wrapped in fabric hanging limp from the ceiling.

She shivered and moved toward the door along the wall, just to the side of the light fixture. She hadn't been inside the room since she'd done a cursory check and realized all of the floorboards needed to be replaced. James told her just the other day that the new floor was laid and stained, and he'd shown her the rotten boards before throwing them into the dumpster. She had never seen anything like it.

The boards were black, stained with some kind of mold or disease that had seeped and warped the wood, eating away at it. And they reeked—a coppery tang mixed with mold and rot.

Poppy pushed the door open, noting the new boards, originally a bright, light wood that had been stained the same mahogany as the built-in bookshelves spanning from floor to ceiling on three walls. There were no windows, and the room gave off an unsettling feeling. She stepped inside, a slight chill raising the hair on the back of her neck.

She stood there, pondering what she would do with the room. It would take her ages to fill all the bookshelves. But lately, when she'd decided she wouldn't allow Jack to keep her from living, she toyed with the idea of going back into home restoration. Trying her hand at building her own business up here in Wisconsin. She had planned to discuss it with James once the project was done. Now, she was wondering if it was a foolish idea.

As she was visualizing a desk in the center of the room, she heard a dull thumping coming from behind the bookshelves on the left wall.

She narrowed her eyes. Poppy knew the upstairs bathroom was on the other side of that wall. *Was Colton running water downstairs?* Poppy knew that sometimes, in old homes, you could hear water banging through the pipes, but this sound was almost rhythmic. Tap, tap, tap. Then, a pause. Then another tap, tap, tap. The pounding became more insistent, and the tapping grew in volume until the bookshelves themselves began to rattle.

Poppy stumbled backward. "What the fuck?"

The sound moved down the wall, rocking the newly laid floorboards beneath her feet. She gasped, lunging for the door and yanking it open. On the other side, Colton paused mid-knock. His brow furrowed as he peered around her to the empty room.

"What's wrong?"

"Didn't you hear that?" Poppy gasped, shooting a cautious glance behind her. The rattling had ceased. The room fell stagnant, as if no one had entered it in years.

"Hear what?"

It was the stress. It had to be. From Jack coming to town and destroying Colton's bike, to the fire at the diner this morning, and the electrician getting injured at nearly the same time, it was no wonder Poppy was imagining things.

It was laughable, Poppy told herself as they shared a meat lover's pizza in the living room, a game show playing quietly on the television. Coming down from the stress of the day, she'd conjured a scene straight from an Edgar Allan Poe story.

Colton must have been using the bathroom on the main floor or washing up some dishes in the kitchen, causing a clanging in the pipes, as she'd originally thought. *That's all.* There was no banging on the walls, no rattling of the bookshelves, just the pipes on the other side. The floor hadn't shook.

"Are you sure you're all right?" Colton asked, holding a piece of pizza halfway to his mouth.

"Yeah, I'm fine." Poppy sighed. "I think I'm just finally grasping all that happened today: the fire, helping Everett out of the diner, and the electrician getting hurt. It really was... a lot."

Colton set the pizza back onto the paper plate balanced precariously on a box and gathered Poppy into his arms. He smelled faintly of cigarette smoke and the outdoors. His skin was warmed from the sun. She knew he had snuck outside for a smoke while she grabbed a couple of beers.

"You were amazing today," Colton murmured into her hair, "going back into the diner like you did. Foolish and reckless, but amazing, nonetheless."

"Don't tell me you wouldn't have done the same if I had tripped and couldn't get out on my own." Poppy grinned into his chest.

Colton kissed the top of her head. "I'd walk through a thousand burning buildings for you."

Poppy's muscles relaxed as she leaned into him. "Just tell me tomorrow will be a better day."

"It will be," Colton said, though they both know he couldn't promise that. "And then this weekend, we'll go to the fall festival, and you'll meet the old ladies, and you'll see you belong here. Belong with us."

"I'm not sure I'm ready for that." Poppy pulled back to look Colton in the eye.

"Come on." Colton ran his fingers through her hair. "It's for charity. Della and Len are running a chili stand, and everyone in town goes all out for it. You're not scared to meet the old ladies, are you?"

"I'm scared that being with you means being called an *old lady*." Poppy smacked his stomach lightly.

Colton laughed, tickling her ribs as he kissed her neck, leaving the pizza forgotten for the moment.

He kissed the column of her neck as his deft fingers slid the hem of her t-shirt upward. Pleased to find her braless beneath the thick cotton shirt, he groaned and took one hardened nipple into his mouth. Poppy's eyes rolled back in ecstasy. Colton kissed across her sternum before turning his attention to her other nipple, then kissed his way to where her yoga pants sat at her waist. He kissed her warm skin, then slid Poppy's yoga pants and panties down.

Once she was bared to him, he hooked one of her legs over his shoulder, spreading her open. His gaze was ravenous, like a starving man presented his favorite meal. His lips descended onto her wet folds, and she was lost in a sea of ecstasy as he eagerly dragged his tongue over her core.

His gaze met hers as he tasted her, driving his tongue deeper and deeper inside her as the wave of pleasure grew. She was sure her heart was going to burst from her chest, unable to take the sensations for a single second longer. And then the wave crashed over her as she screamed his name.

CHAPTER TWENTY

POPPY

It was the morning of Peshtigo's Fall Festival, and Poppy had slept better with Colton beside her than she had since she had moved to town. They climbed into his truck, and it chugged to life; the opening bars of *Kickstart My Heart* by Mötley Crüe blasting through the speakers, startling her.

"What?" Colton laughed. "We can't all listen to sugary pop."

"I don't listen to pop," Poppy scoffed. "In my car, we 'dig through the ditches and burn through the witches.'"

Colton barked out a laugh. "I was not expecting that."

"Who knows what other surprises I have up my sleeve?" Poppy teased.

Colton patted her knee. "I can't wait to find out."

"This must be what it's like when the south tries to celebrate fall," Poppy said wryly as Colton parked on Northwest Front Street. As they got out and turned the corner onto French Street, the pharmacy sign read the temperature as 91 degrees.

"It's definitely not a day to be dressed like that." Colton tipped his head toward a woman wearing knee-high boots over her dark wash jeans, a flannel shirt over a t-shirt, a scarf, and a beanie.

"She must be roasting." She snorted, looking down at her shorts and fall-themed T-shirt. He opted for cargo shorts and a gray T-shirt to ward off sunstroke.

Poppy stopped short when she glanced ahead to French Street and gasped. The street stands transformed. White and yellow tents lined both sides of the street as people wandered and browsed the vendors. Every four feet stood an artificial potted tree with leaves of vibrant red and orange. A metal canopy extended six feet over the top of each tree, with the support posts fastened to the light posts. The canopy was woven with swags of fall leaves, from which dangled bell-shaped lanterns and cloth jack-o'-lanterns. The whole structure was lit with string lights that made it look like the sky was ablaze.

"This is amazing," Poppy said breathlessly. "It must have taken all night to do this."

"Almost."

It was nearly four in the morning before he returned to the house and crawled into bed beside her. He only managed to get a meager three hours of sleep after he'd woken Poppy with his head between her legs, bringing her to orgasm before driving her to two more with his cock buried inside her. Colton gazed over at Poppy. Her gaze was fixed on the purple banner hanging just before the entrance to the festival, her expression stricken.

2023 PESHTIGO FALL FESTIVAL, SPONSORED BY THE BURNING BLOOD RIDERS MOTORCYCLE CLUB and THE PESHTIGO CHAMBER OF COMMERCE BENEFITING DOMESTIC VIOLENCE AWARENESS.

"Did you do that?" Poppy pointed at the banner, her finger shaking as tears gathered in the corners of her eyes. Her voice grew louder and angrier, "Did you do that because of me?"

"No." Colton shook his head. "Relax, baby. It has nothing to do with you. I haven't told anyone what you told me. The charity we're giving to this year was chosen back in January, long before I met you. October is Domestic Violence Awareness Month, after all."

"It's also Breast Cancer Awareness Month," Poppy muttered through gritted teeth.

"Yes, and we did that one last year." Colton nodded. "We choose a different charity every year. Well, not in 2020 or 2021. Things were pretty shut down with COVID."

"I'm not sure whether to believe you," Poppy said, narrowing her eyes at him.

"Poppy," Colton gathered her hands in his, his thumbs rubbing across her knuckles. "If and when you tell people about your past, it's no one's decision but yours. I would never steal that from you. Do some people suspect they know? Sure, but they're not going to push you."

"You're sure you didn't do this?" Poppy's voice wavered.

Colton nodded, not breaking eye contact. "I promise."

She sighed, hugging his middle. "I'm sorry. I don't mean to sound paranoid."

"You don't." He held her tight. "It's understandable, but I swear to you it's just a coincidence."

"Okay. Let's go have a nice day."

"You sure?" Colton asked, concern warring across his face.

"Yeah." She nodded. "I love fall, even when it feels like the hottest circle of hell. Let's go bob for apples or something."

Poppy allowed Colton to weave his fingers through hers as they joined the throng of people meandering up and down French Street. Len and Della's chili tent was the busiest, despite the early hour. There were also stands for hot apple cider, which unfortunately didn't have a large crowd due to the heat, colorfully decorated caramel apples, and pumpkin donuts with cream cheese frosting from Fire Roasted Coffee Shop.

"Do you want to come back later for chili?" Poppy asked. "It will take us forever to get to the front of the line, and I'm eyeing up those pumpkin donuts."

"Sure." Colton laughed. "But if you want chili, you won't want to wait too long. They tend to sell out early."

"That must be some good chili," Poppy said, eyeing the tent.

"Della's own recipe," he said proudly, as if she were his own mother. "With a few of Lazarus's embellishments, of course."

"Lazarus?" Poppy furrowed her brow, trying to remember if she had met him or not.

"His real name is Silas Talbot. He's on the fire department. You'll meet his wife, Naomi, today, and probably Mina Collins. She's married to Freddy, or Wolf, as he's known to the club."

"Okay," Poppy replied nervously, not so sure if she wanted that donut after all.

They strolled past a group of heavily tattooed adults sitting outside a tent, painting animal faces, leaves, jack-o'-lanterns, and other designs on the faces of children and adults alike.

Officer Michelson nodded to them from where he was working a dunk tank, and the female officer who responded the night of the break-in sat dressed like a witch. She struggled to remember the woman's name. Officer Mutton? Officer Munion? Finally, it clicks as the woman glanced over and waved at Poppy, recognizing her or not. Officer Mullins. Poppy smiled and waved back.

A local farmer was selling pumpkins at the tent next to the pumpkin donut tent. Pumpkins spilled out into the street along with an assortment of gourds in pastel blues, pure whites, and blacks.

"Two pumpkin donuts," Colton told the donut vendor as they stepped up to the tent. Poppy reaches for her wallet, but Colton waved her hand away. "Allow me, I insist."

"But-"

"You can get the chili if you want." Colton shrugged, though she suspected he'd insist on paying for that as well.

The vendor handed over the donuts wrapped in wax paper,

and they moved out of the line and down the street a little as Poppy took the first bite. Fall flavors exploded on her tongue, and she closed her eyes, savoring the taste.

Colton laughed and took a bite of his donut. Poppy opened her eyes in time to watch him lick the frosting off the top in an obscene manner. Her cheeks flushed as her core melted.

"Mmm," Colton moaned appreciatively. "It's sweet, but not as sweet as you taste."

"Colton!" she shrieked, admonishing him as she glanced around to see if anyone heard him.

"Don't be embarrassed, baby." Colton pulled her toward him, licking a wayward bit of frosting off her top lip.

"Get a room," someone teased as they pulled apart.

Poppy looked over and saw two couples as different as can be. She recognized the men from the diner, one short and dark-haired, the other slightly taller with graying brown hair. A woman in her early to mid-twenties with pink hair stood beside the taller one, while a homely soccer mom type with blonde hair and glasses cuddled up to the shorter man.

"Leave them alone." The blonde swatted the short, brown-haired man in the stomach. "I think it's sweet, don't you, Mina?"

"It's nice to see Fox with someone; I have to admit." A teasing grin spread across the pink-haired woman's bright red lips. A hint of silver shone in the sunlight as Poppy noticed the stud in her nose.

Colton groaned, gesturing to his friends. "Poppy, this is Silas *Lazarus* Talbot, the chili expert I was telling you about." The shorter man straightens proudly. "And this is his wife, Naomi."

"It's such a pleasure to meet you." Naomi crossed the distance in a second, pulling Poppy into a bone-crushing hug. Poppy stood awkwardly for a minute before hugging Naomi back, patting her on the back awkwardly.

"Not a hugger?" Naomi laughed as she pulled back.

Poppy shot a look at Colton before turning back to Naomi. "Um, not really."

"Don't worry," Naomi winked and patted Poppy's arm. "We'll fix that."

Colton cleared his throat, gesturing to the other couple. "And this is Freddy *Wolf* Collins and his wife, Mina. Mina works at the Curl and Cut."

"It's nice to meet you." Mina waved. "Don't worry, I'm not a hugger either."

"Nice to meet you, too," Poppy echoed. Mina was studying her oddly, tilting her head and rubbing her chin. "What is it?"

"Your hair. What color is it naturally?"

"Oh, um," Poppy stalled as she touched her ponytail.

"Come on, don't be shy," Mina coaxed her. "I have a sixth sense for a dye job."

"It's red." Poppy frowned.

Colton gaped at her, a little shocked, but wisely didn't say anything.

"Ah yes." Mina smiled as if she could picture it. "That makes so much more sense with your coloring. This light brown color washes you out. It makes you look sickly."

"Mina!" Naomi admonished her.

Poppy bristled. "Uh, thanks."

"Ignore her." Naomi rolled her eyes as Freddy shot his wife a look. "She's such a hair snob. Comes with the occupation."

"Are you enjoying the festival, Poppy?" Silas asked, smoothing out the tension in the group.

"Yeah, the decorations are beautiful." Poppy smiled gratefully. "I haven't had a chance to try your chili yet, though."

"You better hurry before it's all gone." Silas winked. "You work at the diner, right?"

Poppy nodded. "I do."

"It's a shame what happened yesterday with the fire." Silas sobered. "Della and Len are great folks, and I hope they're able to reopen soon. In the meantime, they know the club has their backs if they need anything. The same goes for you and the other girls, of course."

"I'll remember that," Poppy said politely.

The group moved over by the pumpkin tent as Colton, Freddy, and Silas explained different events they'd done for charity and their upcoming Christmas toy drive. From the corner of her eye, she noted a young child running past, followed by an embarrassed-looking older woman speed-walking to the nearest PortaPotty. As the men talked, Naomi eagerly tried to enlist Poppy in a fundraiser the high school was having and her book club.

Then Michael, with a hand clamped over his mouth, his eyes wide, and sweat beading on his forehead, ducked around the side of the pumpkin tent. A violent retching sound followed.

"Is he okay?" Poppy pointed in the direction Michael disappeared.

Colton pulled his attention away from the conversation he'd been having with Silas about the insurance company's argument over replacing his motorcycle. "Huh?"

"Michael." Poppy gestured in the direction he went again. More people passed, clutching their stomachs and running for PortaPotties. She felt her stomach start to churn. And she clearly wasn't the only one.

"I don't feel so well," Colton groaned, clutching his toned stomach.

Poppy shook her head. "Me either."

Around them, the beautiful, atmospheric festival devolved into people getting sick, some right in the middle of the street.

Silas scanned the crowd. "This looks bad."

"At this scale, it looks like food poisoning." Freddy turned to Poppy and Colton. "What did you guys eat?"

Colton winced. "Just the donuts."

"Excuse me," Poppy announced urgently as she clutched her

gut and rushed to a PortaPotty, just as one of Colton's club brothers stumbled out.

Locking herself inside, Poppy gagged and pulled the neckline of her shirt over her mouth and nose as she shoved her shorts down as fast as she could. After three false starts and several rattles of the door handle from someone outside, Poppy emerged, blinking in the suddenly harsh daylight. The heat made the cramps worse as she stumbled out in a daze, sweat dripping down her face.

"Poppy." She heard Colton call her name, and she turned toward the sound of his voice.

Colton looked as rough as she felt. His face was pale and sickly. He clutched his stomach as he came toward her. "Are you okay?" Poppy asked him. Her mouth felt dry, and her stomach was still churning, though not as bad.

"I threw up a couple of times." Colton frowned as though admitting it made him weak. "Silas went to get Ben Michelson and Officer Mullins to get some ambulances paged out for the worst off. The festival is shutting down, and Michelson is calling in the health department. They think it's a mass case of food poisoning, and they have to lock everything down until they can pinpoint if only one food vendor was affected or if they all were."

"Is it because of the heat?"

"It shouldn't be." Colton shook his head. "Nothing that's being sold is at risk of going bad in hot weather, but that's a case for the health department. Are you okay to get to my truck? The officers have called ahead to the nearby hospitals. They want everyone checked out."

"I think I'm okay." Poppy followed Colton through the sea of sick people and other citizens trying to escape the chaos.

❧

"As expected, it's food poisoning," the doctor announced to Colton and Poppy as he read the results off his tablet. They refused to be separated once they reached the hospital in Marinette, which had worked out for the better, with the volume of people coming in.

"You're luckier than some of the others, though," the doctor continued. His round wire frames caught the light, obscuring his eyes. He adjusted them as he scrolled down the screen. "It's just a mild case. Keeping hydrated and sticking to a brat diet once you feel up to eating should clear up in the next day or two."

"Thank you, doctor." Colton squeezed Poppy's hand.

The doctor humphs grumpily as he filled out the discharge papers, undoubtedly irritated that his day was upended in such a way. All trauma transports were diverted to Green Bay or Menominee, Michigan, leaving him with case after case of food poisoning.

A keening wail sounded from the next exam room as they were leaving. Colton turned his head toward the sound as they passed. The curtain was pulled back just enough to see a middle-aged woman crying over her elderly mother. He'd seen them both at the festival, and it appeared the older woman had more than just a mild case of food poisoning. She was dead.

"How awful," Poppy whispered as she peered around Colton. "I didn't realize food poisoning could be fatal."

"She must have had a compromised immune system already or something." Colton looked away, taking Poppy's hand in his. "Come on, we shouldn't intrude on the daughter's private grief. Let's get back to the house."

Poppy nodded, falling into step beside him. As they passed the registration desk, Poppy recognized the nefarious figure from earlier. .Clad in all black, he leaned against the desk, a satisfied smirk on his lips—disappearing in a blink.

CHAPTER TWENTY-ONE

POPPY

"You know, they say you don't really know your significant other until you see them sick," Colton mumbled drowsily as they lay tangled up on opposite sides of the uncomfortable couch in the living room.

Poppy cocked an eyebrow. "Yes, it's absolutely horrifying to find out the man I've been sleeping with is a closet fantasy show geek who likes burnt toast."

"Hey!" Colton snorted. "Admit it. You were getting into Game of Thrones, too."

Poppy rolled her eyes as her stomach growled idly. "It is slightly more exciting than my home renovation shows."

"That's the spirit." Colton smiled weakly. His eyes widened for a minute as he reached blindly for the plastic popcorn bucket he'd set beside the couch that morning. After a minute, the nausea passed, and he slumped against the side of the sofa.

They'd been holed up at Poppy's house for two days, alternating between bouts of sickness and taking care of one another.

Poppy allowed Colton to pick up Large Marge on the way home from the hospital since he didn't have the energy to go back and forth to feed her. The large feline was now curled up on her chest, making biscuits in the light blanket she had put over herself before her fever broke.

Poppy knew they were luckier than most. They'd watched the news the night before and learned that ten people had died from food poisoning at the fall festival. The victims were all either elderly or already suffering from a compromised immune system. In all, nearly one hundred people were sent to nearby emergency rooms and convenient care to be diagnosed with the same thing.The health department's investigation was ongoing, but they believed all the food stands were affected by some sort of bacteria.

"You okay?" Poppy asked as she watched Colton. Absently, she scratched Large Marge's soft head, and the cat preened, pushing her head more into Poppy's palm.

"Yeah," Colton nodded as he reached for a soda cracker. "It passed."

"Good." Poppy's head lolled to the side against the back of the couch.

"You know what we've never talked about?" Colton asked as he studied her through tired, half-lidded eyes.

"What's that?"

"The real you." Poppy frowned as Colton continued, "I don't know whether I'm supposed to call you Poppy or Fallon. I don't even know what you really look like beneath the hair dye and whatever else you use to disguise yourself."

"This is me." Poppy glanced away.

"You know what I mean," Colton pressed. "I didn't even know you were a natural redhead until Mina called you out at the festival."

"She is a blunt one," Poppy muttered.

"Poppy," Colton said, raising an eyebrow.

Poppy sighed. "What do you want to know?"

"What else are you hiding?" Colton challenged lightly.

"Well, I'm not faking my skin color, height, or body type." Poppy rolled her eyes. "You know as well as I do that this isn't padding beneath my clothes."

"But you are a natural redhead," Colton said blandly, studying her as if he could picture her natural color.

"Yep," Poppy said dismissively. "Bright red, somewhere between carrot red like Jessica Chastain and dark auburn like Debra Messing. It was a bitch to cover up, and the sad thing is, I really love my hair. But brown is boring. It blends in better than red."

Colton nodded. "And your eyes?"

"Contacts," Poppy popped one gray contact out of her eye to reveal the emerald green beneath.

"Holy shit!" Colton's eyes widened. "Beautiful."

"Thanks." Poppy smiled sadly. "You can call me whatever you want. It's just easier to stick to Poppy in public since nobody else knows the truth except Officer Michelson and probably the rest of the police department at this point."

"I understand." Colton reached out and took her hand. "Do you ever think you'll tell them? Go back to being Fallon?"

Poppy shrugged. "I don't know. Honestly, a part of me feels like Fallon is dead, and I'm someone else, risen from the ashes of her corpse. I would love to go back to my old job, restoring homes professionally. But the rest I could take or leave."

Colton nodded. "That's understandable."

It took another day of rest, bad reality television, and bland eating before Colton and Poppy felt like leaving the house. Colton talked her into meeting James, Vlad, and Trixie at The Watering Hole for drinks.

"What can I get you?" Michael asked from across the bar.

Trixie pouted. "I thought you were joining us, Vlad."

"I will." Vlad frowned. "I'm just waiting for my night bartender to come in. Bear's running late coming from physical therapy."

"Just a 7 Up for me," James orders.

"I'll have a beer," Colton told him before turning to Poppy. "What do you want, babe?"

Trixie "oohs" when Colton used the term of endearment. Poppy rolled her eyes. "I'll have a Numbskul and lemonade."

"I can respect that, city girl," Vlad teased. Turning to Trixie, he asked, "Your usual?"

"I guess." Trixie shrugged, playing with the plastic cocktail skewers on the bar.

Vlad gave her a long look before pouring himself a finger of whiskey. He pulled out a bottle of microbrew beer for Colton, opened a can of soda for James, mixed Poppy's drink, and made a fruity drink for Trixie.

Poppy had taken a single sip of her drink when she spied something across the nearly empty bar. Her face paled and her eyes widened with terror. Colton craned his head to see what she's looking at.

A blond man walked through the door. He wore a gray button-down shirt and black slacks. He was tan, though it was artificial from a tanning bed. He had an average build and average height, definitely shorter and trimmer than Colton. His green eyes narrowed into a glare as he stared at where Colton's hand was on Poppy's thigh. He looked like an angry Ken doll.

"Who is that?" Colton whispered to Poppy.

"Jack." Poppy gasped as she started to hyperventilate. Jack starts crossing the bar, his hands curling into fists. Poppy shrank back against the bar.

Colton's temper flared as he stood and crossed his arms. "You're not welcome here."

Jack ignored him, reaching one small, callous-free hand past Colton's shoulder to grab at Poppy. "I'm not leaving without her."

Colton swatted his hand away easily, like he was nothing more than an annoying mosquito. Vlad glanced around, assessing the situation as Jack attempted to shoulder Colton out of the way. It clicked. He shot James a look, but he was already rising from his stool.

"My friend here was being nice." James came to stand beside Colton. "But I won't be. You have no business here or with her. Leave before we call the police."

"You think I'm scared of you?" Jack sneered, having to tilt his chin up at the two men. "An old fucker with a dad body and a low-level thug? As if." Jack's voice was higher in pitch, almost feminine, in the way all slick fast-talkers tend to speak.

"Fallon, get your ass off the stool and get over here," Jack commanded. "I'm taking you home."

"No," Poppy protested, her voice reed-thin.

"You fucking whore." Jack snarled, losing his tether as he lunged for her. "What, do you let them share you like some biker whore?"

Colton blocked him, throwing himself in front of Poppy. Her fingers fisted the back of his t-shirt, her breath labored.

"That's enough," Vlad growled, yanking Jack back by the collar of his shirt. "This is my establishment, and I won't have my friend talked to that way. Get the fuck out. Trixie, honey, call Officer Michelson and let him know that we have the suspect in Colton's motorcycle vandalism here, and either he comes and arrests him, or we'll take care of it our way."

Trixie nodded and reached for her phone as Vlad dragged Jack out of the bar, protesting the whole way.

Clearly, Trixie called more than the police. By the time Officer Michelson and another officer arrived at The Watering Hole, the parking lot was packed with motorcycles. Bikers, wives, and girlfriends were everywhere, spilling out of the bar and milling in the parking lot. Colton and James stood sentry at Poppy's side as Jack was handed over to Officer Michelson, who handcuffed him and placed him in the back of his squad car.

The second officer, a short, heavyset man with a bald head and a gray-black beard, took Michael's statement as Officer Michelson headed over to Poppy, James, and Colton.

"Are you all right, Ms. Isles?" Officer Michelson asked as he pulled a notepad out of his vest.

"A little shaken up," Poppy admitted., "But the guys didn't let him get close enough to actually touch me."

"Good, good." Officer Michelson made a note of that. "But verbal comments were made."

"A few," Colton added, his jaw ticking, undoubtedly thinking of Jack calling her a whore.

Officer Michelson nods, writing that down as well. Poppy noticed, belatedly, that he had a purple folder tucked under one arm. "I have some paperwork to fill out with you if you want to, Ms. Isles. Right now, we'll have him on the violation of the restraining order at least. We'll most definitely be questioning him about the vandalism to Colton's motorcycle. Still, I can already see right front-end damage to the Escalade he pulled up in this evening, so that's not in his favor. It would be very weak, as you state that it was only verbal, but we can try to charge him with disorderly conduct with a domestic abuse enhancer, as you had been living with Mr. Richards in Chicago. Is that correct?"

"Yes, up until I had help to move away."

"We'll at least give it a try," Officer Michelson said as he grabbed the folder. "It's up to the district attorney whether they'll charge it out or not."

"I understand." Poppy felt her breath even out for the first time since she saw Jack walk into the bar. Her heart rate slowed.

"He did try to grab her and lunged at her," Colton points out.

"But he didn't actually touch her?"

"No." Colton frowned as he crossed his beefy arms over his chest.

"I'll add it to the report, Ms. Isles, is it all right with you if we go inside to complete this packet?"

"Sure." Poppy nodded as she led Officer Michelson back into The Watering Hole.

James and Colton followed Poppy and Officer Michelson to a table by the front window of the bar, but Poppy reassured them, "I'm fine; I just need to fill out some paperwork with the officer." James nodded and returned to the bar to finish off his forgotten soda, but Colton lingers a moment longer. "It's okay, Colton," Poppy insisted. "This isn't anything I haven't done before."

"Alright," Colton said reluctantly before heading to the bar to speak with Della and Len, who had just arrived.

"He's a good guy," Officer Michelson told her. "Loyal and protective to a fault, but he'd never lay a hand on a woman."

"That's good to know," Poppy raised an eyebrow. "Though sometimes the ones you'd never expect it from are the worst of all. Look at Jack. He didn't seem like the type at first, but I have the scars to prove it."

"True," Officer Michelson conceded.

"Though I agree," Poppy continued. "Colton looks tough on the outside, but on the inside, he's all heart."

"Shall we get started?" Officer Michelson opened the folder and pulled out a thick sheaf of papers.

It's all standard paperwork. Did Poppy give Jack permission to verbally abuse her or attempt to strike or tackle her, which Poppy always found to be a ridiculous question. Who would *give someone permission to do that?* The forms also went through past history, and Poppy detailed, as thoroughly as she could, all the times and ways Jack has abused her over the years. At one point, Officer Michelson paused in his notation to look at her, raising an eyebrow as if to ask, "After all that, why did you stay?"

"I honestly thought if I attempted to leave, Jack would kill me,"

Poppy admitted. There were no more tears to cry. She cried them all. Now, all she felt was bone tiredness. "He nearly succeeded on that final night. The night that Detective Milbauer helped me start my new life here."

Officer Michelson's face is flushed with chagrin. "I suppose it's impossible to pass judgment when you haven't been in that situation or lived through the things that you did."

"Thank you." Poppy accepted his apology. She knew what most people thought of women in abusive relationships. She heard all the nasty comments. But the truth was, once you lived through the things she had and made it through to tell the tale, the nasty remarks of others tend to bounce off like rubber bullets. The damage was already done; nothing else could hurt her more than she's already been hurt. "Do you think they'll keep him locked up for a while?"

"It's hard to say," Officer Michelson said slowly. "By state statute, he could face up to nine months in jail and/or a one-thousand-dollar fine. But it depends on the judge, how strict or lenient they may be, and the extent of the violation."

"But he wouldn't get out today yet, would he?" Poppy presses.

"I wouldn't think so." Officer Michelson shook his head. "But we can have the jail notify you if and when he is released."

"I'd like that."

"I'll need you to fill out this form." Officer Michelson pulled out a sheet of paper and handed it to Poppy. "You'll need to use your given name."

"Of course." Poppy grabbed the pen Officer Michelson offered and filled out the form. She signed the rest of the forms that she was required to fill out, as well as her written statement.

Once Officer Michelson and his partner left, Poppy rejoined Colton and her friends at the bar. It strikes Poppy for the first time. Her friends. She'd come to town with plans to keep to herself and keep everyone shut out. Still, the people in this town had wormed their way in, anyway. From the older gentlemen at the diner, even

Shirl and her gaggle of ladies, to Della and the other employees of the diner, and Colton and his club friends.

"Hey." Colton pulled her to his side and kissed the top of her head. "Everything go okay?"

"Yeah." Poppy tilted her head to look up at him. "Just standard paperwork. Officer Michelson doesn't think Jack will be getting out tonight, which is a relief."

"Good." Colton nodded before sharing a look with Michael behind the bar and Gomez on his right side. "He'd better stay away, or we'll take care of him."

"Colton." Poppy sighed, leaning into him. "Don't say that. Don't do anything stupid. He's not worth it."

"But you are," Colton murmured in her ear.

Poppy swallowed hard and reached for her abandoned drink, taking a deep swig. Turning to Della and Len, James, Trixie, Michael, and the rest of the friends she'd made since coming to town, she said, "I think I owe everyone a few explanations."

Their corner of the bar was quiet by the time Poppy finished her story. Della looked stricken. Colton's friends looked as enraged as Colton did when he first found out.

Trixie was the first to cross the barrier and pull Poppy into a tight embrace. "I'm so sorry, girl," Trixie whispered in her ear. "I'm so, so sorry."

James reached out to her next. "I knew it was something, kid; I just wasn't expecting it to be this bad."

"What did you think it was?" Poppy forced a smile, curious as to what they all thought she was running from.

James shrugged. "I thought maybe you were running from the mafia or something."

Poppy barked out a startled laugh. "What?"

James blushed. "I think I've been watching too many movies."

"Probably." Michael clapped him on the shoulder good-naturedly as everyone cracked up.

"So what should we call you?" Della asked, pushing forward and taking Poppy's hands in her own.

Poppy bit her lips, uncertain. She looked at Colton, and he nodded his support. Who do I want to be? The shy girl with the silly name? Or the woman who lived through hell and came out stronger on the other side? "Fallon." *She decided, shedding her new identity to claim who she really was.* "You can call me Fallon."

CHAPTER TWENTY-TWO

FALLON

Fallon gripped the phone harder. "What do you mean, they let him go?"

"I'm really sorry, Ms. Isles." Officer Michelson sounded as disgusted with the situation as Fallon was.

"I've gone back to my real name," she sighed as she slumped down on a barstool at the kitchen island. Colton paused his preparation of their morning coffee. He stood across the island, gesturing for her to put the phone on speaker. She pushed a button, and Officer Michelson's disembodied voice filled the kitchen.

"Alright, Ms. Boseman, then. From what I've been told, his attorney, Mr. Kemp, pulled quite a few strings to get Mr. Richards released late last night. He was supposed to have a hearing this morning, but he failed to appear at that."

Fallon rubbed the skin between her eyes, feeling a headache blooming there. "What are you doing to find him?"

"The court has placed a body-only warrant for him with

statewide extradition as well as with adjoining states," Officer Michelson explained. "That means -"

"That means if he's picked up in Wisconsin, Minnesota, Michigan, or Illinois, he'll be brought back here and placed in jail," Poppy finished for him. "But he has to do something wrong for law enforcement to have contact with him first. Do you really think he's dumb enough to get caught again?"

"That's not necessarily the case," Officer Michelson said. "We've put out an APB statewide as well as in those neighboring states with Mr. Richard's physical description as well as the make, model, and license plate information on the rental car that was delivered to him outside the jail last night. We were able to trace the rental back to his attorney."

"And in the meantime, what am I supposed to do? Am I supposed to just wait around for him to ambush me again?"

"We are doing everything in our power to track him down." Officer Michelson's calm tone grated on Fallon, but she bit her tongue. "We'll have extra patrols sweeping past your house several times a day. In the meantime, we suggest that you have a friend staying with you if you don't already. I understand that you have a security system set up?"

"I do."

"Good," Officer Michelson said. "Keep that armed and keep all of your doors and windows locked at all times. If you receive any calls from unknown numbers that call more than once, let us know. Also, let us know immediately if you receive any more threatening notes."

She sighed. "I will."

"I wish I had better news." Officer Michelson's tone bled with regret. "I really do. I'm as frustrated by this as you are, Ms. Boseman."

She focused on a tree through the kitchen window, using it to anchor herself as she controlled her breath. "I understand."

"Stay safe, Ms. Boseman."

"I'll try." Fallon's tone was hollow, disappointed.

Colton raised an eyebrow as he braced his hands on the island. "They let him out?"

Fallon nodded. "That's the American justice system at work."

"You don't seem surprised." Colton observed as she wiped imaginary crumbs off the countertop.

"Should I be?" she asked as she looked up at him. "The legal system is rarely on the victim's side, no matter what they show on television. Why do you think I fled Chicago in the first place?"

"Maybe I shouldn't go to my club meeting," Colton sighed as he scrubbed his hands over his face. "I hate the thought of you being here alone when nobody knows where Jack is."

"Don't be ridiculous." Fallon shook her head dismissively as she straightened, crossing her arms over her chest. "It's an emergency meeting, especially after what happened at Fall Fest. You can't miss it. I'll be fine. I'll lock the door, arm the system, pour myself a glass of wine, and flip through some design magazines while you're gone."

Colton rubbed the back of his neck, and she could practically see the tense, bunched muscles inflamed beneath his skin. "Are you sure?"

"I'm sure." Uncrossing her arms, she leaned across the island and kissed Colton.

He groaned as he wrapped his hand around the back of her head, drawing her in deeper as he nibbled on her bottom lip. The thumb of his other hand traced and caressed her jawline. "You're not making it easy to go," Colton murmured against her lips.

Fallon laughed. "But you should."

"Fine, I won't be too late."

"No after-meeting parties with biker chicks?" Fallon teased.

"Nah, those get old fast." Colton winked as he grabbed his leather vest off the bar stool next to her and shrugged it on.

After Colton left, Fallon poured herself a big glass of red wine, grabbed a stack of interior design magazines, made sure he locked the door behind him, and armed the alarm. Plopping down onto the couch in the living room, she got ready to hunker down for the evening. Flicking the television on idly, she turned on Unsellable Homes for background noise as she flipped through the pages of Victoria magazine and reached for her glass of wine.

She lost track of time, making notes in the margins of the magazine with ideas on how to decorate the home and where she could find period furniture on a budget. She wanted the house to look authentic, but comfortable, when it was finished, so she switched over to Country Living. As she reached for last month's issue, her phone rang.

No Caller ID flashed on the screen. Fallon hesitated. Usually, when Officer Michelson or one of the other officers called, it came up with *No Caller ID.*

"Hello?" Static crackled in Fallon's ear. "Hello?" she asked again, her tone not as friendly.

"I'm right across the street," a voice hissed. The tone was odd, neither male nor female, and the connection broke apart as the person spoke.

"What?" Fallon gripped the phone a little tighter. "Who is this?"

The line went dead.

Her palms were slick with sweat as she set the phone down on the couch. Her heart rate increased, thump-thump-thumping in her ears as she stood and wandered to the kitchen. She grabbed a butcher knife from the block and peered out the kitchen window overlooking the front lawn and the street. Craning her neck, Fallon couldn't see anything or anyone. The road was quiet and empty.

Setting the knife down on the small kitchen table that she never used, she crossed to the entryway and disarmed the alarm before opening the door. The wind picked up, blowing hot air in her face like a furnace. Still, she pulled her light hoodie tighter around herself as she took a few steps out onto the porch, shutting the door behind her so Large Marge wouldn't get out.

It was unnaturally quiet outside. Even the wind was silent as it pulled at tree branches and knocked leaves to the ground. The cemetery at the end of the block was still; not a single visitor. Not that Fallon has seen any visitors placing flowers or mourning the dead since she moved to town. Down the street, she saw no movement from her nearest neighbors. Nothing stirred, not an animal, plant, or a person.

Finally, a squad car pulled onto her street and headed toward her house for its late afternoon patrol at shift change. Checking both ways by habit, she crossed the street and approached the squad.

"Afternoon, Ms. Boseman," Officer Mullins greeted with a friendly smile.

"Afternoon," Fallon echoed, forcing a smile. "Hey, did someone from the department try to call me a little while ago?"

Officer Mullins frowned. "I don't think so. We just did a shift change, though, so sometimes, when officers come on duty for the night shift, we catch up on calls from earlier in the day or from the last shift. Were you expecting a call back from someone?"

"No." Fallon shook her head. "I just got a weird call from a No Caller ID number."

"Oh?" Officer Mullins parked on the curb and stepped out.

"Yeah." Fallon crossed her arms over her chest. "It was a bad connection, but someone said, 'I'm right across the street,' and then the call dropped."

"That's odd." Officer Mullins's frown deepened. "That definitely wouldn't have been anyone from the department. Do you think it was from your ex?"

"I don't know." Fallon bit her lip. "The connection was terrible, and I couldn't even tell if the caller was male or female."

Officer Mullins muttered thoughtfully, placing a hand on her duty belt. "I want you to go inside and lock the door while I check around the house. Don't open the door until you see me come back, all right?"

Fallon nodded. "Okay."

Officer Mullins peered past Fallon toward the driveway. "Are you home alone?"

"I am," she confirmed. "My... friend had to go to a meeting with the motorcycle club." Officer Mullins hummed again, the sound making Fallon even more nervous. "What is it?"

"Probably nothing." Officer Mullins tried for a breezy tone, but failed. "You head on inside. I'll check things out around the house."

~

Colton

All the club officers were in attendance, as were Len and some of the retired members, including Colton's boss, George. "This meeting is called to order." Vlad banged the gavel on the scarred wood.

Across from Colton, Igor sat poised, pen hovering over paper, ready to take minutes.

Vlad rubbed between his eyes tiredly before looking up at the assembled members. "We have to discuss what happened at Fall Fest."

"It was a tragedy," Len said from the opposite end of the long table. "Has the health department given any updates as to the source of the food poisoning?"

"That's just it." Vlad sighed. "They tested everything, and all the food vendors were contaminated."

"That's impossible." Colton shook his head, voicing the disbelief of everyone in attendance. "How could all the vendors be tainted? They weren't prepared in the same space or by the same people. How could the chili have the same contamination as the cider or the donuts?"

"I have no idea." Vlad shook his head. Colton could tell the stress was starting to take its toll on him, between the fire at his parents' diner and now this. "I'm just telling you what the health department told me."

"What are we going to do?" Spike asked quietly. All traces of humor were stripped from him, leaving him somber and subdued. He was no doubt thinking of those who died and those who were sent to the hospital.

"The good thing is we have short-term festival insurance." Vlad flipped through some forms in front of him. "They should cover all or most of the medical expenses for those who were sent to the hospital and the death claims of those who passed."

"How much money had we raised before everyone started getting sick?" Wolf asked as he steepled his fingers in front of him.

"After the vendors are paid." Igor checked his notes. "We brought in about $2000."

"What do you say to us donating that to those affected?" Silas asked, looking around the table. "I know it isn't much, but I just feel awful about what happened."

"I think that's an excellent idea," George said, and the other retired members nodded in agreement.

"Of course," Colton chimed in, along with the other active members. "It's the least we can do. We can always make the domestic violence charities the beneficiaries of our next event after the Christmas toy drive. I'm sure they'll understand."

"Then that is settled," Vlad said.

"What if someone put something in the food?" Colton mused aloud, thinking of the strange look on the new prospect's face when they locked eyes in the emergency department.

Wolf scrunched up his face. "How? When?"

Colton glanced over to Len and Lazarus. "Was there ever a time when the chili stand was ever unoccupied? Maybe while you were setting up?"

"Not that I can recall." Len scratched his chin. "Lazarus?"

"I don't remember." Lazarus shook his head. "I just helped

Della with my addition and then was walking around with Naomi, Wolf, and Mina."

"But who would want to sabotage us?" Igor shook his head at Colton, like the very idea was absurd.

"Well, how else do you explain all the vendors ending up with contaminated food?"

"I don't know." Igor shook his head, spoiling for an argument.

"Is someone smoking in here?" Vlad interrupted them as he sniffed the air.

"What?" Spike asked, sniffing as well.

Soon, everyone was looking around, sniffing the air. There was a faint scent of burning leaves in the air.

"Maybe one of the neighbors is burning brush," Wolf offered as they pushed aside the partition.

"With gasoline?" Colton coughed as the scent hit him.

"Fuck." Vlad pointed, as they all spotted the source of the burning smell at the same time.

Thick black smoke poured under the clubhouse door as flames began licking up the wall. A six-inch-wide puddle flowed in through the opening where the door met the concrete floor and caught fire, cutting off the back end of the clubhouse, and the only exit, already blocked by flames and thick smoke.

"Call 911!" Colton yelled over his shoulder as he and Vlad jumped into action, overturning the table as a blockade from the flames.

Lazarus was already on his phone, making the call.

"We need to get these garage doors open," Vlad ordered, as he and the other active members moved to the doors.

"How?" Len asked, appearing at Vlad's elbow. "We sealed them shut when we converted the garage to the clubhouse."

"We have to try," Vlad argued. "You and the other retired members get down by the ground so you're not breathing in the smoke."

"No. We're not a bunch of old geezers. Let us help."

"Fine," Vlad gave in. "You guys work on that door. We'll work on this one."

The men got to work on the doors, trying to bust them loose. In the distance, wailing sirens were approaching. Colton, Wolf, and Lazarus picked up an antique gas pump they had as decoration and ran it into the door like a battering ram.

"We should have had a fire extinguisher and an axe in here," Lazarus said through gritted teeth as he tightened his grip on the pump.

Colton grunted. "We'll think of that next time."

"Again, on three," Spike commanded. "One... two... three!"

They ran at the door, smashing the heavy pump into the wood. This time, they heard a satisfying crack. "Once more!" Vlad yelled, joining them.

Over by the second door, George crouched, coughing from smoke inhalation. This time, the men broke through the door, creating just enough space to slip through single-file.

"Retired members first." Vlad waved the older men through the opening. Wolf supported George through the opening as they heard the fire truck pull up outside.

"Colton, you go next," Vlad instructed.

Colton coughed, feeling his lungs filling with smoke as the ceiling started to groan and crack overhead. Vlad shoved him through the opening, followed immediately by Spike. They were whisked away by the EMTs arriving on the scene. Firemen swarmed the building, ready to cut a bigger opening and put out the flames.

Colton stumbled, letting the EMTs assist him as they placed an oxygen mask over his face. He felt dizzy; his head was throbbing and his vision narrowed to pinpricks. He needed to lie down, exhaustion suddenly stealing over him.

As Colton fought to keep his eyes open, he heard the most awful noise he had ever heard in his life. A loud groan roared over the neighborhood, followed by the sound of the clubhouse roof caving in.

Colton had to help. He had to get back there. He had to—the world went black as he was dragged under.

Fallon

"If it's not one of you, it's the other." Officer Michelson shook his head as he walked into Colton's hospital room.

"I honestly am getting sick of seeing you." Fallon sat up, rubbing the kink out of her neck from leaning at an odd angle beside Colton's hospital bed. "No offense."

"None taken." Officer Michelson chuckled. Gesturing to Colton, he asked, "Is he going to be okay?"

Fallon glanced at Colton, laying still with the clear oxygen mask over his face, held in place with yellow rubber band-like straps. She nodded. "He's going to be fine. He just had some smoke inhalation. They're keeping him for observation until his oxygen level comes back up."

"That's good."

"Be straight with me, officer," Fallon said, looking at him tiredly. "What the hell happened tonight?"

Officer Michelson's jaw ticked.

Fallon heard the fire call come over Officer Mullins's radio and recognized the address immediately. Officer Mullins advised her to stay put and let the firemen do their job. She went anyway, standing with Della and Trixie at the perimeter of the scene as the firemen fought the blaze and the EMTs checked the men out. She was there when the roof collapsed, trapping two men inside. And she had been there when Michael Just was carried out of the building over a fireman's shoulder.

Another figure was brought out in a body bag once the fire was extinguished. She didn't know that Colton had already been transported to the hospital along with his boss, George, and his friend, Gomez.

Her heart broke when the fire chief had approached Naomi Talbot, standing at the other end of the perimeter between Mina Collins and Nova Miller. She watched the woman's legs buckle beneath her. Mina and Nova swooped in to catch her before her knees hit the asphalt as the fire chief removed his helmet and gave her the bad news. Fallon didn't think she'd ever forget the sound of the woman's banshee wail.

Silas Talbot, who had earned his club name "Lazarus" by cheating death after three serious injuries while on the fire department, flatlining twice, had finally succumbed to death's embrace.

"The Fire Marshall has just begun his investigation, but he found traces of an accelerant, and the only door in and out of the clubhouse had been barricaded shut." Officer Michelson finally said.

"So, arson."

"It looks that way."

Fallon gripped Colton's hand. "Do you think Jack did this?"

"He's definitely a person of interest. We've updated the ATL with the new information."

"He never should have been let out of jail." Fallon rubbed her eyes. "Arson, murder, attempted murder. What's next?"

"I hope we don't have to find out." Officer Michelson clenched his jaw. "Will you be staying here with Mr. Sterling until he's discharged?"

"Yes." Fallon glanced down at her hands. "It's the least I can do. I wish Colton had never met me. None of this would be happening to him and his friends if I'd never come to town."

Officer Michelson looked uncomfortable. "I'm not sure if you could go back if Mr. Sterling would have had it any other way."

She snorted. "His motorcycle was totaled, his club's clubhouse was burned to the ground, and one of his best friends died in that fire. Oh yeah, I'm the best thing that's ever happened to him."

Officer Michelson opened his mouth, then closed it, unsure of what to say. "I'll stay with him until he wakes up and is able to be discharged," Fallon said. "Then I'm breaking things off—for his own good. I'd never forgive myself if something were to happen to him."

∼

Colton

"I'll stay with him until he wakes up and is able to be discharged," Fallon said. "Then I'm breaking things off. For his own good."

Her words broke through Colton's fatigue, pulling him back to the surface. His lungs hurt; each breath filling and deflating his lungs like a vacuum, filling up and sucking away his oxygen. But it was Fallon's words that froze Colton's heart.

Fuck. Here we go again. Fallon was getting ready to cut and run. *But who was she talking to?* Colton tried to open his eyes, but his eyelids felt weighed down. He began to panic, his breaths coming out in ragged bursts. His fingers scratched the fabric beneath him, feeling scratchy cotton beneath his calloused palms.

"Nurse!" Colton heard Fallon call out anxiously. "Hey! We need help in here."

It came rushing back to him all at once. The fire at the clubhouse. The smoke he'd breathed in. Collapsing by the ambulance. The bubble in his mind burst, and the beeping monitors and machines came rushing back. He could feel someone gripping his hand as the scuffling of sneakers on linoleum floors and rushed footsteps filled the room.

A buttery yellow glow flashed in front of his closed eyelids. Colton tensed, his eyes involuntarily squinting against the glow. "He's coming to," an unfamiliar female voice announced.

Colton's eyelids fluttered a few times, as if the weight had been removed. The bright fluorescent lights bothered his eyes as he stared up at a white and gray mottled ceiling and the masked face of an unfamiliar woman. Over the stranger's shoulder, Colton spied Fallon looking on worriedly, and Officer Michelson, standing awkwardly with his hand resting casually on his holster.

That's who Fallon was talking to, Colton realized as he blinked, trying to clear away the rest of the fog. Colton wished Ben would just unholster his weapon and put him out of his misery after the grimness of Fallon's decision.

"There he is," the nurse announced, the smile coming through in her voice, despite being obscured behind the mask.

Fallon sighed audibly as Colton tried to yank the clear oxygen mask away from his mouth.

"Now, now, Mr. Sterling." The nurse stilled his hand. "It's best to keep that on for a few minutes longer until the doctor gets here to check on you. You inhaled a lot of smoke." The nurse moved to make a note of his vitals on his chart as Fallon cautiously leaned over him.

"I'm so glad you're okay." Her eyes were heavy with unshed tears.

"Sure is good to see you waking up," Officer Michelson said gruffly, as his grip tightened on his holster and duty belt.

A million questions ran through Colton's mind, but the mask kept him from asking. As if sensing Colton's worry, Officer Michelson cleared his throat. "There'll be plenty of time for questions and explanations once the doc's given you the all clear."

They only had to wait a few more minutes before the doctor bustled in, a female doctor this time, instead of the dour-looking man from the food poisoning incident. The doctor checked over Colton's vitals and flashed a light in his eyes twice before telling the nurse, "It's okay to remove the oxygen now. His levels are back near normal, and his pupils are normal and reactive."

The nurse gently removed the mask. Colton coughed a couple of times and laid his head against the thin pillow on the hospital bed.

"The good news is that you're going to be just fine, Mr. Sterling," the doctor announced. "But you'll have to take it easy for a few days. If you experience any dizzy spells, I want you to come right back to the emergency room."

"I will." Colton's voice was rougher than usual.

The doctor seems satisfied with his answer. "I'll start getting your discharge papers ready."

"Is everyone okay?" Colton asked once the doctor and nurse left the room. The nervous look Fallon shot Officer Michelson gave Colton enough of an answer.

"I'm afraid there was one casualty," Officer Michelson told him regretfully. "Mr. Silas Talbot died when the roof collapsed on him."

Colton smashes his eyes shut against the onslaught of Officer Michelson's words. He could see it—the roof caving in beneath the weight of the flames, crashing down onto Silas's form. Colton hoped that he went quick and didn't suffer the torture of the fire charring away his flesh.

"What happened?" Colton bit out. "Who did this?"

"It's still under investigation." Officer Michelson's response was vague. "There was an accelerant used, so we believe it was most likely arson."

A choked sob escaped Fallon's lips as she turned away, burying her face in her hands. Colton understood now. Fallon believed Jack was responsible for the fire, and she was planning to force distance between them

"Fallon." Colton reached his hand out for her, but she shook her head, keeping her back to him. Her shoulders shook with silent tears.

"I can't," Fallon choked out, her meaning unclear.

Officer Michelson cleared his throat. "I'll get your statement at a later time. I'm glad you're on the mend, Mr. Sterling."

Colton watched Ben excuse himself from the room as quickly as he could extricate himself.

"I'll take you back to the house for your things and pick up Marge, but I think it's for the best if you go home."

"Don't," Colton said. "Don't do this again."

Fallon refused to look at him. "I have to."

The ride back to the house was painfully silent. Colton opened his mouth a dozen times to try to work this out with Fallon, but he didn't know where to begin. She was stubborn as the day he met her, and once she set her mind to something, it was nearly impossible to convince her otherwise. Eventually, Fallon turned on the radio, raising the volume so that it was impossible for Colton to say anything without shouting over the angry metal music piping through the speakers.

At the house, Colton waited in the front hall, suddenly feeling like an intruder as Fallon jogged up the stairs to get his duffle full of clothes. He stepped into the living room and found Marge curled up on one of Fallon's sweaters. The cat slept soundly, with a hint of what looked like a contented smile on her face.

"I'll get her carrier." Fallon startled him as she set his duffle down in the doorway before turning tail. Her boots clicked on the wooden floors as she disappeared into the dining room, where they had stored Marge's cat carrier.

"Come on, Marge." Colton sighed as he bent to pick the cat up. Marge mewled in protest, digging her claws into the soft fabric of the sweater, bringing it up with her. "Sorry," Colton said, carefully detangling the fabric from Marge's claws and dropping the sweater onto the couch as Fallon set the carrier down.

"It's okay," Fallon said softly, as she watched Colton urge the cat into the carrier.

The car ride back to Colton's house was nearly as silent as the ride from the hospital, save Marge meowing unhappily from her carrier. Fallon stayed in the car as Colton got out.

"I'll see you soon," Colton told her as he bent down to look in the window.

"I don't think that's a good idea." Fallon sniffled, staring blankly ahead, refusing to meet his eye.

"Come on, Fallon." Colton sighed. "Don't let it end like this. I thought you were done letting Jack scare you away from living life."

Fallon shook her head and pulled away.

Colton sighed again, defeated, as he looked down at the cat carrier. "I guess it's just you and me again, Marge."

The cat mewled her dissatisfaction as Colton slung the duffle over his shoulder and lifted the carrier off the ground as he dug in his pocket for his house keys.

CHAPTER TWENTY-THREE

FALLON

A deafening emptiness engulfed Fallon as she let herself inside, locking the door behind her and arming the alarm. She hung her purse and keys on a hook by the door and kicked her shoes off. The stillness slithered up, wrapping around her throat as an overwhelming pit opened within her. The house seemed to mimic her loneliness as she wiped her eyes and entered the kitchen.

In the sink, two sets of dishes, utensils, glasses, and mugs sat on the drying rack, mocking her. Half a dozen times on the short drive home, she contemplated turning around and going back for Colton before stopping herself. Even now, her fingers burned to pull her phone from her pocket and call him, asking him to come back.

Then she'd remember the Burning Blood Riders clubhouse burning, see the roof collapsing in on itself. Silas's body being carried out of the wreckage covered in a white sheet, and Naomi collapsing as her world came to a crashing halt in the blink of an eye.

Colton was better off without her. Until Jack was rotting in a dark cell somewhere, Fallon had to stay away. Maybe if Jack saw she was no longer with Colton, he'd stop targeting him and focus on her so the police could catch him slipping up.

Fallon swallowed hard, standing straight as she forced herself to leave her phone alone. Her throat was dry from all the screaming and crying she'd done. Her eyelids were weighted, burning, and itching from wiping away all the fallen and unshed tears.

Headlights lit up the driveway, and for a minute, she thought Colton had chosen to ignore her cold shoulder and come back to her. Her heart soared, restarting after what felt like a prolonged interval. Then she heard the sound of a car horn beeping once, then the sound of boots on gravel, then another car door shutting, and finally Colton's truck roaring to life. Her hopes and heart turned into a heavy stone in the pit of her stomach.

It was just Michael and Trixie coming to pick up Colton's truck, like she'd asked. Fallon hadn't wanted Colton to drive himself home after he'd inhaled all that smoke. The doctor cleared him for discharge after giving him some oxygen. However, he was still advised to avoid operating heavy machinery for the next twenty-four hours.

Fallon turned from the front window, grabbed one of the glasses from the drying rack, and filled it halfway with the end of a bottle of Moscato she'd found in the door of the refrigerator. The one they had split over a dinner of salmon and asparagus only a few days prior.

Fallon took a healthy swig of the wine as she listened to the crunching of gravel as Michael and Trixie pulled away. Drifting toward the back window beside the pantry, she rested her forehead against the cool glass as she swirled her wine.

The shadows were stretching longer across the yard, making it look like the trees were creeping closer to the house. She heard the cawing of a pair of crows perched in a dead oak tree, halfway between the house and the forest, and felt the chilling fingers of unease down her spine. There weren't any rabbits rambling about the yard. The grass was yellow and dead from the dry heat, and the squirrels had mistaken the unseasonable weather for a false summer and slowed their gathering for the upcoming winter.

Fallon's eyes drooped, and the exhaustion of the evening started taking its toll. Just as she went to put her glass on the kitchen island and go upstairs and wash off the day, she caught something dark passing between the trees. Something that looked vaguely human.

Narrowing her eyes and cupping her hand over her brow to block away the glare from the overhead light, Fallon pressed her face up against the glass. Her eyes scanned the forest. She looked back and forth for any sign of what she'd seen, but there was nothing there—nothing but the trees and the gathering darkness. She shook her head and downed the last of her wine before setting the glass in the sink and going upstairs.

Colton

Colton sat on the couch with his head tilted back and his eyes closed. Large Marge laid next to him, making biscuits on his leg, when he saw the flash of headlights come across his living room windows. For a split second, he thought she had changed her mind and came back until he saw the second set of headlights and heard the twin slamming of doors and the crunching of boots on the loose gravel. Vlad and Trixie didn't knock or ring the doorbell but let themselves in.

"Thanks for bringing the truck home," Colton mumbled without opening his eyes.

"Are you all right?" Vlad asked, as he dropped the keys on the coffee table in front of Colton.

"No." Colton snorted as he cracked one eye open.

Vlad sat down on the arm of the couch across from Colton as Trixie sat down on the cushion. They both looked as exhausted as Colton felt. "It's been a run of shit luck lately." Vlad shook his head in disgust. "That's for damn sure."

"I can't believe Laz is gone." Trixie's eyes filled with tears. "I mean, that was his whole club name; he always came back from the dead."

"Not this time." Colton frowned. "I want to do something for Naomi and the kids."

"I'm calling everyone together at the bar tomorrow to talk about just that," Vlad said, already a step ahead of him.

"Good." Colton closed his eyes again. "Just tell me the time, and I'll be there."

"Should you even be driving?" Trixie asked, her tone laden with concern.

"Doc said not to operate heavy machinery for twenty-four hours. I should be fine by then." Colton waved off her concern as he idly scratched Large Marge's head. The cat purred her approval.

"I'll pick you up," Vlad said.

"Dude, no need. I'm fine. It was just a little smoke inhalation. It's no big deal."

Vlad crossed his arms over his chest. "Well, then, what else is wrong with you?"

"Fallon broke things off again." Colton rubbed his temples, feeling a headache forming. "She's afraid her ex will keep coming after me and that it's all her fault that Laz is dead."

"I know Michelson said the fire was started with an accelerant, but her ex being a psycho doesn't make Fallon responsible for his actions." Sadness bloomed over Trixie's face. "I should call her and make sure she's all right."

"I hope you get through to her better than I can," Colton muttered.

"Did you know that women find men who have cats less attractive?" Vlad said out of the blue as he took in Colton and Large Marge huddled together on the couch.

"Fuck off." Colton grunted, trying not to crack, and let a smile shine through.

"Seriously, though, she's been through a lot. I'm sure her first instinct is to bolt. She'll come around." Vlad patted Colton on the shoulder. "Trix and I will let ourselves out. I'll pick you up tomorrow before the meeting. If you need anything in between, call us."

"I've already set up a GoFundMe," Della announced once Vlad quieted everyone down to start the meeting.

The bar was full of club members, past and present, and their wives. Half the members of the nearest chapter were also in attendance.

"I'll get it circulating on social media," Mina said. She handled most of the social media for the club.

"We'll share it on our pages as well." Glen "Hagrid" Harrison, who mightily resembled his club moniker, nodded. He was the president of the Sheboygan chapter of the Burning Blood Riders.

Vlad thanked his mother, Mina, and Hagrid. "I don't want Naomi to have to worry about paying for the funeral."

"Is there anything else we can do for Naomi and the kids?" Spike asked. "I know the holidays are coming up, and that's going to be rough on the kids so soon after losing their dad. We could get them presents when the time comes. And Halloween is coming up. If Naomi doesn't feel up to taking the kids around trick-or-treating, one of us could do it. I don't mind. Or if they prefer to go with one of the women, I'm sure Trixie and Della don't mind, or even

Nova or Fallon. We could even organize a sort of trunk-or-treat and invite the local kids."

Vlad nodded in agreement. "Those are all good ideas."

Igor, Wolf, and Della pipe in with a few more ideas as Colton's gaze drifts over the crowd. Fallon isn't here, but he didn't really expect her to be. He was sure she was somewhere, blaming herself. Toward the back wall, his gaze landed on the new prospect, Damien. His head was down, and in his hand, he flicked an engraved silver lighter open and shut, the flame winking on and off.

Itching from the weight of eyes on him, Damien tucked away the lighter, his head coming up as he scanned the room through narrowed eyes. When he caught Colton watching him, he smirks. The grin was unhinged, evil. It made Colton's stomach clench.

From the first time he laid eyes on the prospect, he'd sensed something was very wrong with him. And now he wondered if there wasn't more to it. At every turn, there was Damien, looking like he was enjoying himself. Like he was in on a joke that nobody else was privy to.

Colton decided it was time to dig a little deeper into Damien Dogoode.

Fallon

"Coffee or wine?" James asked as he joined her in the kitchen and set down his clipboard and laptop.

Fallon scrunched her nose. "Coffee, I think. I've been dragging all day, not knowing what to do with myself when I'm not working."

"Do you know when the diner will reopen?" James stole a bar stool as Fallon started preparing the coffee.

"Not yet." Fallon shook her head. "I hope it's soon. I feel so restless, and I also think that the community could use some good news after everything that's been happening lately. How is your dad doing?"

"The same." James smiled wryly. "You can take the diner away from the grumpy old man, but you can't take the grumpy old man from the coffee clutch. Dad, Alfred, and Edgar have been meeting at Fire Roasted and driving the girls that work there crazy."

Fallon smiled. "I miss those guys."

"They miss you too." James tapped his pen on the island counter. "Believe me, they can't wait to get back to the diner to pester you about hiding your real identity. You're in for an earful."

"I know." Fallon laughed. "I hope they're not too mad at me."

"Mad?" He scoffed. "Never. Curious is another matter." James's phone rang. He pulled it from the pocket of his shirt and glanced at the screen. "Speak of the devil. Excuse me, I have to take this."

"No problem." Fallon nodded as she poured the water into the coffeemaker.

"Hey, Dad, what's up?" James answered the phone. "Do they know what the cause was?" Fallon turns to face James, curious. "You're kidding me?" James furrowed his brow. "Don't they do annual inspections for those sorts of issues?"

"What's wrong?" Fallon mouthed to James. He shook his head, holding up one finger.

"Well, keep me updated on how he's doing, and tell him that Fallon and I are both thinking of him," James said. Fallon's heart pounded as she strained to hear any fragments of Everett on the other end. "Yeah, we're going over a few things at the house. Of course, I'll pass on your regards."

By the time James hung up, Fallon was chewing on her thumbnail nervously. "What's going on?"

"There was a carbon monoxide leak at the church," James sighed. "All the vents were clogged up. Edgar's been hospitalized. He collapsed with a case of carbon monoxide poisoning."

"Oh no. I saw a fire truck and an ambulance pass when I was coming out of the grocery store earlier, but I didn't think anything of it." Fallon covered her mouth, shaking her head in disbelief. "Is he going to be okay? How did this happen?"

"They're giving him oxygen at the hospital and monitoring his heart overnight because the carbon monoxide gave him an elevated heart rate," James explained calmly. "He should be okay in a day or two. Dad and Alfred are at the hospital with him. Apparently, the church has been skipping its yearly carbon monoxide checks since COVID-19 started. I'm sure the fire department is going to have an issue to take up with them later."

"Definitely. I'm glad Father Edgar is going to be all right. With everything that's happened in the past few weeks, it's like a snowball effect. I can't help but wonder what is going to go wrong next."

"At least we can say that the house is finished." James sounded relieved. "Or mostly anyway. My guys will finish putting the rest of the fixtures in tomorrow. You wanted to talk about the furnishings, right?"

"Yeah." Fallon nodded. "I was curious about the house. I know the first house on this land burned during the fire in 1871, and this house was built in its place, but do you know how close the house was to the original? I can't find the original blueprints anywhere."

"I'm not sure." James scratched the stubble on his chin thoughtfully. "The original blueprints might have been donated to the Peshtigo Fire Museum if they survived the fire. Have you checked it out yet?"

"No."

"You should start there. And do it quickly; they're only open a few more days until they close for the winter. I thought you didn't want to do the furnishings to period authenticity."

"I don't." Fallon shook her head. "I was actually trying to figure out how to furnish it now that I have a little money leftover since we came in under budget."

"You've come to the right person." James grinned. "I actually have a few ideas."

CHAPTER TWENTY-FOUR

FALLON

Fallon stepped out of the afternoon sunshine and into the air-conditioned church building. "Welcome to the Peshtigo Fire Museum." An elderly woman, sitting on a folding chair in the narthex, greeted. "Would you like a guided tour, or do you want to just wander around?"

"Actually, I'm looking for information about the house I bought that I've been renovating." Fallon tucked a lock of hair behind her ear. "Or rather, the house that originally sat on the land before the fire. I live on the hill on North Splake Court."

"Ah yes." The woman nodded sagely. "The land where the old Sorenson mansion stood."

"You know it?" Fallon asked eagerly.

"Oh, yes." The woman nodded again. "Everyone who's lived here for any period of time knows the story of old Zachariah Sorenson. Rumor has it that his mansion was where it all began. That and the strange man who arrived in town one day. Let me show you around. I'm Iris, by the way."

"Fallon." She stuck her hand out to shake the old woman's wrinkled one. "Fallon Boseman."

Iris took Fallon to a display case containing a few artifacts that had made it through the fire and were subsequently donated by the survivors' families. A Civil War powder flask that came from Fort Sumter, South Carolina, and made it through the fire unscathed, a burnt clump of blackberries, a broach and set of earrings, some crockery, broken and intact, and a bible that was found scorched and opened to a specific passage.

She directed Fallon to read through several accounts written by survivors, as well as articles from local and faraway newspapers, and showed Fallon drawings and photographs of the destruction. The devastation made her feel slightly ill.

"Only one house in town survived the fire." Iris gestured to several boards and said, "These were taken from the house when it was remodeled in 1983." Fallon leaned in closer to peer at the wood, which looked almost petrified. "It was conditions like these," Iris said quietly. "Scorching temperatures for October, a lack of rain, and tinder-dry grass and crops."

She met Iris's gaze; the elderly woman was conveying something to her with her gaze that Fallon didn't want to consider. That was then. More than one hundred and fifty years had passed since the fire decimated the area. Things were far more advanced now. Fire departments could get to a fire in minutes, calling in other agencies at a moment's notice. *Surely, what happened in October 1871 could never happen again.*

Fallon swallowed hard. "And Zachariah Sorenson?"

"There was a man to be feared," Iris said, moving them over to sit on an antique couch.

Fallon gestured to the sign that stated to kindly not sit on the couch. "Is it okay to sit?"

"It's fine." Iris waved off her concern. "It's circa 1920s and was donated by a local family. Two women aren't going to send the chair legs crashing out from underneath us."

Fallon sat as Iris set a few albums and books onto the floor next to them, then grabbed the top one. "Some say the troubles in Peshtigo began with the arrival of a stranger in 1871. But really, Peshtigo started on a darker route the day Zachariah Sorenson moved to town."

~

Zachariah Sorenson had always been an intimidating man. He'd worked his way through the ranks in construction and architecture down in Milwaukee, gotten his hands roughened as he grew his fortune. Some of the city's most ornate buildings were attributed to Zachariah's vision. There, he met Isabeau Wildemere, an immigrant from France. She'd been an actress in a play Zachariah attended to win the business of a potential client.

Instead, Zachariah had been utterly captivated by the beautiful brunette with porcelain skin and large, bewitching eyes. He'd talked himself backstage and demanded that she have a drink with him. There was something about Zachariah, a commanding presence with an overabundance of charisma, that made it impossible for Isabeau to refuse.

By month's end, they would be wed, aged twenty-seven and nineteen, respectively. Isabeau left acting, never to step foot on a stage again. Six weeks after their marriage, Isabeau was expecting their first child, a daughter who would be named Bridgett. Zachariah decided it was time to expand their horizons north, in the tiny logging town of Peshtigo, where he would build his empire.

In Peshtigo, Zachariah designed and built the most beautiful, ornate house the town had ever seen. He quickly established his reputation as the man everyone envied and whose favor they all curried in one way or another. Zachariah soon bought into the woodenware factory, the largest in the whole country, as well as the sawmill and foundry. He quickly became one of the most powerful and influential businessmen in town.

Men sent their wives and daughters to sidle up with Isabeau, hoping their names would be brought up in conversations with her husband. Farmers and merchants alike flocked to Zachariah, begging for loans and investments.

It had all gone relatively well. Zachariah had become the most feared and adored man in town. His wife was rarely seen out of their home, except for church services at the Roman Catholic Church on Sunday, but she was less important. An excellent hostess for the lavish dinner parties Zachariah held, to be sure, concocting feasts of delicacies ordered specially from specialty markets in New York and Chicago. Overall, from the outside, the Sorenson family looked like the picture of American industrial success. Life was good. Until the summer of 1871.

Zachariah invested heavily in buying farmland beyond town and brought up Irish and Belgian immigrants from Chicago to live on tenant farms and work the land that year. Zachariah also wielded his influence over the sawmill and woodenware factory to sell their lumber and building materials directly to his associates in Milwaukee and Chicago. The materials were used for mansions Zachariah himself designed. Everyone was supposed to get rich, but Zachariah was set to sit atop them all in terms of wealth and power.

And then the drought came.

Crops withered within days of sprouting. The soil was dry, cracked, and useless. It seemed as if each morning the sun rose and, with it, the temperatures, soaring higher than anyone could remember it being in their lifetime.

The fear was palpable in every part of the tenant farmers' beings. You could smell it, taste it. Every time Zachariah came to survey the crops, lips pursed and turned down in dismay, eyes hard and blaming as though the tenant farmers were turning up nothing on purpose, the farmers' hearts would stutter and leap to their throats with fear. Each night, they would kneel at the end of their bunks, stomachs empty, bodies worn, weary, and stinking of the day's sweat, no matter how much they washed.

There they'd stay, praying for rain until their knees were sore and imbedded with sawdust from the unfinished floors. The Irish immigrants crossed themselves superstitiously as they remembered the Great Hunger of their childhoods.

With no crop, there would be no yield to sell, and no earnings to return on Zachariah's investment. And Zachariah did not intend to be on the losing side of anything. So, by October 1st, tempers were frayed and brittle. Neighbors turned on neighbors, only worsened by the blistering heat that had no interest in going away.

Some tenant farmers began to meet in secret in the backrooms of the local tavern and the basement of the Roman Catholic Church, trying to figure out what to do. Zachariah had already begun putting pressure on them to come up with something, anything, from the barren fields, even though their stores were largely depleted. They had nearly nothing stored for the coming winter. Things were becoming desperate; starvation and death had already claimed some of their fathers, wives, children, and friends - and they feared this was only the beginning.

Then, on the morning of October 1st, when the stranger, clad head to toe in black, sauntered into town with a cloud of dust billowing in his wake, the townspeople narrowed their eyes in suspicion, tracking his every move. Head held high, he marched through town, whistling a chilling tune that sent shivers down the townspeople's backs even in the swelling midmorning heat.

Past the Roman Catholic Church, then the Congregational church, ignoring the parishioners standing gathering outside, watching him. He acted as if he didn't see them, as if they weren't even worth his attention.

Along the river, the stranger walked, pulling branches from trees just to hear them crack over his knee like brittle bones snapping beneath his boot.

Some of the townspeople, those who had renounced their higher power, feeling as if they had been abandoned, watched his procession. He walked right up to Zachariah Sorenson's grand home, sitting proudly by the river in the middle of town, taunting the starving and worried townspeople. Later, they would say when the stranger all in black walked into Peshtigo, he signed the death warrant of more than twenty-five hundred souls and brought a plague upon the land, the likes of which would echo through time forever.

The stranger had walked every inch of the countryside. From down east Maine to San Francisco and beyond. There was something about the man that set folks wrong. He never stayed anywhere for long, a few weeks here, a month there. And everywhere he went, he left despair in his wake. Famine, disease, earthquakes, tornadoes that flattened entire counties. He was destruction. He was horror. He was the Four Horsemen of the Apocalypse, all rolled into one. Peshtigo, Wisconsin, was already well on its way to destroying itself that fall. The stranger wouldn't have to do much at all.

A dark cloud hovered over the aura of Peshtigo. An aura of corruption and cruelty that led the stranger to Zachariah Sorenson's house like a siren's song.

A young Irish girl came to the door when the stranger knocked. When she swung the door wide and took him in, her eyes widened in terror. Her legs shook, her skin cooling by several shades as she swore quietly under her breath and crossed herself, begging for salvation as she attempted to slam the door in the stranger's face. The stranger shoved his worn boot into the door's opening, his wrinkled hand curling around the door. "I'll have a word with your master."

The girl gulped, the workings of her throat visible through her thin, pale skin. The stranger licked his lips, envisioning ripping that throat open and feasting on the tissue beneath as boils and pustules sprung up on her face and decay set in upon her limbs.

Not waiting for the girl to step aside and grant him entry, the stranger shoved the door wider with his elbow, shoving the girl deeper into the hallway. "I'll expect him in the sitting room momentarily, so you better go fetch him."

The girl, terror clawing up through her stomach, quivered as she watched the man pull his black, wide-brimmed hat from his head, seeing him fully for the first time. The stranger's eyes were empty pools of black, his lips cracked and peeling, revealing sharp yellow teeth that didn't quite fit into his mouth. His skin was sunken, pulling tight over his bones. A rash covered the exposed skin at the stranger's throat, disappearing into the neckline of his shirt. His hands were gnarled, his nails far too long, and blackened beneath as though he'd just come from digging in the dirt or perhaps digging himself from the grave. A coin-sized dome of flesh rose up on his skin, seeming to skitter around and down the back of his neck, a creature or an insect below the flesh.

"What are you waiting for, girl?" The stranger sneered, slammed the door at his back, and sauntered into the sitting room like he owned the place. "Go."

The stranger's voice was possibly the most startling part of him. His accent was from everywhere and nowhere at once, loud as a shot and soft as a hiss into the ear, commanding and demanding no less than absolute submission.

Gathering her skirts, the serving girl rushed up the stairs to her master's study, where she rapped on the door three times before hearing, "Come in," droned impatiently from the other side.

Zachariah Sorenson sat behind a massive desk, a spread of invoices and contracts laid before him. At his elbow stood a nearly empty bottle of whiskey; in his hand two sips of the fiery liquid rolling around the bottom of the mostly empty rocks glass. "What is it?" Zachariah demanded. "Why are you interrupting me, girl?"

"There is a man downstairs," the girl felt close to tears. "He demands an audience."

"Tell him to go away," Zachariah growled dismissively as he turned back to his papers.

"He's most insistent master," the girl whimpered, tears streaking down her face, unbeknownst to her master. "He won't go away."

"Fine." Zachariah glared at her as he shoved away from his desk. He stood and opened the top drawer of the desk, removing a pistol from the depths and quickly confirming that it was loaded. "I'll handle this, you useless whore. You're fired. Get out of my house."

The girl didn't protest, didn't beg for her job, or allow herself to worry about what the loss of wages would mean for her struggling parents and siblings living in a cramped room in the boarding house owned by the woodenware factory. She skittered back down the stairs and flew out of the house, not bothering to shut the door behind her.

Zachariah's boots thudded down the stairs as he took them one by one. Any other unexpected and unwanted visitor would be shaking in their boots by the time Zachariah walked into the sitting room, but not the stranger. The stranger had made himself at home, leaning back on the couch, arms slung over the back proprietarily, one foot thrown up on the low table, the other booted foot grinding mud into the Persian rug.

Zachariah opened his mouth to demand the meaning of this intrusion, but the stranger beat him to it. His dark eyes bore into Zachariah's, and a flush of heat rose Zachariah's neck. "You will let me stay here," the stranger stated flatly. A demand, not a request.

And Zachariah found himself nodding, "Of course, sir, anything you wish, only say the word."

~

Not a soul in Peshtigo had seen Zachariah Sorenson or his family in two full days. This was both a relief and a cause for concern, keeping the town on the precipice of collapse. Zachariah missed the town council meeting on Monday and blew off his Tuesday night poker game at the saloon, where he played weekly with the other elite businessmen; swindling them out of their cash and valuables.

Bridgett Sorenson missed two days of school and several arranged play times with friends that her nanny was supposed to escort her to.

Isabeau Sorenson, who had been absent from mass on Sunday with a note sent by a maid excusing her with illness, remained out of view. However, this was the least unusual absence.

The stranger in black had not been witnessed leaving the Sorenson home. Not on Sunday evening after supper, not on Monday morning, or at all that day. When another full day was nearly spent without movement from the house, including the servants that came and went daily, people became fearful.

Though not a single townsperson had exchanged words with the stranger in black, they noted an off-putting sense of menace emanating from the man. He had not greeted a single person the day he stalked through town, nor had he made eye contact or even a nod as he passed by. He was mysterious in the way that all unexplained things were. Enough to make anyone curious and have tongues wagging all over town with theories and imagined backstories, but also giving a sense of unease that no one dared come any closer.

Once he disappeared through the doors of the Sorenson home, only one person had come out. A young Irish maid named Siobhan fled to the boarding house where she lived with her parents and many siblings. She refused to speak to any of them when she returned, trembling. Then, under the cover of darkness, she stole a rope from the shed and hanged herself from a tall oak tree behind the boarding house.

Inside the Sorenson home was another nightmare entirely. The servants lived in terror of the stranger in black. The stranger's presence loomed over them like a slick, humid mass. His shrewd eyes seemed to follow their every move, and he was ever there, ever watching, omnipresent.

Zachariah Sorenson forbade the servants from leaving after the first night. They were completely cut off from their family, friends, and loved ones. The blocks that separated them might as well have been a continent away, for that is what the house had become: a hostile territory cut off from all else.

Zachariah's cruelty was no longer restrained; he openly beat his servants and his wife over the smallest infractions as the stranger in black watched on, his thin lips pulling away from his sharp, yellow teeth in a terrifying grin. With a broken arm and a bruised neck, Isabeau Sorenson retired to the master bedroom upstairs, cradling a bottle of laudanum, as she had on too many nights throughout her marriage, slipping away into a drug-induced haze and leaving her only child to her husband's whims.

Bridgett was a bright child, curious and observant, tall for her age, and turning into a beauty like her mother. In her six short years of life, she had seen her father's whims, moods, and cruelty far too often. She had adapted, finding nooks and crannies in the home where he would never find her. But even tucked away, the cries of torment and the sound of switches across bare skin managed to reach Bridgett's young ears. Tears streaked down the child's face as she covered her ears in a fruitless attempt to block out the sounds. She resolved to stay hidden as long as it took until the stranger in black was gone and her father snapped back to some semblance of humanity.

The stranger fed on the torment. The howls of pain and open weeping were music to his ears. The tearing of flesh and the darkening bruises upon the pale skin were a visual masterpiece, a stage production just for him. Zachariah Sorenson was a cruel, hard man before the stranger in black arrived. Now, with a bit of manipulation, he would reach his full potential. The stranger in black had walked upon the thread of time. He'd cast malice, famine, pestilence, and death across the land as though a mighty hand swept over the map and made it so. And this was only the beginning.

The unyielding heat wave was making the people of Peshtigo crazy. At least, that was the official story.

On the night of October 4th, a group of men had been playing cards at one of the three local saloons. These were different from the well-to-do businessmen who played weekly with Zachariah Sorenson. The assembled group consisted of two tenant farmers, three men from the woodenware factory, Edward Drees, the blacksmith, and Albert Phillips, who was a partial owner in the livery stable.

The seven men sat around a too-small table, complaining about the weather, the dying crops, and the state of the local economy if the weather continued. They placed bets and spit tobacco into the spittoons beside their seats. The stakes were high, though a month or two earlier, they might have laughed at such a win. The last man standing at the end of the game of poker would use the winnings to buy himself a meal from the saloon. Nothing fancy, just a beef stew and a heel of bread, but for several of the men, it was a banquet compared to the scraps they'd eaten in the past two weeks.

The moon rose higher in the sky, a waning gibbous edging toward the dark new moon ten days away. Five of the men folded, nursing watered-down Schlitz as they watched the remainder of the game play out, their stomachs growling and their tempers thin.

A young man named John Brodt, who worked at the woodenware factory, and a middle-aged man named Spence Townsend, a tenant farmer with a wife and six children at home, were the last men standing. Both men were thin, on the brink of starvation from a hard summer and an un-bountiful fall. Spence worried for his children and his wife, who was expecting their seventh child. They had no animals to slaughter, and small game was scarce, only enough meat to stave off the hunger pains when split between a family of eight.

His youngest daughter was sickly and unable to get out of bed. She barely had the strength to open her eyes that morning, and her wrist felt skeletal beneath Spence's hand. He'd do anything to win. Anything to bring that bit of stew and bread home to his family.

Nineteen-year-old John Brodt lived in the boarding house owned by his employer. He lived in a ten-by-fifteen-foot room with his parents and his two much younger siblings. His father had been crippled in a sawmill accident two years ago. His mother was a tailor, and this year had been challenging for her. When the crops floundered over the summer and the drought began, people stopped spending their coin, even for the necessities.

Women went back to mending their clothes. There was little need for a tailor when people learned to make do on their own. It was up to John now to support his family and make sure his younger brothers were fed. He'd make sure his brothers ate tonight. His mother and father, too. Even as his stomach growled, his determination steadied him. He would win for them.

In the corner, the stranger in black watched the game, an odd smile on his face. No one noticed him, nor did they question how he could afford a lager and a steak and potato dinner. In fact, few except the barkeep registered the stranger's presence at all.

After a few more hands, John set down a royal flush to Spence's two pairs of threes and fives.

John smiled, pleased with himself, but before he could gloat, Spence rose from the table, his face purple with barely restrained rage. "You cheated! I saw you!" Spence upended the table. The buttons they'd been using as chips *plinked* to the ground, along with the pot. The other men sprung away as their chairs tipped backward. "Don't deny it, you louse!"

John started to laugh it off, then his eyes bulged as Spence pulled a pistol from his pocket with a shaky hand and aimed it at him.

"Cheaters don't get the pot; now get your ass out of here so I can claim my meal." Spittle flew out of Spence's mouth as he glared at John.

"Don't be a fool." John shook his head, his hackles raising. "I won fair and square; you just can't accept it. It will be me taking that meal home with me."

John bent down to sweep together his winnings, counting his bounty as he did, until he felt the cool metal of the pistol on his forehead.

"You go to hell." Spence's tone was deadly calm. Before anyone could stop him, he pulled the trigger. John's head exploded as the bullet pushed through his skull and buried itself into the floorboards as the body slumped to the floor. A shower of blood coated Spence's arm and the winnings scattering the floor.

The other men rushed Spence, wrestling the gun from his hand as another patron ran to fetch an officer. The stranger in black strode out of the saloon, whistling a tune to himself.

The next morning, the barber opened his shop as he did every day. It was on this hazy morning that Eli Feldman, the jeweler, sat in the barber's chair waiting for Don "Dewey" Lassiter to give him his weekly shave. The early morning sun was already hot, rising along with the temperatures in the eastern sky.

Dewey prepared his shaving kit as he mopped at his brow. He hadn't slept well the night before, with no relief from the heat, even in the dead of night. He'd finally resorted to sprawling out on the wooden floor of his bedroom, hoping for the wood to give some cooling relief. Instead, he woke with a backache and a stiff neck, sweating right through his sleep clothes.

As he turned toward Eli, the bell over the door jingled. Without turning around to greet the new customer, Dewey called out, "Take a seat; I'll be with you shortly." The newcomer grunted his acceptance.

Taking up the straight razor as if in a fog, he didn't notice the stranger in black taking a seat next to the door. Dewey tilted Eli's head back for a better angle as he raised the razor. "Wait!," Eli's eyes bulged. "What are you doing?"

Eli squirmed, but Dewey's hold was firm. Eyes glazed over in a dreamlike trance, he drew the straight razor across Eli's throat, splattering blood on the mirror. The open slit gushed and weeped, drenching the front of Eli's white, button-down shirt.

Eli let out a wet gasp before slumping forward. Dewey raised the razor again to his own throat and sliced it open from end to end. Eyes rolling back into his head, his body thumped to the ground as blood pooled around him. The stranger in black smiled and strode out of the barbershop; job done.

That night, Reed Montgomery, owner of the largest grocer in town, came home from a long day at work and found his wife in bed with his biggest competitor. His wife, Edith, hastily covered herself, claiming she had no idea how it had happened. Carlton Bailey, the competitor, shook his head as if waking from an unpleasant dream, wondering how he had gotten there and where his pants were.

Reed went into a rage and beat Carlton to death with his bare fists before hanging Edith from the large oak tree in their front yard, naked as the day she was born. Reed then grabbed his hunting rifle and knelt in the front yard with it between his knees. He put his mouth over the muzzle, and pulled the trigger.

Neighbors who had run out to see what the commotion was claimed to have seen the stranger in black walking down the street, a spring in his step as he headed toward the Sorenson home.

As the stranger in black let himself into the Sorenson home, he stepped over the body of the butler. Flies laid larvae in the corpse's mouth as maggots crawled over the wound in the back of the man's head. The man paused, tilting his head as he admired Zachariah's work. Then he lifted the man's legs and dragged the corpse toward the basement to join the rest.

It was a well-guarded secret that Isabeau Sorenson had become addicted to laudanum to cope with the many abuses she suffered at the hands of her husband. Zachariah had engaged the services of a doctor from the next town to the north to hide his dirty little secret. The doctor made biweekly visits to the Sorenson home where he would reluctantly deliver another bottle of laudanum, but he was catching on to Isabeau's abuse of the tonic and was trying to wean her off. The doctor noted in his medical journal she was using too much and becoming dependent on it.

But the good doctor wasn't married to Zachariah Sorenson and wasn't subjected to his whims. Then there was their house guest, who ruled the house through terror.

The staff had only seen Isabeau emerge from her room once to lay eyes on the stranger. Her maid had to catch her when she'd nearly fainted as she took in the stranger's sharp yellow teeth that didn't quite fit in his mouth as he sneered up at her. A rash covered his throat like a collar, oozing and dripping yellow pus onto the neckline of his tattered black tunic. When he caught her staring, he mocked her, waving with gnarled hands and fingers tipped with long, blackened nails. The sight of him had Isabeau racing for her chamberpot to throw up her breakfast and the maid almost hadn't been able to catch up to her in time. She'd tried to convince her mistress that the stranger was a figment of her addled brain.

The servants had overheard a roaring row between Zachariah and Isabeau over the stranger. Zachariah's temper flared at her boldness and he'd left her in such a state even her maid was unable to stand the sight of her. The young girl gagged as she applied medicated lotion to her back, ripped apart from Zachariah's belt. His backhand knocked three of her teeth loose as well, making her grateful that he prohibited her from leaving the house and mingling with the locals.

After that beating, Isabeau stayed in bed and barred the servants and even her daughter from entering her rooms except for the maid who brought her food. There was no explanation of what had happened to her most trusted friend and maid, who was not seen after the day of Isabeau's beating.

The servants lost track of Isabeau as much as she lost track of them. She had no idea of the horrors that had been going on down-stairs—the abuses and cruelties Zachariah had been inflicting on their staff with an audience of one.

On the night of October 6th, Zachariah entered her bedcham-ber. He hadn't demanded her wifely duties in some time, prefer-ring to inflict his perverted desires on the barmaids in one of the saloons in town. Zachariah didn't miss how his wife had flinched from his touch, but that night, he wasn't alone.

The stranger entered the room. He stared at Isabeau as if he were starving, and she was a juicy steak. Oh, the plans he had for her.

Zachariah was a puppet. Half of his staff was now stacked like logs in the basement of the home.

The last words Isabeau Sorenson would ever utter were directed at the stranger. "Who are you?"

"You can think of me as the angel of death," the stranger whis-pered in her ear. "I'm here to free you from your gilded cage." Tears leaked from the woman's eyes, dripping down her battered cheeks. "This might hurt a little." The stranger licked his lips as his mind turned over the possibilities.

He opened his mouth, his teeth elongating as his jaw cracked, opening wider as he clamped down on Isabeau Sorenson's throat.

Blood sprayed across the wall. It soaked through the sheet and stained the wood floor. The stranger drank the woman's blood, luxuriating in it like a fine wine. When he finished, he didn't touch the body. It had been shredded enough. The sight alone was enough to please him. Instead, he summoned Zachariah.

Zachariah didn't so much as blink at the carnage before him. In a haze, Zachariah hefted his wife's lifeless body over his shoulder, walked out the bedroom doorway and to his study, as if strings were directing his movements. The remaining staff huddled upstairs in the crawlspace. They didn't dare come downstairs when they heard the hammering and prying of boards on the floor below.

The stranger watched as Zachariah dragged the bookcase free from the wall. With a crowbar, he pulled board after board from the wall until an opening emerged. There, he lifted the body from the floor and placed her standing up in the narrow space. On autopilot, Zachariah replaced the boards, building the wall back up until, at last, all he could see was the wide, lifeless eyes of his wife. Zachariah had paused then, as if the sight made no sense to him. Shaking himself free, he'd grabbed the last board and hammered it home before dragging the bookcase back into place.

Zachariah wiped the sweat from his brow. The armpits of his white undershirt were stained yellow with sweat, and his suspenders hung at his waist. He took a ragged breath, letting the sweat cool his skin as he glanced over at the stranger, waiting for his next instructions.

CHAPTER TWENTY-FIVE

FALLON

Fallon shook Iris's hand. "Thank you for your time."

Iris watched Fallon turn to exit the museum. Fallon's head was swimming from the stories Iris had told her cobbled together from journals and letters of the survivors.

It took Fallon a minute to adjust to the sunlight as she stepped out of the museum. She stood on the steps, glancing out over the town, picturing it the way survivors and those who came to the town's aid would have seen it days after the fire. Everything leveled, nothing more than piles of ash as far as the eye could see.

Swallowing hard, Fallon turned toward the cemetery, steeling herself. A handful or more of the graves had plaques like Iris mentioned. The first few told of people who saved others in the fire, and another told the devastating story of an older brother just trying to save his young siblings. One told of an entire family gone in the blink of an eye.

And then, at the foot of the hill, sat the mass grave containing the remains of over three hundred and fifty people. Some burned beyond recognition, others without a single burn on them - most likely lost to smoke inhalation or suffocation from the lack of oxygen in the air.

Fallon closed her eyes, the sounds of frightened screams and nervous horses filled her ears. She could almost feel the flames licking at her skin. Fallon shivered, forcing the image away and nearly running out of the cemetery.

Later that afternoon, as the shadows started creeping across the hardwood floors of the living room, Fallon sat on the uncomfortable antique couch, knees pulled up to her chest, a half-drank glass of wine in a goblet dangling precariously from her left hand.

A home renovation show played on the television with the volume turned low. Every time she closed her eyes, she could see people burning. People running from homes engulfed in flames. People running into the river, floating like Titanic survivors, waiting to see if they'd succumb to hypothermia before the flames could get to them. Families fleeing the town in wagons, only to become engulfed.

She made the mistake of going on her laptop to learn more about the fire. She learned about a ship full of Italian immigrants who had sailed to Peshtigo to work on the expanding railroad. They arrived on October 7th, 1871, and were never heard from again. Fallon knew from Colton and James that the town had a dark, tragic history, but this was so much worse than she could have imagined.

A sharp, screaming alert shattered the relative quiet in the house, yanking Fallon from her thoughts so hard that it felt like someone had plunged her head into a pool of ice-cold water. Looking down, she scrambled to find her phone and turn off the alert.

She found the offending device buried halfway under the

couch, where she had to strain to reach her arm so she didn't tumble off the uncomfortable piece of furniture. Flipping the phone open, she opens the text alert. It was a county-wide alert, the kind you can't turn off no matter what type of phone you have.

EMERGENCY ALERT: DANGEROUSLY HIGH LEVELS OF ARSENIC HAVE BEEN FOUND IN THE WATER IN THE PESHTIGO AREA. DO NOT DRINK WATER DIRECTLY FROM THE TAP OR USE IT FOR BATHING OR CLEANING. BOTTLED WATER WILL BE DISTRIBUTED AT THE PESHTIGO FIRE DEPARTMENT AND PESHTIGO POLICE DEPARTMENT, STARTING AT 6:00 PM. BOILING WATER WILL ONLY INCREASE THE ARSENIC LEVEL. DO NOT DRINK! IF YOU BELIEVE YOU HAVE BEEN EXPOSED TO ARSENIC POISONING, PLEASE SEEK MEDICAL ATTENTION IMMEDIATELY. SYMPTOMS OF ACUTE ARSENIC POISONING INCLUDE VOMITING, ABDOMINAL PAIN, AND DIARRHEA.

"What the fuck?" Fallon uttered as she stared down at her phone. Fallon turned off the streaming app on the TV and went to a live local news app, and sure enough, there was a bulletin announcing the tainted water.

"Thanks, Boris," the news anchor on the scene in town, took over from the studio. "Early this afternoon, five people were admitted to the intensive care unit in Green Bay, showing signs of severe arsenic poisoning. The five patients were all from the same crew of city workers that had been working on a stretch of Business 41. They claim they just replenished their water bottles at the city garage to stay hydrated from the heat. The health department was sent out to test the water. By that time, the Marinette County Sheriff's Department and Peshtigo Police Department were being overwhelmed with calls for ambulances. All over town, there have been severe symptoms of vomiting, diarrhea, and abdominal pain, with patients flooding emergency rooms and urgent care clinics in Marinette, Oconto Falls, Green Bay and as far away as Shawano. An area-wide alert has gone out to advise residents to only drink bottled water and to avoid bathing and cleaning with tap water until further notice. Now, back to you, Boris."

Fallon's mouth hung open in shock. A buzzing noise filled her ears, and it took her a minute to realize that it was her cell phone buzzing, still open in her palm. She quickly accepted Della's call.

"Have you seen the news? Did you get the alert?" Fallon asked in lieu of saying hello.

"We did." Della's raspy voice was a comforting balm. "The club is helping the fire and police departments gather up all the water they can find at the grocery stores and gas stations to distribute this evening. Do you want us to set aside a pack for you?"

"I'll come down to the police department. What about you guys?" Fallon asked, as her fingers fidgeted with the hem of her shirt. "Do you want me to bring you some? You shouldn't have to run out tonight. I'm sure it will be chaos."

"Thank you, dear," Della rasped. "But we'll be side by side with Michael and the boys where we belong."

"What can I do to help?"

"We could always use another set of hands to give out supplies," Della replies after thinking for a moment.

"Just tell me where I need to be, and I'll be there."

"Thank you for offering to help out," Michael grunted as he hoisted another 40-pack of water onto a folding table. "It means a lot."

"Of course." Fallon tightened her ponytail and wiped sweat from her forehead with the back of her forearm as she stacked another package of water. "Anything I can do. You all have done so much for me. I want to be able to give back."

Neighboring towns had trucked in all the pallets of water they could spare, and the conference room of the Peshtigo Police Department was laden with clear plastic packs of water. The squad cars had been moved out of the garage bays so a distribution line could be set up where the water was stacked. Volunteers handed the packs off to cars waiting in line outside the garage bays. Officer Michelson, Michael, Trixie, Della, Len, and a few of the other club members and officers were manning this station. The other half of the club and the fire department would be handing out supplies in the same fashion over at the fire department.

"Mom, Dad, Trix, and Fallon," Michael gathered them together. "Could you go out to the garage and start getting the first pallets set up by the garage bays? The officers, the guys, and I will carry the rest of these out to the garage bays."

"You just don't want the women and the old geezers throwing our backs out carrying out these pallets." Della patted her son's cheek. "I raised you right."

Michael laughed. "I just think we have enough problems right now without you and Dad slipping a disc."

"Are you ready for this?" Trixie asked Fallon as they started hauling water pallets to the front of the garage.

"Sure." Fallon blew a stray lock of hair out of her face. She could already tell her face was beet red from exertion. "How hard can it be?"

"Remember the rush for toilet paper during COVID?"

"Come on." Fallon snorted. "It won't be that bad."

"You'd be surprised how badly desperate people act in emergency situations," Trixie replied darkly.

Officer Mullins ushered the first car up and instructed the driver to pop their trunk. To ensure supplies didn't run out, each car was allotted one pallet of water for the time being. The first wave of hand-offs went smoothly, with Trixie, Fallon, and Officer Mullins, who insisted on being called Katie, taking turns loading water pallets into waiting vehicles.

Fallon saw Colton helping Michael, Gomez, and Officer Michelson carry pallets of water into the garage, and felt his lingering stare. She kept her attention focused on the long string of cars weaving a U-shape through the police department parking lot and disappearing in a long line down the block instead. Now was not the time for conversation—not that Fallon had anything to say to Colton anyway. She couldn't cave, not now, not when Jack was still out there somewhere.

Forty-five minutes into the distribution, as the lead car pulled out of the parking lot, a car from further behind cut in front of the second vehicle in line. The second vehicle, already inching forward, plowed into the back end of the sleek Dodge Charger, which decided it wasn't going to wait.

A large white man, with thickly corded arms that looked like something off a bodybuilding ad, climbs out of the Charger. His head was shaved, and a white t-shirt stretched to the limit across his broad chest. He snarled, hands curling into fists as he advanced toward the Kia that drove into him.

"Officer Mullins, Officer Michelson," Fallon calls out, standing near the back door of the department. "We need assistance over here."

Officer Mullins and Officer Michelson rushed over, along with Michael and the bikers. By the time they crossed the short expanse of the garage, the Kia driver was out of his car, shouting at the driver of the Charger. Spit flew as the Kia driver yelled, shoving the chest of the much larger Charger driver. The driver of the Charger lunged for the Kia driver as Officer Michelson stepped between them. Colton yanked the driver of the Charger back by the collar of his shirt. The fabric made a sickening ripping noise as Colton tried to hold the man back.

Then other drivers were out of their cars, darting for the open garage bays to grab their pallets of water while the officers were distracted. Michael pulled Trixie and Fallon back. "Go inside with Mom and Dad!"

The scene descended into chaos as Officer Mullins called for backup. Trixie and Fallon raced inside, yanking the door shut behind them as people tried to rip the door open, thinking there was more water inside.

"This is like the Cabbage Patch Riots of 1983," Trixie muttered breathlessly as they leaned against the door.

"You weren't alive in 1983." Fallon laughed through gasps.

"I know," Trixie agreed. "But my mama told me about it."

"Why is it," Fallon inhaled deeply as she fought to get her heart rate back to normal, "that in a crisis, people always devolve into chaos like this."

They're going back to their primal instincts," Trixie commented, and Fallon couldn't tell if she was joking or being serious.

Della and Len appeared in the hallway. Della looked over their disheveled appearance and said, "That didn't take long at all."

"Maybe you should serve them up the batch of chili from the Fall Fest," Len joked. "That will clear 'em out quick."

It felt like hours before the officers and the club members got things back under control. Officer Michelson used a bullhorn he found in a spare locker to announce that no more supplies would be handed out at the department, and they should all go home.

Michael and Colton found Trixie, Len, Della, and Fallon drinking soda in the break room. "Are you all right?" Michael asked, his gaze sweeping worriedly over Trixie first, then his parents and Fallon.

"We're fine," Della said. "Sorry, we missed out on the riot."

Michael groaned. "Mom."

"What? Your dad and I still have some fight left in us. We're not headed for the nursing home just yet."

"I don't want to have to book anyone else for disorderly conduct tonight," Officer Michelson said, looking exhausted. "Half my guys are at the county jail, booking people in. We had to call the sheriff's department for assistance."

Fallon yawned. "I just want to go home and pretend this never happened."

"Can I walk you to your car?" Colton asked quietly, pulling her aside from the others.

"Colton," Fallon sighed. "I don't think that's a good idea." Colton's nostrils flared, but he didn't say anything else.

"Someone should walk you to your car, Fallon," Officer Michelson butted in. "Just in case someone is lingering outside. Katie and I could escort you if you prefer."

"Okay."

CHAPTER TWENTY-SIX

OCTOBER 8, 1871

The church bells were ringing on the morning of October 8, but no one was in a hurry to sprint the last few blocks to the church. Everyone was moving sluggishly. Sweat beaded on their foreheads as the townspeople walked to church. Their good Sunday clothes clung uncomfortably to their skin, chafing with every step. Some of the elderly were helped along to the church, old women fanning themselves, murmuring, "I've never felt heat like this in all my life."

The church was only a brief reprieve. The priest seemed muddled from the heat. He kept losing his place and starting again. People shifted restlessly in the pews as women fanned themselves and babies and small children wailed. During communion, an elderly man collapsed, and the town doctor ambled forward, rubbing his back as though moving was painful. He waved smelling salts under the man's nose, and the old man came to. Two men helped him back to his pew, and the priest came down to give communion to the man.

"Let us pray," the priest's voice boomed after everyone was reseated after communion. "Pray that the fires of hell will stop encroaching on our sleepy little town. Pray that God may forgive our sins and cast a great cooling breeze throughout the land."

"Amen," the congregation echoed.

After church, as the townspeople shuffled back home, a queer moaning could be heard to the west. More than one person crossed themselves at the eerie sound. An old man named Peter Tobbens sniffed the air a few times. "Smells like a forest fire is nearby."

His wife cried in distress. "That's all we need."

Everyone walking near Peter cast their gaze to the sky. Birds were flying toward town in droves, hundreds of dark little bodies streaking through the sky, nearly obliterating the sun. In the forest, the hooves of deer thundered in droves as the herd raced through the trees to escape an unseen force. Rabbits and other small animals scurried through the underbrush, trying not to get trampled. There was an uneasiness in the air, and those that could, hurried home as quickly as their legs could carry them without getting heat stroke.

And in the shadows, the stranger watched. The stranger was always watching.

CHAPTER TWENTY-SEVEN

FALLON

"Alright, last one," James grunted. He and Fallon lifted the new dresser for her bedroom. Fallon backed out of the U-Haul as James guided her. "Okay, slowly take a step back down the ramp," James instructed. "Slowly now."

"I swear this feels heavier than the bed frames and the dining room table combined," Fallon puffed out as she waved her left heel around behind her, looking for a safe place to step.

It was only ten in the morning, but they had already spent the last several hours furnishing the house. They'd lucked out on their expedition to Green Bay the day before. Driving around the city as well as the surrounding suburb towns, they'd stumbled upon a few estate sales where they'd haggled prices on two antique bed frames, an old desk, a dining room set, several dressers, end tables, and other staples.

They'd made out like bandits and barely put a dent in her budget. While most of the pieces were old, likely three or four decades older than the house, and all a bit mismatched, she was pleased with the items they'd found.

Once out of the truck, James turned so that he and Fallon were walking horizontally up the stairs with the mahogany dresser. It was a sturdy piece of furniture. All the drawers were in good working order, and a black swirling design had been etched into the wood. It almost matched the bed frame they'd found at a separate sale. They'd also picked up two nightstands that must have come from the same set.

After much heaving and nearly mislaid steps up the staircase, James and Fallon reached Fallon's bedroom and set the dresser against the opposite wall from the new bed. "I like it," James announced, looking around the room.

"I do, too." Fallon smiled, pleased with all they'd done.

Her mattress had found a new home in a gorgeous mahogany four-poster bed. On either side of the bed were the nightstands she had bought with the dresser. Fallon felt slightly guilty for putting the cheap lamps she'd purchased at a big box store on the antique nightstands. On the floor, an imitation Persian rug covered the refinished hardwood floors. A padded wooden chair she had repurposed from the living room sat in the corner of the room by the window. An oval mirror hung over the newly re-stoned fireplace on the same wall as the chair. Fallon could already picture cozying up with a throw and a book if the temperatures ever dropped.

"Do you want to do a walk-through?" James asked.

"Sure." Fallon grinned. She couldn't wait to see how everything had come together.

"I wish you had an Instagram account," James said wistfully. "This house is a showpiece. Social media would gobble it right up."

"I know," Fallon said, her mood dampening. "I deleted all of my social media accounts when I left Jack."

"Maybe once he's behind bars," James suggested. "It'll be like a rebirth. You coming back out of the shadows and showing off what you've accomplished."

"I'd like that." Fallon could picture it, but like so many parts of her life, she felt stalled in purgatory until Jack was located and put away.

"Maybe you and Colton could find your way back to each other, too," James added casually.

Fallon groaned. "Not you, too."

"What?" James asked innocently. "I just think you two were well suited. A blind man could see how happy you were with him. That's all any of us want for you."

"I know." Fallon fiddled with a loose thread in the pocket of her jean shorts.

"Come on." James threw his arm over her shoulder. "Let's go check out the rest of the house."

The study down the hall was like stepping back in time. Fallon would need to work on adding books and other knick-knacks to the built-in bookcases. The desk in the center of the room gleamed beneath the small chandelier light James had found and installed. They'd salvaged the desk and a luxurious faux leather office chair from a law office in Green Bay that had been redecorated and was selling their old furnishings. On the desk, she had her laptop set up next to an Edison lightbulb lamp she had fallen in love with on Amazon and ordered a few weeks ago.

"You could take up writing in this office," James teased. "Become an academic. Revisit the lost art of letter writing."

"Funny." Fallon snorted. But maybe, if she ever decided to relaunch her business, this would make a comfortable office.

They passed the bathroom and stepped into the spare bedroom at the other end of the hall. They'd gone lighter and airier with this bedroom after they found an ash wood bedroom set at another estate sale. The room gave off a slightly coastal vibe. Fallon already pictured putting up nautical prints on the walls and a navy blue bedspread.

"I like the contrast between this bedroom set and the master bedroom." James seemed to read her thoughts. "You'd think it wouldn't work with the wainscoting and the house's overall aesthetic, but it really brightens up the space."

"I like it when things don't necessarily match, but still work together," Fallon agreed.

They went downstairs and admired the fully-furnished living room. A multicolored rag rug covered much of the floor. Fallon kept the uncomfortable couch, but she'd managed to find a couple of sink-in armchairs that were much more comfortable. They hung her television above the fireplace mantle and set a couple of scratched-up end tables between the chairs and the couch, then placed lamps on them. Behind the couch, they'd placed a console table where Fallon could already picture a small red bowl she'd found at a flea market in Chicago years ago and held onto. It would sit in the center, and she'd place some of her design magazines on either side.

They left the space in front of the big front windows empty. Fallon knew already that she'd get a big Christmas tree when the time came, one that would fill up the entire window, its white lights glittering behind the panes when friends drove up to the house. They'd gone for a slightly larger dining room table. However, only half of the chairs were left when she bought the table, so surrounding the table was a mishmash of chairs from the old set and the new set. A glass-fronted sideboard sat against the back wall, waiting to be filled with a special dining set if she ever found one she liked.

"Are you happy with it?" James asked as they settled into the two wooden rocking chairs they'd placed on either side of the door on the front porch.

"I love it," Fallon gushed. "The house turned out beautifully, and the furniture fits in so well. I can never thank you enough for all that you've done for me."

"That look there." James pointed at her. "That twinkle in your eye and that glow of happiness. That's all the thanks I need. I wish I had more renovations like this one."

"Really?" Fallon laughed. "With the human remains in the backyard and all the mishaps along the way?"

"The bumps along the way are what make it all worth it in the end," James said. Fallon got the impression that it wasn't just the renovation he was referring to.

She excused herself inside to make a pot of coffee, and they sat on the porch for a while in companionable silence. Finally, James stood up and handed her his empty cup. "I should get going. I have to check on my dad, and then I have to pick up my daughter from my ex-wife. It's my week for visitation."

"Have a good rest of your weekend," Fallon said as she got up, stretching out her sore muscles before collecting the mugs.

"It smells a bit smoky out here." James sniffed the air. "I just noticed it. Someone must be burning their dried-out crops north of town."

"I've always loved that bonfire smell." Fallon inhaled deeply. "I wish you could bottle it. It brings back so many memories from childhood."

James nodded. "Of campfires and ghost stories and summer camp."

"I'll talk to you soon." Fallon waved goodbye to James.

After washing the mugs, Fallon decided to take advantage of the sunny afternoon and wandered into her backyard. The old well was still taped off, and Fallon couldn't wait until the university gave her the okay to remove it.

There was a stillness to the air as she wandered through the yard, stacking up twigs and crunching through the leaves. Fallon couldn't hear any birds in the trees, but she could hear the bubbling of the river just beyond the forest. She realized she had never broached the tree line, never walked through the narrow swath of forest, and never laid eyes on the river just beyond her property.

It felt cooler when she stepped under the tree cover. A chill skittered down her spine as she rubbed her arms, both grateful for the sudden temperature change and wishing she was dressed warmer. The forest was eerily silent, as though even the trees were holding their breath, watching her step deeper and deeper. The leaves beneath her feet felt damp and slick; they didn't crunch beneath her shoes like the ones in her yard. No twigs snapped between her feet. No birds sang, and no small prey animals skitter in the brush.

Fallon began to feel uneasy. There was a sudden churning in her stomach as something in the back of her mind screamed that she shouldn't be in the forest. She was about to turn back when something buried beneath the leaves caught her eye. It looks like the sole of a shoe. Fallon stepped forward, careful not to trip over a hidden tree root. The leaves looked elevated, like there was something buried beneath it. Fallon crouched, reaching for the shoe—it is a shoe. As she tugged at it, she gasped, falling back as she realized the shoe was connected to something larger, something heavier.

Something lunged forward, hunching in on itself and hovering inches from Fallon's face. She gasped, shaking her head in disbelief. Her eyes must have been deceiving her. Because if they weren't, she would be face-to-face with Jack's bloodless corpse.

His face was contorted in shock and horror, and bugs crawled in and out of his mouth. Her stomach curled with disgust as her gaze traveled downward. His shirt was covered in a large, rust-colored stain around a three-inch long vertical slit.

"I didn't intend for you to find him so soon." An unfamiliar voice startled Fallon. The voice was male, his accent was foreign and familiar all at once.

Her gaze darted from side to side, looking for the source of the voice. Then, a man emerged from between the trees, dressed head to toe in black. His cheekbones were so sharp they looked painful, and his greasy black hair fell into his eyes. It was the strange man she saw on a motorcycle after the fire at Della's. He looked even more menacing up close.

Fallon stared between Damien and Jack's corpse. Terror clouded her eyes, and she bolted away, crashing through the trees back toward the house on the hill. "You can run!" Damien shouted after her. "Run all you want, but you won't survive!"

Damien's laughter bounced off the trees as murders of crows flew from the treetops, taking to the skies, their caws the only warning sound. But no one knew about such harbingers of danger these days, so the townspeople would pay the warning caws no mind.

Now

Now, boxing the town in like a neatly wrapped present, flames sparked up. A great wind blew down from each direction, driving the flames inward toward the town. A great roar like that of a train built up as an uneasy hush fell across the city. The sky darkened as Damien arced a hand over his head, swiping the sun right out of the sky, and swallowed it down his gullet with a big gulp. Wild animals and domesticated pets fled toward the edges of town, only to realize there was no escape.

Then, a cacophony of screams rose like a rising wave across the town as the townspeople realized what was happening. Like so long ago, bolts of fire fell from the sky, burning houses and barbecuing people where they stood.

The bridge was filled with frantic people, some hopping over the guardrail and dropping into the river. With a twist of his hand, Damien snapped their necks, their bodies hitting the water with a sickening crunch.

More people still climbed down the banks, pushing and

shoving anyone in their way.

CHAPTER TWENTY-EIGHT

COLTON

Colton was in the middle of Call of Duty when, distantly, the town's fire siren began to blare. Pausing the game, he listened for a minute, then shrugged and went back to his game. In the front hall, Large Marge meowed and scratched at the front door. "You are an indoor cat, Marge," Colton called out. "Nobody will hand-feed you shrimp in the wild, old girl."

Marge's mewls became more insistent as she puttered into the living room and rubbed against Colton's legs anxiously. The fire siren hadn't stopped its wailing yet. Curious, he checked his weather app to see if a tornado was headed for town. Nothing. He flicked on the police scanner that he kept on his coffee table. He'd gotten it a while ago and occasionally liked to listen to the chatter. The sheriff's department sometimes dealt with interesting calls, like the time a man was stuck twelve feet up in a tree with his cat while his wife waited at the base of the tree for deputies and the fire department to respond.

"Paging Marinette Fire Department, Marinette Fire Chief,

Marinette Tender, Marinette Pump Truck, Oconto Fire Department, Oconto Fire Chief, Oconto Ladder Truck, Lena Fire Department, Lena First Responders, Coleman Fire Department, Coleman First Responders, respond mutual aid for Peshtigo Fire Department for a wildfire surrounding the town and widespread fires throughout the town. This is a five-alarm fire. Repeat paging..."

"What the fuck?" Colton was on his feet in an instant, yanking up the blinds in his living room. The sky had darkened, and at the edge of town, it glowed red. Across town, he could see flames popping up, licking toward the sky. "Fuck," he uttered, wrapping the cord for the blinds around his hand so hard it burned his skin.

"We have to go." Colton scooped Large Marge off the floor and tossed her into the cat carrier he had left by the front door. He grabbed his truck keys off the hook by the door and darted out into the inferno.

He could hear screaming in the distance as gusts of wind spread the fire from building to building. His only thought was Fallon. He had to get to her and make sure she was safe. He'd pick her up and throw her into the truck if he had to, and then he'd drive them out of town. And if he couldn't find a break in the flames, he would make sure they got to the river like his ancestors did one hundred and fifty-two years earlier.

Hopping into the truck, Colton threw the cat carrier into the passenger seat with a slight protest from Marge. Ramming his key into the ignition, Colton's truck roared to life as he threw it into gear and punched down on the accelerator as he rocketed back out of his driveway, fishtailing once he hit the road as he swung the truck toward the direction of Fallon's street. He had to get there in time. Fallon had to be okay.

The needle on the speedometer climbed higher and higher as he swerved around other vehicles all the way down Oak Street. As he passed an apartment building, a flash of light streaked past him and struck a parked car. Glancing in his rearview mirror, he watched in horror as the car rocked on impact and then exploded, flames and black smoke shooting up toward the sky. The blast threw his truck forward as if someone had picked the road up and shook it out like a rug. The windows shattered in the apartment building, and two streets over, car alarms started blaring.

Colton floored the accelerator as North Splake Court came into view and turned, not bothering to slow down.

~

Fallon

Fallon needed to get to the river. After she encountered the man in the woods, she ran all the way back to the house, only to find a butcher knife coated in dried blood sitting on her kitchen counter. Fallon had gotten sick all over the floor as the realization of whose blood it was hit her like a ton of bricks. Before she could call the police department, she had seen the flames lick up at the edge of town, just beyond the cemetery to the west of her home. It was like lighting a gas fireplace, going from nothing to seven-foot-high flames in the blink of an eye.

Explosions that rocked the ground and threw Fallon to the floor more than once, fires popping up everywhere. All Fallon had to do was get through the woods and into the river. She'd have to swim as far as she could upriver, past the city limits, and then she would be safe. Her car was useless. She'd never get through the blaze.

Fallon took up the butcher knife, gripping the handle hard in her palm as she ran for the front door, cursing herself for taking out the back door in the renovation. She nearly laughed at the irony. She might as well have lit fire to the money she'd spent on the renovation. If the house on this land had burned to the ground not only once, but three times before, it would happen again. History was repeating itself, and she had never been more terrified.

Fallon threw open the front doors and darted out onto the porch, frantically scanning the yard for the man from the woods.

She jumped down the stairs, her ankle screaming and buckling beneath her weight as she fell to her knees, gravel digging into her bare skin and scratching up her palms. She screamed and picked herself off the ground as headlights flooded her front lawn, and then suddenly, Colton was there, leaping from his truck and at her side in an instant.

"Fallon," Colton croaked, his throat thick with emotion as he yanked her into his arms, his hands in her hair, running down her neck and over her shoulders as if he had to prove to himself that she was still in one piece.

"I'm okay." Fallon clung to him. "It will be okay. We have to get to the river."

"My truck," Colton started to say.

"We'll never make it through the flames." Fallon pointed to the flames burning steadily just beyond the cemetery.

"We have to try."

Bolts of flames rained down around them as if the storm was protesting their escape. Fallon's car was struck, exploding, when the fire made contact with her gas tank. The ground trembled, throwing them to the ground.

Fallon blacked out. She wasn't sure how long she was out, but when her eyes opened, she and Colton were in a heap on the ground. Colton's shirt was covered in ash and soot, and his face was dusted with it, too. She figured she fared just about as well. But she was alive, and based on the pulse throbbing in Colton's neck, he was too, and that was the important part.

Rolling off of Colton, Fallon tapped his cheeks, trying to wake him. His eyelids flickered, and he began to cough in earnest as he rolled to his side. "We have to go." Fallon tried to urge him to his feet.

"Have. To. Get. Marge. From. Truck." Colton coughed out.

As Colton got to his knees and slowly pushed himself to his feet, Fallon limped around the passenger side of the truck as quickly as she could manage and wrenched the door open. She yanked a terrified Marge in her cat carrier out of the truck before hobbling back to Colton's side. Her ankle was twisted but, thankfully, not broken.

They supported each other as they made their way around the side of the house. The garage was burning already, and it wouldn't be long before it spread to the house. As they reached the tree line at the edge of the property, a dark figure emerged from the trees.

"You didn't think I'd make it that easy to get away, did you?" Damien Dogoode stepped from the shadows.

"You," Colton rasped, recognizing the man from somewhere.

"That's right." Damien bared his sharp, yellow teeth. Fallon realized now that they were crooked and didn't quite fit into his mouth properly. He was a horror movie villain that stepped right from the screen into real life, and he was advancing on them.

Fallon raised the butcher knife in front of her and said, "Don't come any closer."

Damien laughed, and with a wave of his hand, the knife flew from Fallon's grip and landed on the far edge of the property. "You think I'm afraid of a silly little blade?" He cackled. "I'm death incarnate. I'm the four horsemen of the apocalypse in one bag of bones. I am the cleanser of worlds. You are no match for me."

Damien outstretched his hands, and Colton was ripped from Fallon's arms and thrown skyward before crashing back to the ground fifteen feet away, landing with a sickening crunch and laying still. Marge, in her carrier, was cast further away, yowling and hissing behind the metal grate.

"Why are you doing this?" Fallon asked, edging backward slowly.

"Because I can." Damien shrugged. "Because I am destruction. I go where I'm called. I destroyed this town once, and I'll do it again."

"What did the people of this town ever do to you?" Fallon's voice shook as she took in the enormity of what Damien said. Yards away, Colton still hadn't moved. "Why us?"

"It's about what you do to each other." Damien cocked his head. "Look at how you pathetic humans acted over silly bottles of water. And that's just one example."

"So you're going to kill everyone because of the actions of a few?" Fallon challenged.

"All must face judgment sooner or later."

"And Jack?"

"Hmm." Damien hummed as if he didn't know the name.

"The body in the woods," Fallon reminded him.

"I thought I could find an ally in him," Damien admitted. "But I've been betrayed by humans before. Never again." Bored with the conversation, he raised his hand, and then Fallon flew through the air. She landed hard on her side a few feet away from Colton.

"If we go, we go together," Fallon croaked, feeling like every bone in her body was shattered. Blood dripped from her lips, landing on Colton's shirt. "You were right. I shouldn't have been so afraid to give us a chance. If I had the chance to go back and change things, I would take the leap." Fallon collapsed onto Colton's chest.

EPILOGUE

Perhaps there was hope for humanity after all. Not likely, but perhaps. Damien waved his hand and smirked as the woman's ribs snapped, and she croaked out a pained sound, her eyes slowly closing. Bored with the scene, Damien walked across the burning yard, ready to watch the rest of the town burn. And then it would be on to the next place, the town rotting from the ground it sat on. Judgment came for everyone in the end, and Damien would never stop. As long as humans roamed the earth, there would always be a next town on the horizon for Damien.

Over one hundred and fifty years to the day after what became known as the Peshtigo Fire burned through more than a million acres of land in northeastern Wisconsin and killed an estimated 2,500 people, history has repeated itself.

Fire departments from six different agencies battled flames that surrounded the town for over five hours with the aid of air tanker operators dropping fire retardants from above at regular intervals. Inside the ring of fire, the Peshtigo Fire Department worked tirelessly to put out fires cropping up all over town. By midnight on October 9th, a third of the city had burned to the ground. The death toll steadily rose to 131 fatalities as emergency responders combed the town over the next four days.

In 1871, it took five weeks for news of the Peshtigo Fire to reach the widespread world. In 2023, with social media at your fingertips, news of the fire spread worldwide in less than an hour and was broadcast on national news the next morning. By the afternoon of October 9th, news crews from all over the country were camped out at the edge of town, and coverage was all over the television and the internet for weeks to come.

Peshtigo Mayor Tom Schultz became a daily fixture on the news. In a statement, he remarked that just as their ancestors did before them, Peshtigo would once again rise from the ashes and credited quick thinking and fast responses from other agencies to the relatively low death toll.

While neither as widespread nor as deadly as its predecessor, locals had been left to wonder why this had happened to them and why their sleepy little town had attracted such devastating blazes, though record high temperatures, drought conditions, and low humidity have been sourced as the cause of the fire.

On October 10th, northeastern Wisconsin received its first rainstorm in nearly a month, and temperatures dropped to a seasonable 55 degrees.

Damien Dogoode had spared Fallon and Colton's lives. It was unknown how they had survived, just that they were lucky. Due to the fast response and modern firefighting that had not existed in 1871, two-thirds of the city's houses and businesses had survived. The southeast corner of town was hit the hardest, though the northwest end where Colton's house had stood was mostly gone, too.

Now, two months later, a third of the city lay in charred ruin. Yellow caution tape blocked off businesses and residences the building had deemed uninhabitable. In the middle of the night, if you listened closely, you could hear some of them collapse in on themselves. It would be a slow rebuilding process, especially with winter setting in. Donations of food, clothing, and personal care items had poured in from near and far.

First responders found Fallon and Colton after the flames had been brought under control. Every other house on North Splake Court, along with the swath of forest between Fallon's property and the river, was gone. The lawn was scorched, every tree, bush, and blade of grass was gone. But the house was still there. And in one still-green circle of grass, Colton and Fallon were found unconscious, curled into one another. A few feet away, Large Marge's cat carrier was located. The cat was terrified, and her whiskers had been singed, but otherwise, she was fine.

Colton and Large Marge moved in with Fallon for good after they'd been released from the hospital.

The house was now being transformed for Christmas. A little cheer was needed after the fall they'd all endured. Colton and Fallon were hanging large evergreen wreathes with simple red bows under James's watchful eye. James and Everett had been lucky. They'd gone to Oconto together to pick up James's daughter Anna and had been on the other side of the firewall when it started.

Colton was still hobbling around on his walking cast. In addition to a tibia shaft fracture, he had also cracked three ribs and had a linear skull fracture. It had been a slow healing process, made worse by his smoking habit, but he was taking it in stride.

Fallon was slowly rejoining the connected world. In the new year, with James's help, she would launch her new home restoration business. The home in Peshtigo would be her showpiece. Already people had driven down the road to snap photos of the finished house. James's company, meanwhile, was booked until the following fall, rebuilding homes and businesses around town.

In one week's time, they would all gather to celebrate all they still had and all that was to come with a Christmas open house slash engagement party for Michael and Trixie. They'd survived the fire together and decided life was too short not to spend every morning waking up together. Della was already pestering the couple about when she'd have some grandchildren to spoil.

Fallon was in no hurry to follow Michael and Trixie to the altar. She took things day by day now, reclaiming her life and taking back all the things Jack had stolen from her.

Fallon felt whole once more. She could relate to the town, delivered from the ashes to become something stronger. Jack was gone, never to bother her again. And though Fallon knew that Damien was still out there somewhere, she knew he wouldn't return to Peshtigo, not anytime soon anyway.

Colton only knew bits and pieces of what had really happened the night of the fire. Fallon had pieced together the whole picture —all the accidents and eerie occurrences that Damien had caused. The town, the state, and the media had been quick to believe that weather conditions caused the fire, but Fallon knew the truth. In a way, though Damien claimed to hate humanity, it was through destruction that Fallon found freedom.

Deadwood, South Dakota

Damien Dogoode took the last curve as the town of Deadwood unfurled before him. To onlookers, he was just another biker coming through western South Dakota now that spring had arrived. The tiny village had changed a lot since Damien strolled into town in September 1879 and left nothing but ash at his back two weeks later, but gambling was still king. And where gambling was found, corruption, rot, and darkness weren't far behind. Judgment came for all in the end. And the funny thing about history is that if you aren't careful, it would repeat itself.

Damien threw his head back and laughed, a cruel sound that seemed to reverberate through the mountains.

PESHTIGO FIRE CEMETERY

On the night of October 8, 1871, Peshtigo, a booming town of 1700 people, was wiped out of existence in the greatest forest fire disaster in American history.

Loss of life and even property in the great fire occurring the same night in Chicago did not match the death toll and destruction visited upon northeastern Wisconsin during the same dreadful hours.

The town of Peshtigo was centered around a woodenware factory, the largest in the country. Every building in the community was lost. The tornado of fire claimed at least 800 lives in this area. Many of the victims lie here. The memory of 350 unidentified men, women, and children is preserved in a nearby mass grave.

Erected in 1951 by the people of Peshtigo.

AUTHOR'S NOTE

When I was a child, when he wasn't working outside landscaping, I'd almost certainly always find my great-uncle reading books about history. He'd be sitting in his chair reading about how the railroad was built across America, other times about the Trail of Tears in which the government sent much of the Native American population on a death march west just so they could claim their land, and his personal favorite - the Civil War.

If my grandmother (his sister whom we both lived with), he, and I were on vacation and there was a historical marker, he had to stop at it and read the plaque.

My great-uncle passed this love of history down to me.

The history curriculum in the fourth grade in the State of Wisconsin focuses on Wisconsin's history from the Ice Age onward. I went to a small school district in a small town, and our books had seen better days, perhaps not quite old enough to have been new when my great uncle — who was born in 1923 and only went to school until the 8th grade — had been a student. In that falling apart book, I first learned about the Peshtigo Fire of 1871.

My love of history takes on a slightly darker tone than my

great-uncle's. My fascination with the Cecil Hotel in California inspired No Check Out. My love of shipwrecks and maritime disasters may yet spawn a book. I have a fixation on lighthouses and supposedly haunted places and am drawn to them in my travels. My 4th-grade horror and fascination with the Peshtigo Fire turned into the book you are holding now.

The Peshtigo Fire, The Forgotten Fire, The Deadliest Forest Fire in U.S. History.

While the paranormal elements in this book are entirely fictional, much of what I have included about the Peshtigo Fire in 1871 comes from survivor accounts and other research. The Great Chicago Fire of 1871 did happen on the same night as the Peshtigo Fire, but the Peshtigo Fire was more widespread and far more deadly.

ACKNOWLEDGMENTS

I first have to thank my family. My great-uncle, Robert Fenner, for passing on his love of history. My grandmother, Bonnie Fenner, for always believing in me and encouraging me. And my mother, Deborah Berndt, who bravely battled cancer for four years. They all shaped me into the woman I am today.

I also want to thank my editor, Hannah Cutchin of Charshade Press. You were fantastic to work with and I thank you for helping me make It Rose From the Ashes into the best version it could be.

To my wonderful writer friends: Tyffany Hackett, Chelscey Clayton, Hannah Marae, Beth Weg, Stacy Jane, Katy J. Schroeder, and A.J. Torres for encouraging me every step of the way.

To my coworkers, a lot of whom inspired the officers mentioned in this book.

And finally, to you dear reader. Book number 11! If you've been with me since the beginning or if this is your first book of mine you've read, I thank you for giving my stories a chance!

ABOUT THE AUTHOR

TAYLOR FENNER is the author of eleven Young Adult and New Adult novels and novellas. Her Young Adult Fantasy Retelling, CURSEBREAKER, was shortlisted for the 2017 Ozma Award for Fantasy Fiction, and her standalone fantasy novel, MONSTERS & MIST, is a Literary Titan Silver Book Award Winner and was also shortlisted for the 2021 Ozma Award for Fantasy Fiction.

Taylor is a thirty-something-year-old book junkie who devours books in most genres, although she has a soft spot for thrillers and horror novels.

Taylor lives in Wisconsin with her escape artist cat, Houdini, and a British shorthair cat, Makita, who might have eaten her last owner. Besides writing, by night, Taylor works the night shift as a dispatcher in a possibly haunted police station. When not working on her next novel, you'll find Taylor traveling or planning her next adventure, watching horror movies - she says classic horror is the best - reading or watching shows about creepy history, indulging in sugary coffee drinks, singing badly along to songs on Spotify in the car, and obsessively planning for Halloween starting in July (it's never too early). You can follow Taylor on Instagram, Facebook, or TikTok.

facebook.com/taylorfennerwrites

x.com/taylorfenner

instagram.com/taylorfennerwrites

tiktok.com/@taylorfennerwrites